Aqueel "Al" Athar & Tanya Athar-Jogee

TINY GLIMMERS OF LIGHT

A Novel

Published by River Grove Books
Austin, TX
www.rivergrovebooks.com

Distributed by River Grove Books

Design and composition by Greenleaf Book Group
Cover design by Greenleaf Book Group
Cover images used under license from ©Adobestock.com

Publisher's Cataloging-in-Publication data is available.

Print ISBN: 978-1-966629-26-9

eBook ISBN: 978-1-966629-27-6

First Edition

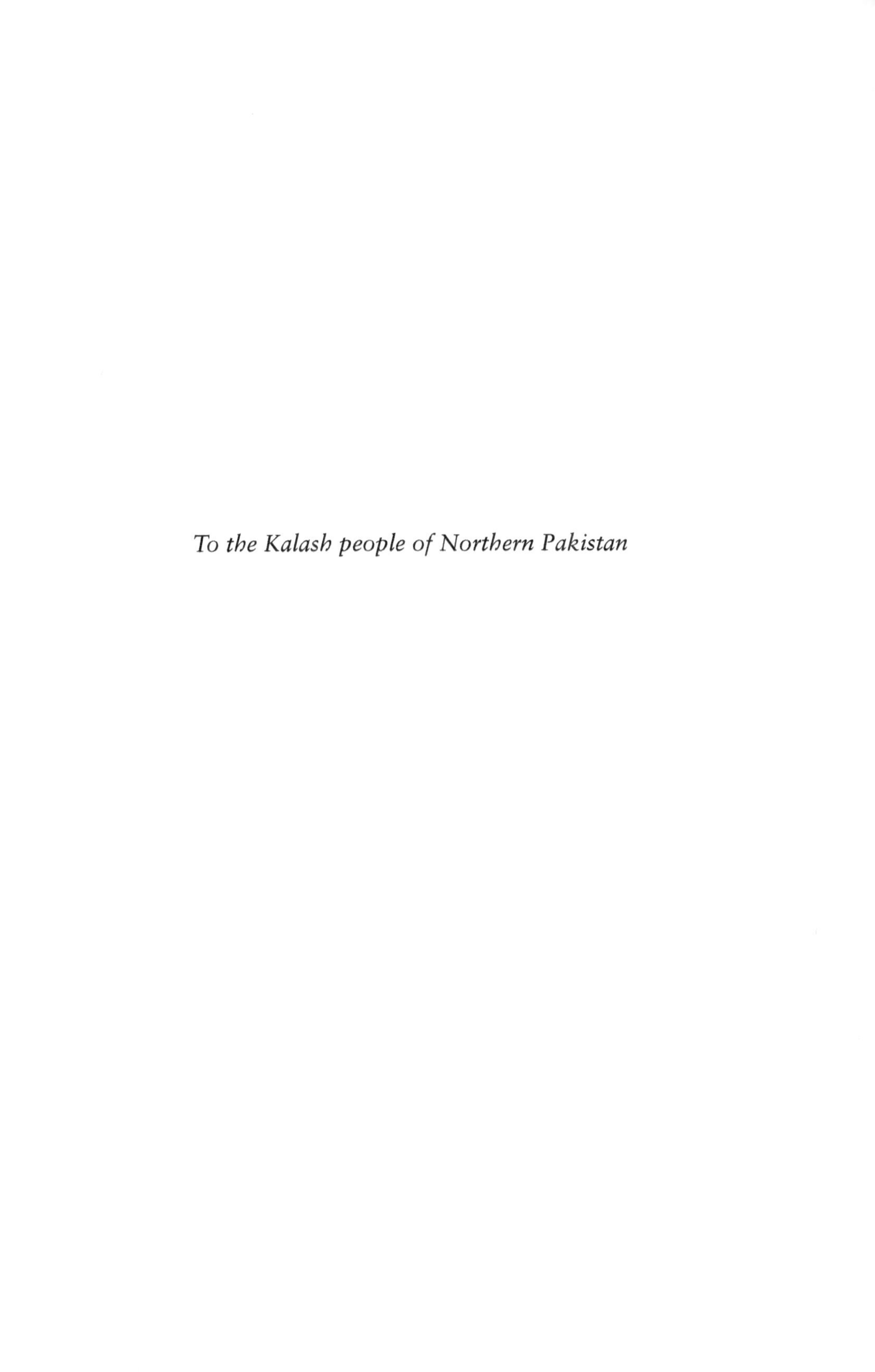

To the Kalash people of Northern Pakistan

CHAPTER 1

Karachi, Pakistan 2014

Bala rolled over in the dim light and squinted at the scratched-up face of his watch. It was 5:30 a.m., right before the break of dawn and much too early for a friend or family member to come calling. But the knocking persisted.

Who the devil is at my door at this ungodly hour? Bala had spent much of the night shivering, even though he had made sure to take out extra blankets for himself, Naseebo, and Goha. He was annoyed at the chilly weather, which was unusual for nighttime in September, and on top of that, his ankle throbbed from being twisted at the construction site across town the day before.

Bala had eventually managed to convince his supervisor to give him a day off, but he still smarted that it had required so much persuasion. After all, he had slogged away without complaining every day for the past two weeks, most days with the sun beating down relentlessly as it approached midday. He had put in ten-hour days without a single day off. And now, when he finally drifted off to sleep despite the cold and his swollen ankle, someone brazenly disturbed his rest.

Maybe it's a greengrocer or a fishmonger getting an early start. But it doesn't take a scholar to know most people are still sleeping.

Whoever it is can come back later. Bala pulled his blanket closer to his face and glanced at his wife, who snored softly on the *charpai* next to his. A wisp of her long, wavy dark hair had fallen across her face, and he watched it rise and fall from her chapped lips with each slow, drawn-in breath.

Bala gently shook Naseebo's shoulder. "*Rani*," he whispered. It was a term of endearment from the day they had first shown attraction for each other two decades earlier. Despite their poverty and their difficulties, she had always remained his queen, his one and only.

"Mmmm." Naseebo turned over and bent her arm into a *V* to cover her eyes.

"Can you see who is at the door? It might be something important—whoever it is isn't leaving. I would go myself, but my ankle and foot are killing me." As if the injured ankle weren't bad enough, Bala still hadn't recovered from his previous work injury a month ago, which had severely bruised three of his toes when several bricks in a cart transported by a worker at a construction site came loose from the pile and landed on him.

Meanwhile, his beloved nineteen-year-old son Gohar, who as a baby had quickly acquired the nickname Goha, slept in an adjacent room Bala had built out of wooden planks he found discarded on the side of the road. When Goha had started high school four years earlier, he mentioned that sleeping in the same room as his parents prevented him from having a good night's rest, and Bala had witnessed firsthand his son's irritability and inability to concentrate on his studies. He'd hauled the wood home, proud of himself for being able to remedy the situation right away.

Though just as incongruous and dilapidated as the rest of the shack, the private room made Goha oblivious to the world outside when he retired for the night, in part because he habitually shut his windows and door before bed to keep the constant shouting, motorbike engines, and blaring *adhan* in the *katchi abadis*, low-income housing settlement, at bay. Bala was pleased with how the separate room helped raise his son's grades; he wanted to do everything in his power to give his cherished flesh and blood a shot at securing a good job and better future for their entire family.

Naseebo pushed herself up with her elbows and rubbed her eyes. "Okay, I'll go," she said sleepily. She wore the same two-piece, modest *shalwar kameez* she usually wore to bed, the faded green one stained in some places and threadbare in others. She rose slowly from the rickety bed, the wooden floorboards creaking from her weighty feet, and picked up the patterned cotton *dupatta* she had hung over a peeling wooden chair the night before. She draped the fabric loosely over her head and bosom.

Bala had left his ratty *chappals* outside the bedroom door, and she slipped her feet into them. She trudged across the unpaved courtyard. *Who on earth would come knocking even before the muezzin has called the fajr adhan?* The gravel crunched underneath her feet; the sound amplified in the early morning darkness. She cracked the door open and squinted until she made out the silhouette of a man. Speckles of gray peppered his brown facial hair, and an embroidered beige *topee* neatly covered the crown of his head.

"*Assalam-o-alaikum,*" he whispered gruffly, pushing the creaky door open and entering the courtyard.

"Excuse me," said Naseebo. "Where do you think you're going?"

"Woman, get out of my way. Do you have no shame talking to a *na-mahram*? What's the matter with you? And where's the man of the house?"

"And do you have no shame in forcing yourself into a stranger's house? Please get out." Throughout her life Naseebo had encountered misogynistic, ill-mannered, and lecherous men, and she had quickly figured out how to stand up for herself. She prided herself on being outspoken and fearless; however, in that moment, jolted rudely out of her slumber, she drew her *dupatta* tighter over her chest, an act more out of habit than intimidation.

"Bala, come here quickly. *Dekho ye kon hai.* I have no idea who this man is or what he wants."

By this time, Bala had splashed water on his face and was fully awake. He limped over to Naseebo and the stranger at the door.

"*Assalam-o-alaikum.*" The man's harsh voice was at odds with the Islamic greeting of peace.

"*Wa 'alaykumu s-salam.*" Bala tried to be polite. "*Aap kon hain?*" Who are you? "*Sahib*, you have barged into our property without permission. Can you please tell me what you're doing here so early in the morning?"

"*Suno meri baat.*" Listen to me carefully, the man responded. "We need to have a man-to-man talk."

Bala frowned. "It is practically the middle of the night. *Meray paas baikar baton ka waqt nahi hei.*" I don't have time for a useless discussion right now.

The man's posture grew rigid. He snorted. "*Chupp karo.*" Shut up. "You better stop talking now and do as I say."

Bala bristled. He eyed the belligerent stranger suspiciously, figuring he must either be a drunk hoodlum or a nasty beggar determined to steal their few meager possessions. The stranger was average-sized and looked a few years older than Bala, yet he somehow still evoked intimidation. Bala was afraid. He had been around long enough to know people in his low social strata were easy targets for those with bad intentions. He waved Naseebo away sharply.

Naseebo, too, sensed the man was up to no good. *Who is this man, and why is he harassing us? Did he make a wrong turn? Can't he see we're paupers?* She scowled at the man and reluctantly walked back into the adjoining bedroom.

By then the man's gruffness had subsided, but he inspected Bala cautiously. "Just listen to me, please. I have an opportunity for your son that will get you and your family out of these miserable conditions."

Bala narrowed his eyes at the man, again confounded at how and why he'd ended up inside his shack in the middle of the night. "What are you talking about? And how do you know I have a son?"

"*Madrasa mein Gohar ka naam kissi ne bataya thha.*" I know about Gohar from the local *madrasa*.

"Who from the *madrasa* told you about Gohar?"

"I have my sources." A shadow crossed the man's face, and his light brown eyes grew darker. "Don't waste my time or yours with idiotic questions," he snarled.

Without warning, his tone quieted again. "I'm sorry. Forgive me. Please, let me take you to the *Chaaye Khana* by the main road." They could have breakfast and talk privately there, he said. "I promise you won't regret it. I have a legitimate lucrative offer that will guarantee your family a comfortable lifestyle in the future."

I'll believe it when I see it. Bala shook his head as he heard voices of workers at the construction site commiserating about a spate of con artists roaming the city, intent on stealing money from laborers like themselves. But his painful ankle and never-ending rut of poverty convinced him it wouldn't hurt to hear the man out.

Even if he's a phony, I have nothing to lose except the shirt on my back.

Sunlight cast its first delicate rays through the cracked windowpane onto the man's light brown, unblemished complexion. He was dressed in a spotless, dark gray *shalwar kameez* and brown leather sandals with buckles on the sides. He spoke impeccable Urdu, the kind many of Bala's elite clients spoke when they told him what needed to be done for their home projects or renovations, but Bala could tell from his appearance and accent he wasn't a local Karachiite; he likely came from up north. Bala occasionally met men from that area, mostly Pashtun youngsters who spoke Urdu in varying degrees of fluency, who had left everything behind and ventured hundreds of miles south to the gigantic coastal city in search of less arduous, more lucrative work than what they were used to in the mountainous areas.

Bala spent several minutes in uncomfortable silence with the stranger, deliberating his request. "Okay. I'll come with you," he said finally. "But if you pull a fast one on me, I know people who will make your life hell." Bala couldn't think of even one influential contact he possessed, but he attempted the trick anyway and gave the man his most threatening glare. He ordinarily wasn't a rude man, and a part of him wished he could snatch the words and discard them the moment they came out. But Bala was skeptical of the stranger's motives and concerned he knew so much about his precious Goha.

"*Rani*, I'm going out for a while," he said loudly, hoping his emboldened tone would make the stranger think twice about any untoward motives. "I'll be back soon."

When Bala followed the man out of the house, the crisp air hit his cheeks like a whip, and he held up his hand to shield his eyes from the sun. Someone had disposed of their dinner leftovers on the ground a few feet away from his door, and flies swarmed around the dirty plastic soda bottles; stale, molding bread; and rotting chicken bones. He held his breath and scrunched his nose.

A gray Toyota Corolla parked at a distance shone like reflective silver in the sun. As they walked toward it, he recognized it as one of the current models at the car dealership he passed by often on his way to some grueling contract job or another. The man waited for him to get into the front passenger seat, then started the ignition without a word and pulled out of the dusty, half-paved street onto the main road.

Although it was early, the *Chaaye Khana* was bursting with its typical clientele—truck, taxi, and auto-rickshaw drivers, a diverse medley of men who were tall and short, fair-skinned and dark, bearded and clean-shaven, young and old. They talked loudly over each other in different dialects and accents, opining and complaining about the high price of gas, the rising costs of living, and the government's inaction in improving the status quo.

Bala positioned himself to sit on a wooden bench on the pock-marked cemented porch.

"No. Not here," the man said in his characteristic hoarse whisper. "Not where so many people are coming and going. Let's go to the back where it's less crowded."

Behind the restaurant, the man pointed to a rickety metal bench under a large banyan tree. He pulled out a page of newspaper from his *shalwar* pocket and attempted to wipe off the pigeon droppings and leaves. He eventually gave up, sat down, and motioned for Bala to sit beside him. The bench, cold and hard against Bala's skin, was insulated only by his thin *shalwar kameez*. In his haste to oblige the man, Bala had forgotten to bring a coat or woolen blanket to wrap around his shoulders.

The man cleared his throat. "First, let me introduce myself properly. My name is Dabir Khan, and people call me Lala Dabir. I recruit young men, like your son Gohar, to work in Northern Pakistan." Much of the work was top secret, and his organization was working hard to bring about systemic social, educational, cultural, and political changes to the country. "I'm sure you agree that since Pakistan was born out of carnage when the British left in 1947, there's been an onslaught of foreign influences, and most of them haven't been positive. A lot of work needs to be done to preserve our unique Pakistani heritage." He paused for a minute, looking at Bala intently as if to figure out whether he agreed.

Bala remained expressionless. With his rudimentary education, he knew little of the history or geography of Pakistan, much less the systems that apparently needed changing.

Dabir said the organization was making changes up north that would gradually spread across the entire country. "If your son joins us, your family will be well compensated for his service."

Is Dabir waiting for me to respond? Bala tried to think of a question that wouldn't expose him as a *gadha*, an uneducated fool.

"What do you mean by Northern Pakistan? Peshawar?" he said finally. Peshawar was more than eight hundred miles north from where Bala's family lived in Karachi, a major commercial and industrial city on the Arabian Sea. From what Bala understood, Peshawar was a relatively prosperous frontier city known for its unique dishes, culture, and history.

"*Peshawar se bhi aagay.*" Even farther north than Peshawar, Dabir said.

"Okay. But before I commit to anything, I need to know what type of work Goha would be doing." Bala crossed his arms and silently commended himself for prioritizing his son's safety even as a golden carrot dangled in front of him.

"Bala, be patient. I told you, the work we do is confidential."

Bala observed Dabir suspiciously, convinced he hadn't told Dabir his name and yet somehow not surprised he knew it.

"One thing I can tell you is how much your family will receive up front if your son joins us." Dabir peered over his right shoulder and his left, then discreetly pulled out a pen and paper from his *kameez* pocket, wrote down a figure, and handed the slip to Bala.

Bala's eyes widened. *Naseebo and I wouldn't be able to make that kind of money if we worked day and night for a hundred years.*

"And that's not all," Lala Dabir continued, the corners of his mouth turning up a smidge at Bala's reaction. "You and your wife will live in a furnished house in a nice suburb of Karachi. Believe me, it'll be a world of difference from your shack in that God-forsaken *katchi abadis.* You can pick out furniture and decorations yourself. And all your expenses—rent, gas, water, electricity—will be handled by the organization."

Bala's head spun in an effort to convince himself that his companion was an honest and trustworthy man who meant no harm.

From the moment he joined the organization, Dabir said Goha would receive two hundred and fifty thousand rupees a month. "As I'm sure you know, that's about ten times what most day laborers make. He'll also get a stipend to visit you every three months."

"Visit us? Where will he be going?"

"I told you, north of Peshawar. Aren't you listening? Gohar will be stationed in remote places where he'll carry out secret missions to further the cause of our organization."

Bala's brow creased. "My wife Naseebo won't be happy if our son leaves us. I need to talk to her—"

"Wife?" Dabir sneered. "No. No, no, never. We never involve women in our work. Don't you know what our religion says about women? It says they have feeble minds, bad memories, and can't be trusted!" Lala Dabir frowned and shook his head.

Bala was perplexed. *Who is this guy? Doesn't he have a mother, sister, daughter, or wife?* Some of Bala's coworkers had talked that way about women before, and it always perturbed him how they used Islam to justify their superior male attitudes.

Bala considered mentioning a few strong, powerful well-known female figures in Islam—namely Mary, the mother of Jesus; Khadija, the wife of the holy prophet Muhammad; and Fatima, the daughter of Muhammad and Khadija. But he feared Dabir would get angry again and rescind the offer, and he might lose out on what was surely a once-in-a-lifetime opportunity. At the very least, though, he needed reassurance that Goha's life wouldn't be in peril.

"These secret missions sound risky." Bala's body was rigid as he anticipated Lala Dabir's reaction. "My son is very dear to me, and I don't want him involved in dangerous activities."

"*Kiya baikar baat kar rahay ho?*" What kind of crazy talk are you spewing? Dabir growled. "Is there any guarantee you or I won't be overrun by a truck and crushed like a stray dog when we cross the street after we leave this place? What kind of Muslim are you? Do you have any idea what our religion says about life and death?"

Dabir clenched his fist on the arm of the bench, his knuckles turning white. "Nobody knows where or how they will die. It's already written and can't be changed. It's known only to the almighty Allah!"

The next moment, his posture relaxed, and his voice became level, almost cordial. "Bala, I assure you that everyone who follows the rules of the organization will be just fine. You and your family can avoid trouble if you do what I say."

"All right then." Bala nodded slowly. "What do I need to do?"

"*Abhee kuch naheen.*" Nothing right now. He instructed Bala to meet him next Friday by the thicket of trees on the left of *Kati Pahari*, a bypass through the hill that had been cut in two to make room for the highway near Qasba.

"Dabir *sahib*, I've lived in this area for a long time. I know the neighborhood well." Bala laughed. "You don't have to tell me where *Kati Pahari* is."

Lala Dabir pursed his lips and gave Bala a hard look. "None of this is a laughing matter. Our assignments are top secret. Everything I tell you is strictly confidential. If you and your son take this lightly and make wrong moves, you'll regret it—and you'll miss out on the chance to relieve your financial burdens and make your life easier."

The number on the paper flashed through Bala's mind, and he felt his face get warm. "Sorry, Dabir *sahib*. I understand. You can trust me and Goha. We won't betray you."

"Good. Remember this conversation is also under wraps." He ordered Bala to tell Naseebo that Goha was offered a job as an office manager trainee in a multinational corporation based in Peshawar. "If she asks for more information, just say you don't know anything else. I'll talk to Gohar myself when the time is right."

"Okay."

"Then it's settled. Let's leave here separately. I'll go now and you can follow in a few minutes. See you on Friday."

Dabir's frame vanished into the dense, noisy sea of people outside the restaurant. Bala waited for a few minutes, then got up, exited, and crossed the road. With the back of his hand, he wiped the sweat from his forehead. As the rich smell of cardamom, cloves, and other spices lingered in his nostrils, combined with the pungent smell of petrol from the mélange of motor vehicles, he only then registered that Lala Dabir hadn't bought him breakfast as he had promised.

CHAPTER 2

The uneasiness Bala felt from meeting Lala Dabir was like someone had turned him upside down, and now the pieces were in all the wrong places. He fretted over lying to Naseebo; from the beginning of their relationship, he had been honest with her, and he was confident she was equally forthcoming with him. However, with Dabir's strict warnings reverberating through his mind, he decided to keep his commitment to the strange man. Dabir's unpredictable mood swings were like puffs of wind aimlessly tossing around garbage from one place to the next. At the same time, Bala was exhilarated at the prospect of securing a more comfortable life for his family, and the last thing he wanted was to sabotage it. On the express bus home, he constructed a plausible explanation for the man's visit that his smart, perceptive wife would believe.

Naseebo was crouched by the door, sweeping dust out of the house with a *jharu* she ordinarily used for cleaning other people's houses. When Bala approached, she stood and bombarded him with an onslaught of questions. Where was the man from? Did someone send him? What business did he have with them? Had he approached other houses in Qasba? Why did he come knocking so early? And why was he so discourteous and abrupt?

Bala shrugged. He told Naseebo that the time he spent with the man turned out to be a waste, just as he had suspected. He said the man claimed to be a land developer, but Bala soon discovered he was a total fraud.

"He said he wanted to buy our house, but his offer was way below fair market price." Bala focused on a flock of birds that had gathered around a pile of garbage nearby. "I know our shack isn't worth much, but he was clearly trying to swindle me. I rejected his offer, and then he tried to lure me into buying an undeveloped plot several miles north of Qasba."

The land was in a godforsaken place with no paved roads, Bala said. Getting there required plodding through rocks, boulders, and overgrown vegetation. There was no running water, electricity, or gas, and the closest paved road and bus stop were at least half a mile away.

"He told me a special government grant will pay for developing the area, and when the work is done, the land will be worth its weight in gold."

"How do you know he isn't telling the truth?" As Naseebo tucked a wisp of hair behind her ear and adjusted her *dupatta* over her chest, her eyes shone. For as long as she had been a domestic helper, she had dreamed about living a comfortable, carefree lifestyle like the madams of the houses in Clifton and Defence Housing Authority where she worked. On several occasions while dusting dressers in the master bedrooms, she had been tempted to pocket a solid gold chain or ring. One time, she had even squeezed her hand into unnatural contortions to pry a thick gold bangle onto her wrist when the family was downstairs eating lunch in their ornate dining room.

She had overheard them talking about the Pakistani government and its foreign policies, discussions she automatically and subconsciously tuned out because they were too confusing and intellectual. She had opened the madam's deep red velvet jewelry box and taken the piece out, her heart pulsing through her *kameez* as she determinedly pushed it over the thickest part of her hand, the hard, shiny metal pressing against her dark skin. The bracelet had been stenciled with intricate designs, and she couldn't stop staring at it. She loved how it made her feel like she had been born into a life of privilege and affluence.

But she didn't have the guts to take it, mostly out of fear. She only had the bangle on for a few seconds before hastily stepping into the master bathroom and quickly lathering her hands with soap to make it easier to slide off. A couple of female servants she knew had lost their livelihoods after they became known for stealing, and some had forfeited even more. One woman's spouse left her after she got caught with stolen items in her home. The husband refused to have his honor tarnished by being associated with a *chor*, thief, and a disgraced female one from a lower class at that.

Naseebo had spoiled her reputation once before, and she vowed it would never happen again. *Never again, especially at the risk of losing Bala and Goha.* Being a house servant wasn't a mentally stimulating or exciting job, but she could spend her days among classy, educated people in comfortable environments while her son was in school. The madams readily exchanged information about their servants, and she dreaded that a soiled name would force her into a seedier working condition like a factory, where many women she knew regularly complained about sexual harassment and abuse.

"Naseebo," Bala said in an uncharacteristically sharp tone, "what has happened to you? You're usually the cautious one. Trust me, the guy's a con man. Let's forget about him."

He went inside and turned on the sink in the courtyard, waiting for the pale brown water that spurted out to run clear and hoping that changing the subject wouldn't raise alarms with the woman he held dear, the mother of his child who knew him so well. "On a positive note, I have good news for you, *rani*," he said, wiping water off his face and hands with a thin, fraying towel. "Goha told me he was offered a job as an office manager trainee at an international company in Peshawar."

Naseebo's face brightened. She had seen her clients' *bachay*, children—many around Goha's age—pack their bags and leave for faraway, exotic lands to study or work. From everything she heard, those places were like heaven compared to her world. Most of the time, the kids didn't come back to live in Karachi. They stayed abroad, far away from their parents, grandparents, and extended family, and only visited about once a year. They spoke proudly of living abroad, describing how modern, clean, and organized things were, and they didn't hesitate to openly and confidently criticize their own country and culture. She envied those families and longed for her prized Goha to escape the destitute conditions he had grown up in.

"Who offered him the job? I'm so proud of our *baita*. He's such a smart boy. Maybe his name will become his destiny after all." Even before she had met Bala and gotten pregnant, Naseebo was determined that if she had a boy, she would name him *Gohar*, gemstone, so that it might miraculously change her fate and bring her future family wealth and good fortune. Now a tear formed in Naseebo's eye, and when she dabbed it with the corner of her *dupatta*, it started as a small dark spot and spread outward into a jagged blotch. "Where is Peshawar?"

"It's far, Naseebo. Up north, on the other side of Pakistan. I don't know how he got the job. But *subhanallah*, at least he'll be in Pakistan and not traveling across the world like so many young people from rich families these days."

The following Friday afternoon, Bala went to the neighborhood *masjid*, mosque, for *jummah namaz*, the afternoon Friday prayers required for all Muslim males. As he knelt in *sajda*, prostration, with his forehead pressed to the prayer mat, an avalanche of emotions—fear, apprehension, excitement, dread, relief, uncertainty, and exhilaration—swept over him. He bowed for a long time, praying earnestly for God to help him make the right decisions, for Lala Dabir to be a man of integrity, and for his treasured Goha to stay safe. His beloved parents had passed away a few years ago in a fire at the cardboard factory where they worked, and his estranged only sibling, his younger brother, had stopped talking to him when Bala inherited most of their parents' few belongings. He wished he had a confidant with whom he could share an honest account of his encounter with Dabir.

While he prayed, an image of Goha hunched over applications for government college scholarships, working earnestly in dim lighting in the squalid conditions of his room, appeared in his mind. His son badly wanted to go to college and land a respectable clerical job in a clean and safe working environment that would help their family financially. However, his dream vanished when he learned most endowments had been usurped by influential families with no conscience or misgivings about bribing corrupt politicians who allotted them.

Now, as Bala waited at the thicket of the trees near the *Kati Pahari*, he surveyed the area cautiously. Lala Dabir ambled toward him from the opposite direction. A woolen cap had replaced his *topee*, and he appeared older and unkempt. After each step he leaned into a tan wooden cane, and a woven canvas bag was slung carelessly over his shoulder. Bala hardly recognized him when he gestured to follow him into a restaurant.

The dining room was playing high-pitched popular Bollywood and Lollywood movie songs. The music was grating, and Bala pressed his hands to his ears as a greeter led them to a remote corner of the large dining room. A few minutes later, a waiter approached their table with two menus and a metallic jug covered in condensed droplets. Without picking up the menu, Dabir immediately placed an order for large servings of beef *korma*, chicken *biryani*, and kebabs. Bala had never ordered those sorts of dishes from a restaurant—he rarely ate out, except occasionally from street vendors when he worked long hours and Naseebo didn't pack him enough food to satisfy his appetite. He wasn't used to eating so much meat, especially not all at once, and ordering it from an outside venue always felt far too extravagant for his scant earnings. As he smelled the braised spices from the kitchen, he salivated.

Dabir took a sip of water. "*Meray dost.*" My friend. He placed his hands on Bala's. His tone was gentle and more conciliatory than during their previous encounter. "Before we go further, let me apologize for forgetting to buy you breakfast the other day. We were so busy talking it slipped my mind. As a gesture of goodwill, I want to compensate you for the time you've spent with me so far."

He scanned the restaurant, pulled out a large brown wallet from his *kameez* pocket, and handed Bala a stack of bills.

Bala's heartbeat quickened. The money consisted of Pakistan's largest currency—1,000- and 5,000-rupee notes.

"It's two hundred and fifty thousand rupees, or roughly one thousand U.S. dollars," Dabir said.

Bala's hand trembled as he took the cash. He pretended to be composed, but his insides had turned to jelly. He had never seen so much money, let alone possessed it. He couldn't even fathom how he would spend it and what he'd be able to buy. He skittishly shoved the bills into his *kameez* pocket.

When the food arrived, Bala piled spoonfuls of the fragrant *biryani* and meat dishes onto his plate and started shoveling them into his mouth. The spices hit his tongue like fireworks going off in all directions, and he nervously grabbed his glass of water to stifle their intensity. *Please, Allah, don't let Dabir have second thoughts and demand the money back.* When the heat in his mouth subsided, he leaned back with a fullness he'd never experienced before and decided he would use the funds to treat himself to more expensive meals and an extended reprieve from his back-breaking manual work.

Dabir wiped his hands on his napkin and reached into his bag. "This is for you." He handed Bala a black flip phone. The device was for him or Naseebo to answer calls from Dabir or a person approved by him; they weren't allowed to make outgoing calls without Dabir's approval. Given Dabir's derogatory earlier comments about women, Bala was a little surprised that Naseebo had been given access to the phone, but he didn't dare mention it and risk having the privilege withdrawn from his wife.

Glowering, Dabir pulled in, his face only a couple inches away from Bala's, his voice low and menacing. "The ringtone is disabled, and this phone will only vibrate. Make sure you answer calls discreetly. The vibrate setting is fixed and can't be changed."

Bala's eyes enlarged and he nodded dutifully. *I wouldn't know how to change the setting even if I wanted to.*

"Also, this phone's being tracked. If it's lost or misplaced, or if you give it to someone else, I will know. The account will be canceled, and your chance for a better future will disappear. Keep the phone with you at all times and protect it like it's made of gold and studded with rubies. Is that clear?"

Bala gulped. "Yes, sir. I understand everything you said. I guarantee I will follow the rules." Bala had never owned a cell phone but occasionally borrowed them from his friends or supervisors, and he marveled at how they connected people together without wires or plug-ins. He was entering another world whose doors, until now, had been slammed shut and bolted. He put the phone in his left breast pocket and held his right hand over it protectively.

"One last thing." Lala Dabir's eyes were slits, and he leaned in even closer. "You have a lot of money on you. If you try to run away with it, the organization will hunt you down. When we find you, you'll regret it. But if you're honest with me and I see I can trust you, many more good things will come your way."

Bala nodded and smiled faintly as Dabir pulled back.

Dabir told Bala to bring Goha along the next time they met. They agreed to reconvene three days later, after *maghrib namaz*, on the sidewalk at Lasbela Bridge. "Use scarves to cover your faces so nobody recognizes you. People are doing that to avoid pollution these days, so you'll blend right in and won't look suspicious."

CHAPTER 3

Lasbela Bridge and the surrounding streets were constantly overflowing with traffic, people, and rubbish. Bikes, cars, buses, auto-rickshaws, trucks, and pedestrians thronged together, a jumble of chaotic movement and activity in every possible direction. Unless people stopped in their tracks and looked closely, they wouldn't recognize even the most familiar faces.

That evening, soon after the *muezzins* called the *adhan* from the minarets of nearby mosques, Lala Dabir rested against the fence on the bridge above the squeaking, growling, grinding, and honking vehicles crammed onto the street below. He waved discreetly when Bala and Goha approached from the opposite direction and signaled them to follow him. Through the throngs of passersby, Bala and Goha held hands tightly as they pushed and maneuvered their way to Nishtar Road, where Dabir led the way into a roadside café.

Dabir appeared similar to the first time Bala saw him, well-groomed and tidy. He wore a smoky gray *shalwar kameez* and sandals, and he greeted Bala and Goha warmly before placing an order for several pricy meat-based items. He raised his voice to be heard above the drone of people and traffic, reiterating to Goha the same information he had given to Bala.

"*Baita, meri baat ghor se suno.*" Son, please listen to me carefully, he said gently, placing his hand on Goha's shoulder.

Goha flinched from the unexpected gesture.

"There's strict secrecy involved with our organization and work. It's so confidential it needs to stay between the three of us for now—you can't even tell your mother. I know that'll be hard for you. Pakistani boys adore their mothers." He smiled knowingly at Goha, who shifted uncomfortably.

"That's a good boy. So tell me, have you ever traveled by train?"

"Yes, sir." Goha straightened and rested his arms on the table. "I went to Hyderabad once with my class to participate in a high school debate competition. I was captain of the club, and I coached younger kids on how to effectively argue their position. We came in first place."

"That's great. You didn't travel first class, though, did you?"

"No, Dabir *sahib*. We didn't think we'd be able to go. But at the last minute, the government and a couple of NGOs paid for the trip. We rode economy, not first class. But it was still a great experience."

"I'm sure it was. Next week, you will travel to Peshawar on the Rehman Baba Express. It's a long ride from Karachi, so we're giving you a first-class ticket plus money for expenses to make your trip more comfortable. Believe me, most of the boys we recruit don't get anywhere near that kind of treatment."

Dabir pulled a ticket and an envelope out of his *kameez* pocket and handed them to Goha.

When Goha peered inside the envelope, his eyes bulged at the stack of 1,000- and 5,000-rupee notes.

At Goha's expression, Dabir's lips formed the brink of a smile.

Dabir said a young man named Babrek Azam would meet him on the city station platform. Babrek had greenish-brown eyes and would be dressed in a black *shalwar kameez*, a dark green vest, and a brown Chitrali cap.

Goha glanced anxiously at his father. "Dabir *sahib*, I appreciate your trust in me. But before I accept your proposal, can you please tell me what type of work I'll be doing?" His debate club experiences and constant encouragement from his parents had given Goha the confidence to ask hard questions and speak up for himself, even with strangers or acquaintances.

"I already told your father you'll be working for a welfare organization that will make our country better in every possible way. Aren't you interested in doing noble work?" Dabir abruptly placed the napkin from his lap onto the table. "You'll get more information from Babrek when you arrive in Peshawar. Also, in case I wasn't clear earlier, if anyone—including your mother—asks what you're doing, your answer is you're working for an international company as an office manager trainee. Okay?"

Goha hesitated. "*Jee*, Dabir *sahib*." Yes, Dabir, sir.

Lala Dabir stood hurriedly and slapped a few bills on the table. "I need to go now." Then he walked briskly out of the restaurant and disappeared into the hordes of people, vehicles, and smog.

Amid the mayhem on the street, Bala somehow managed to wave down a rusty, three-wheeled, doorless auto-rickshaw painted in lime green with swirly orange patterns. It pulled over and halted close to them, black smoke sputtering from its tailpipe. A poetic Urdu couplet was painted in white above the taillights. Poetry verses were common on Karachi's public vehicles; they could be funny, lighthearted, ridiculous, outrageous, or just as often, dark, poignant, or serious. To Bala, they were a creative, albeit inconsequential, way for people like him to amplify their presence in a status-conscious society where lower classes were rendered invisible. The words on this particular rickshaw gave him pause; it was like a sage had posted them down from the heavens as a timely message intended solely for his eyes: *Mohabbet na kar ameeron say jo barbad kartay hain; mohabbit kar ghareebon say jo hameesha yaad kartay hain.* Do not love the rich who only ruin you; love the poor who always remember you.

"Don't worry, son," said Bala as he shifted to make room for Goha on the hard seat behind the driver. He shouted to be heard over the vehicles of every possible size and shape whizzing by at breakneck speeds. "I'm sure everything will be fine. *Inshallah*, you'll have a chance to make a name for yourself in the organization. And if the work isn't right for you, you can always come home. You know your *ammi* and I will always be waiting for you." He patted Goha's thigh.

As the rickshaw jerked forward in stops and starts through the congestion, Bala turned his head toward the street. He knew he was trying to justify his decision to himself as well as his son. After all of Dabir's warnings, Bala wasn't convinced Goha would be able to easily pick up and leave, even if—God forbid—he was in a dire situation. It sounded like Goha was going to be staying in isolated areas hundreds of miles away from Karachi, without his own transport or means to communicate regularly.

But Bala reassured himself that a short-term stint, even a risky one, would ensure his family—himself, Naseebo, Goha, and hopefully soon a new *bahu*, daughter-in-law, and *potay*, grandchildren—lived comfortably in the long-term. He could envision himself and Naseebo playing with their grandkids in a house that was abundantly safer, cleaner, and more peaceful than the slums of Qasba. His obliging and respectful *bahu* would make him chai and serve him homemade samosas and chaat as he sat with his feet up on the veranda, watching TV. As he fantasized about living the kind of life he had only dreamed about until then, he marveled at his good luck that Lala Dabir had come knocking on his door that fateful morning. *Alhamdulillah*. Praise be to God.

As Bala anticipated, Naseebo was anxious about sending Goha away for an unspecified time and equally nervous when she found out about the twenty-eight-hour journey to Peshawar. Her brow wrinkled when she carried out mundane tasks, and she tossed about restlessly at night, muttering incoherently in her sleep. Her worry intensified when she learned that bandits and robbers routinely attacked passengers, and poor maintenance and negligent workers had resulted in several train derailments.

However, the day before Goha left, Bala saw his *biwi*, wife, trying to be brave and cheerful for her son's sake. She put on a flowery pink *shalwar kameez* and a little makeup that she had, as usual, bartered for a few hundred rupees with a local vendor in the *katchi abadis*.

"*Inshallah*, everything will go well, and the work you do up north will bring honor and prosperity to our family," she said to Goha as she crouched on the ground, scrubbing his socks and underwear in a scratched-up red bucket in the courtyard. The water had turned a dull brown, and it sloshed around in the pail with the sad, floating garments spilling out the sides. Her voice quivered.

"Goha, my *baita*. You are my world. Everything I do is for you. Don't forget about your *ammi*, okay? Please take good care of yourself. Your father and I will be so worried about you. We'll miss you so much. Stay happy and healthy. *Jeetay raho*." Stay blessed. Her sentences came out as staccatos, each one ending in a high, emotional lilt. Her tears finally broke through, smudging her eyeliner and creating splotchy black rims under her eyes.

Goha had to swallow several times before he could speak. "Don't worry, *ammi jaan*. I'll be fine. *Inshallah*, I'll be back soon." He put down the shirt he was hanging on the clothesline, walked over to Naseebo, and draped his arm around her shoulder.

Goha's kindhearted old *madrasa* teacher and imam of the local *masjid*, Sheikh Samir, was a tiny, saintly man who had taught him off and on throughout his childhood. The sheikh stooped when he walked and had gnarled hands and crooked yellow teeth that frequently, and without apparent reason, transformed into an infectious, enrapturing smile. Unlike Goha's other *madrasa* teachers, he had insisted on translating his Arabic lessons into Urdu so his students could grasp the meaning behind divine teachings and learnings.

At that moment, one of his profound lessons floated through Goha's head: *Prophet Muhammad said heaven lies beneath the feet of their mothers*. Goha heard the sheikh's voice as if he were right there in the courtyard, and as he hugged his *ammi*, he wanted nothing more than to give her a better and easier life. Her fleshy body surrendered to his lean, muscular frame, and he told himself he would do everything in his power to make that happen.

Despite being exhilarated about his upcoming adventure, his eyes welled at the thought of leaving his parents and friends in

Qasba and saying goodbye to the gigantic, no-nonsense, gritty metropolis that was the only home he'd ever known. As he let go of Naseebo, he vowed never to forget the smell of blooming flowers, herbs, spices, and bark from the *attar*, perfumed oil, she had applied in her son's honor.

The next day, Bala, Naseebo, and Goha stood solemnly on the platform waiting for the train. Naseebo's eyes were bloodshot, and she kept pulling forth the edge of her *dupatta* to wipe trickles from her eyes and nose. She was quiet and downcast save for her frequent sniffles, and as she held Goha's hand, she made him promise, over and over again, to be in contact with them as often as he could.

That morning Goha had washed up extra well with a special lavender-scented soap he had bought in the market. He gingerly put on the new navy *shalwar kameez* that Bala had ceremoniously presented to him the day before, taking great care not to soil it. It was made of one hundred percent soft king cotton and had a designer label with cursive writing stitched on the back collar. From how it caressed his skin with even Goha's slightest movement, it was undoubtedly far better quality than any of his other *shalwar kameezes*. He could imagine this was the type of clothing worn by legendary Mughal emperors he had learned about in school, who had ruled over the Indian subcontinent for hundreds of years.

"How could you afford this, *abba*?" Goha had asked his father. But Bala simply told him to wear it in good health as he embarked on his trip up north. Goha figured Lala Dabir must have been responsible; he had never known his parents to buy such expensive garments. Granted, some of his clothes were exceptionally nice for people of lower, working-class status, but they were almost never new. For as long as he could remember, he had relied on hand-me-downs—everyday outfits, shoes, socks, and even underwear—that his mother accepted from owners of the houses she cleaned.

The low whistle of the train sounded in the distance, and minutes later, the winding green-and-yellow locomotive pulled into the station. Goha hesitatingly waved to his parents one final time, then climbed the platform steps. As he hoisted his bag onto the overhead rack, he resolved to dry his tears and replace his sadness and dread with excitement and wonder at his upcoming adventures.

As Goha wandered through the aisle searching for his seat, the air-conditioning ran full blast, and the car was uncluttered and clean. Unlike the economy section he had traveled in before—where the air was profuse with bodily smells and masalas, where it wasn't uncommon to hear scruffy people engage in crude, loud, or brash discourse—there were few passengers in first class. These travelers were well-dressed and smelled fresh, and they mostly kept their gazes out the window or their noses buried in a book. The chairs were plush and well-padded, and when Goha found his spot, there was enough room for him to stretch out his legs comfortably and recline all the way back.

This is incredible. I could get used to a lifestyle like this. The whistle blew, the train jerked forward, and he pulled a glossy U.K.-based fashion magazine out of the pocket in front of him. Moments later, his attention waned as a pang of hunger coursed through his belly.

As the train accelerated, Goha walked unsteadily through several passenger cars, grabbing the handrails for support. As he approached the dining car, glasses and silverware clinked amid amicable chatting. Selecting a chicken tandoori sandwich, masala fries, and a Coke, he reached into his *kameez* pocket, pulled out his wallet, plucked a few bills from the wad Lala Dabir had given him, and picked up his tray. Most tables were occupied, but a slender man in his early twenties caught his eye. He was wearing slim-cut Levi's jeans and a trendy, fitted red T-shirt with a Coca-Cola logo, and he was sitting by himself at a table for two.

"Care to join me?" he asked.

"Sure, thanks," Goha replied, pulling out a chair. "I didn't really want to eat while standing on a fast-moving train."

"I don't blame you."

"Look, we have something in common. You're wearing Coke and I'm drinking it." Goha pointed to the logo on the man's shirt.

The man laughed, dimples forming on the sides of his mouth. "Where are you headed?"

"Peshawar." Goha took a big bite of his sandwich and gestured for the man to help himself to fries.

The man picked one off the plate, looking pleased at Goha's generosity. "That's great, *yaar*. I'm going to Multan. My family has a business there, and I'm going to help them out." His eyes lingered on Goha's. "Why don't you plan to stay in Multan for a little vacation? This train stops there before it goes on to Peshawar. It won't cost you anything extra, and I'd love to show you around. The Sufi tombs are architectural marvels, and hearing *qawwalis* echoing off the walls of the shrines is super cool."

Goha had heard Multan was full of interesting Sufi history. But he was a little bewildered by his lunch companion's overt friendliness. "Thanks for the offer, but I'll pass. There's someone waiting for me in Peshawar."

"Oh, I see," the man replied. "Do you have a girlfriend there?"

"No, I don't, and I'm not looking for one. I am going to Peshawar for work," Goha responded dryly.

"Are you looking for a boyfriend? I could show you a good time." The man winked and reached over to touch Goha's hand.

"No, I'm not." Goha yanked his hand away. "I think I need to leave now. Excuse me."

Goha rose swiftly, leaving his half-eaten lunch on the table. He quickly crossed through several cars, his hands shaking as he pried open the latches and nervously pushed through the doors.

He finally sank into his chair and reclined, gazing out the window. *Maybe I should have given that guy the benefit of the doubt. Maybe I misunderstood him.*

As he dozed on and off for the next few hours, the man in the Coca-Cola T-shirt kept reappearing. In one dream, the man sat beside Goha on the train and put his arm around him. In another, they were hanging out together and chatting congenially at a seaside restaurant shack in Karachi. In the last dream, Goha had taken him up on his offer to go to Multan, and the man introduced him to a group of friends. They all traveled in a rickshaw to a beach far away, and the rocky ride and darkness left Goha dizzy and disoriented. He couldn't see anyone or anything, and all he could hear was the deafening sound of waves crashing relentlessly against the shore.

Goha woke up from the last dream with a start and jerked his head around, half expecting the man to be hovering over him, his dimples scarily recessed like a maniacal demon in a horror movie, laughing at his naivety and gullibility. But there was no one there except the same passengers from the beginning.

Roughly twenty-seven hours and twenty-six stops later, when the train finally reached the Peshawar station, Goha stood up cautiously, still nervous about a second encounter with the man in the Coca-Cola shirt. He had heard about unsuspecting young people being abducted by gangs and only released to their families if they were able to hand over ridiculously enormous ransoms, and he knew his parents would never be able to rescue him if that happened. *I'd better keep my eyes wide open from now on.*

As Goha stepped off the platform with his luggage, a cool, dry wind hit his face, one that was markedly different from Karachi's sticky, steamy air. A tall, handsome young man with shaggy hair and wide-set hazel eyes stood at a distance, his outfit exactly as Lala Dabir had described—a Chitrali cap, black *shalwar kameez*, and green vest. The man's eyes were slightly glazed over, and in his right cheek was a small, engorged lump.

"*Assalam-o-alaikum. Aap Goha hain?*" Peace be upon you. Are you Goha?

"*Jee. Wa 'alaykumu s-salam.*" Yes, peace be upon you too.

"*Mein ne aap ke baray mein bohat kuch suna hai.*" I've heard a lot about you. His Urdu was flawless, yet slightly accented, like Lala Dabir's. "It's nice to meet you. I'm Babrek." He wrapped his arms around Goha and gave him a kiss on the cheek.

Goha recoiled at the rich, woody smell of tobacco. While he was grateful for the warm welcome, Goha was simultaneously, once again, confused by the visible affection from a total stranger. *What's up with the guys around here?*

Babrek spit his chewing tobacco off to the side and grabbed Goha's bag. He walked over to an outdoor tea stall, gesturing with a flick of his head at Goha to follow. He put the bag down, pulled a wad of rupees out of his *kameez* pocket, and handed them to the chai *wallah*. "A cup of *kahwa* and two samosas."

Babrek put his arm around Goha's shoulder. "It's a long way from Karachi to Peshawar. You must be hungry. And exhausted."

Goha stiffened at Babrek's touch, and after the lengthy train ride, he didn't think he could stomach anything at all, let alone spicy, rich food and a hot drink. But he changed his mind when the vendor held out fresh, flaky triangular pastries and a steaming cup of tea emitting scents of saffron, cinnamon, and cardamom. He heard his mother telling him the importance of being respectful and *tameez-daar*, well-behaved, in particular toward people he had just met and was trying to impress. Sheikh Samir, too, frequently quoted a *hadith* about manners: *The Prophet Muhammad said the best among you are those who have the best manners and character.* So he politely accepted the snacks.

Babrek seemed to read his mind. "Here in Khyber-Pakhtunkhwa, it's our tradition to offer our guests refreshments after a hard journey."

"The trip was long, but it wasn't hard," Goha replied. "It was actually really comfortable. I sat in a first-class air-conditioned car with a reclining seat. I've never experienced anything like it."

"Oh, that's great." Babrek laughed. "I heard you graduated high school at the top of your class, plus you've come a long way to join us. Maybe that's why our leadership is giving you VIP treatment. Most people we draft aren't pampered like that."

Babrek pointed to a remote corner of the parking lot, where a mustached man with a dour expression stood beside a black Toyota SUV. "That's our car, and he's our driver."

As they strode toward the vehicle, an unfamiliar sensation washed over Goha. In Qasba, he had never once been on the passenger end of a driver-passenger relationship—his people were always the ones driving and serving others. It was like someone had flipped a switch and rotated his life 180 degrees to the other side.

As they got closer, Goha slowed his pace. A handgun was strapped around the driver's waist. "Why does he need a gun?" he asked Babrek when the driver was still out of earshot.

Babrek shrugged. "Everyone carries one around here."

He handed the driver Goha's bag and opened the back door for Goha to slide in, then sat himself down in the front passenger seat. When they reached the congested, winding streets of the old city, Babrek pointed out their accommodations near the historic Qissa Khawani Bazaar, a Western-style midrise that seemed at odds with the traditional clothing and customs of the region.

At the hotel, the driver took Goha's bag out of the trunk and gave it to an overly eager young porter while Babrek escorted Goha into the lobby. When Babrek approached the clerk at the front desk, he seamlessly switched from Urdu to the regional language, Pashto. Goha stood a few feet behind them, oblivious of their exchange. Babrek addressed the hotel employee with clear authority, and Goha could sense from body language that he was going out of his way to please Babrek. Then Babrek reached into his pocket and maneuvered a sleight of hand, and Goha's pulse quickened. He guessed some shady transactions were underway, and he desperately wished he understood Pashto so he was more clued in to what was going on.

When they reached the room, Babrek took his time peering into the corners and opening all the drawers and closets. "It smells kind of musty in here," he said. "This hotel is usually up to par, but once in a while, they fall short. Anyway, if you see anything that's missing or needs attention, let me know. I'll make sure they take care of it right away."

"It seems totally fine to me." It was a basic hotel room but luxurious compared to his family's residence in the *katchi abadis*, a shack constructed of mismatched bricks, mud, wood planks, and tin sheets beaten out of large oil canisters, with a thatched straw roof that leaked during heavy rains.

Babrek sat on the bed, casually slung his ankle over his knee, and picked up the phone to order room service. He put down the receiver. "I have to attend an important meeting across town this evening. I'm sorry you'll be eating on your own your first night, but I think you'll like the food. I'll be back tomorrow morning. Good night, Goha. *Shab-bakhair.*"

Babrek got up swiftly and kissed him again, this time on the lips.

CHAPTER 4

That evening, Goha became increasingly uncomfortable with Babrek's sexual advances. He paced the hotel room thinking about a BBC documentary, *Pakistan's Hidden Shame*, that he had watched at his friend Ali's house a few weeks before he left for Peshawar. He told Ali about it after he heard rumors at *madrasa* about sketchy, so-called religious teachers who sexually abused their students, and Ali had managed to promptly secure a pirated copy from a contact who regularly dealt in the black market. As troubling as the gossip was, Goha wanted to know what was going on beyond his world; hiding from it wouldn't make it go away. *The pursuit of knowledge is a duty upon every Muslim*, Sheikh Samir repeatedly said.

The documentary turned out to be depressing and disheartening. It revealed how men, mostly long-distance bus and truck drivers, shamelessly took advantage of unwilling boys, most of whom were abjectly poor, some even homeless. It showed how sexual abuse was pervasive throughout Pakistan and most prevalent in northern areas. At overnight truck stands along highways, a few hundred rupees could buy abusers a night with a boy as young as eight or nine. The video revealed how predators used the boys as cheap sexual commodities and easy means of sexual gratification. To attract customers, most boys had been trained to perform seductively by sleazy, flesh-peddling pimps.

Plenty of boys throughout Goha's childhood came from extremely impoverished conditions and didn't have anywhere near the same kind of love and support from their parents as he did. The boys from those families were worse off in practically every way. He shuddered at the thought of people he knew falling prey to such predators.

The documentary upsettingly concluded that politicians and authorities had plainly and simply failed to control the country's rampant child prostitution. He couldn't begin to comprehend how or why the sex offenders remained beyond reproach, and the more he pondered the film's takeaways and his own experiences since arriving in Peshawar, the more upset he became.

Goha lay in his bed for a long time, restless and agitated. *Should I try to escape? Lala Dabir didn't sound like he was bluffing with his strict warnings. If I try to leave, I could end up in a worse position than I'm in now. Or put my ammi and abba in grave danger.*

Emotionally exhausted and frustrated, he finally fell asleep.

Goha woke up early the next morning and jumped into the shower first thing, vigorously scrubbing his body with a small bar of hotel soap until he was covered with thick, foamy streaks. He wanted urgently to cleanse himself from the *napaki*, impurity, of Babrek, but as he stood under the showerhead and the cool water eventually rinsed off all the white residue, he couldn't help but think there was likely more to come.

The phone in Goha's room rang exactly at nine. It was Babrek.

"Goha, *salams.* I'm waiting for you in the lobby."

"*Salams*, Babrek. I'm getting dressed. I'll be there in a minute."

Babrek inspected Goha up and down and let out a soft whistle as he approached him in the lobby. "I hope you had a good sleep," he said with a wink.

Goha's stomach plunged.

Since the driver wasn't feeling well, Babrek would drive them to the rooming house in the tribal area. "The accommodations there are simple but adequate," he said. "I've made arrangements for two."

On the way to the vehicle, a middle-aged man approached them from the opposite direction. He addressed Babrek in Pashto, then pointed directly at Goha. Goha didn't care for his suggestive expression. He frowned and scowled at the man.

"Pashtun men have a reputation for preferring men, and you're nice to look at," Babrek told him, keeping up his stride and casually waving the man off.

Oh. So that explains it. The man on the train, Babrek encroaching into my physical space, and now this salacious stranger. Goha slouched forward, put his head down, and pretended to be invisible until they reached the car.

Babrek's car was a souped-up model with smooth contours and digital components. Goha had occasionally ridden in the cars of his friends' parents, but those vehicles were generally old, scratched, and dented. Sometimes the windows were jammed shut, the upholstery was filthy and torn, or the air conditioner merely served to recycle the hot, dusty air of Karachi summers. Other times the spark plugs malfunctioned or the rackety engine made it impossible to talk without yelling. His parents never owned a car, and Goha had gotten used to riding his bicycle or piling onto a public bus with masses from the lower classes.

They drove on several highways surrounded by scenic mountainous vegetation, making small talk and stopping frequently for refreshments. Locals recognized and greeted Babrek at every stop. Every time they were about to leave, Babrek picked up a piece of *paan* for himself—a skillfully folded chewy bitter betel leaf filled with areca nuts, herbs, spices, and chewing tobacco—which he kept pocketed in his mouth until he spat it onto the ground at the next stop. Although *paan* was widely consumed in Pakistan and throughout the subcontinent as a stimulant and palate cleanser, Goha had never acquired a liking for it. The few times he'd tried it had made him want to gag.

When they arrived at a small town near the Indus River, just outside the bustling city of Mingora, Babrek parked the car in front of a brick building surrounded by towering oak and pine trees. Goha inhaled the sweet, sharp, woodsy scent; it was a refreshing change from the rank air pollution he'd been exposed to all his life in Karachi. At the entrance, a small sign in Urdu indicated the property was meant for tourists and visitors.

"You'll be staying here for at least the next few weeks, but you could be here for months," Babrek told him. "I'll mostly be staying here, too, to make sure you're comfortable and understand your duties."

They entered a small hallway, and Babrek stopped at the first door and took a key from his pocket. The room was sparse but adequately equipped with a small kitchen, breakfast table with four wooden chairs, full bathroom, queen-size bed, artificial leather recliner, upholstered sofa, TV, and two shelves lined with magazines and books. Like the hotel room in Peshawar, it was a world away from Goha's primitive residence in Qasba.

Babrek opened the closet door, revealing five *shalwar kameezes* in various neutral shades hanging on the rack. Three woven head caps and two pairs of leather Peshawari sandals were arranged neatly on a shelf beside two folded prayer rugs. "These are for you," Babrek said.

Also in the closet was a long, silver safe. The door was slightly ajar, and Babrek knelt to open it all the way. Inside the safe was a thirty-five-inch-long, shiny black Kalashnikov rifle and a large box of cartridges. Babrek carefully lifted the weapon out with both hands and set it on the table. Goha's eyes doubled in size.

"You may need this to carry out your duties. It's an AK-47. It probably looks intimidating now, but you'll get used to it in no time. Isn't it incredible?" He ran his hand over the smooth barrel. "This was made close to here, in my hometown of Darra Adam Khel. It's like the original Russian Kalashnikov, but believe me, the ones we make are better quality. I have one too."

Babrek extended his arm into the farthest reaches of the safe and retrieved a compact automatic Smith & Wesson–style handgun. "This one is for your everyday use," he explained. "Around here everyone carries a pistol for protection. Like I told you before, it's part of our culture up north and no big deal. You should take it with you whenever you leave the room. The cartridges are already loaded, so it's ready to go."

Goha stroked the rifle's cold metal trepidatiously. He picked up the gun and was surprised at how lightweight it was—Goha had never touched or even seen a firearm up close, let alone used one. *What will I need these for?* He was about to ask but stopped—he wasn't sure he wanted to know.

"I can see you're excited to try these out," Babrek said, examining his face and grinning. "Tell you what. Tomorrow morning, we'll go to the forest, and I'll show you how to use them."

Babrek pointed at the bulge in the side pocket of his *kameez*. "My handgun is right here. There are large, reinforced pockets in the clothing that's stitched in this part of the country, and now you know why." He put the guns back into the safe and closed the door.

"It's been a long day for you. Why don't you rest for a while, and I'll see you after *maghrib* prayers?" Babrek rose to leave and, to Goha's immense relief, did not turn around to kiss him.

Goha opened the window. In the distance stray dogs barked, cars honked, and motorbikes screeched. The discordant mixture of sounds made him yearn for the *katchi abadis*, his parents, friends, and the busy, bustling streets of Karachi.

When he peered outside, the scene was disconcerting. Men and young adolescent boys who appeared no older than ten or eleven were holding hands behind trees and along property fences. He caught glimpses of them stopping frequently to grope and kiss each other in the waning light. *Are these people Muslims? This doesn't feel like the Pakistan I know. What in the world is going on here?*

In Karachi, men walked in the streets or hung out in social gatherings with their arms locked together or wrapped around each other. But as far as he knew, that was as far as it went. Open demonstrations of affection between men and boys were common in Pakistan's segregated society, but he was confident he hadn't seen explicit homosexual behavior out in the open, and certainly not with kids who hadn't yet reached puberty.

He sat on the edge of the bed with his eyes closed and his hands cradling the sides of his head. He brooded over the BBC documentary, which many of his friends had dismissed as Western propaganda against Pakistan and Islam. It pained him to think the boys outside his window may have been coerced into sexual relationships.

The sun is setting, and it's almost time for maghrib prayers, but no one around here seems to know or care. In *madrasa*, Goha had studied Qur'anic verses about the dire outcomes that came from Prophet Lot's followers adopting a homosexual lifestyle. He stood up, surveyed the books on the shelf, and found exactly what he was looking for—the Holy Qur'an in Arabic with an Urdu translation. He leafed through the pages until he found the Lot story. Sheikh Samir had interpreted the scripture for his students, telling them how Prophet Lot continually warned his tribe to stop their promiscuity, but they refused to listen and made fun of Lot instead. As a result, the sheikh emphasized, they became the subject of God's wrath: A shower of rocks killed them and destroyed their towns.

From the onset, Goha had been taught to be a good Muslim, and he couldn't remember even one time he questioned the Holy Qur'an to be the word of God received by his messenger, the revered Prophet Muhammad. He knew other religions and belief systems existed, but he suspected their followers simply hadn't found their way to Islam yet.

Goha's head was light as he put the holy book back on the shelf. *How do I get myself out of here?* He deliberated over his predicament until his nerves popped out of his skull, but he couldn't work out a feasible way to leave, at least not for the time being. His father's words rang in his head: *Inshallah, you'll have a chance to make a name for yourself in the organization.* He heard his mother, too, saying how his work up north would bring honor and prosperity to their family. His parents would be utterly disappointed—worse than that, crushed—if he gave up on the lucrative opportunity before he even got started.

Goha shut the window tight. He unfolded a prayer rug and recited his *maghrib namaz*, praying earnestly for Allah's guidance, for the health and safety of his loved ones, and for the people of the town to find a moral path. Then, laden with apprehension, he crashed on the bed and closed his eyes.

Goha was drifting off to sleep when he heard the door latch click. It was well past 10:00 p.m.

The door creaked open, and an irksome light spilled into the room.

Goha jostled awake, squinting from the glare. When his eyes finally adjusted, Babrek emerged carrying an oversized duffel bag. His hazel eyes were glassy and unfocused, and the butt of a cigarette dangled from his lips. He removed it with his thumb and index finger, squished it, and tossed it carelessly onto the floor.

"What are you doing here so late, Babrek?"

"I'm staying here with you tonight." His words were slow and slurred.

"But . . . you told me there would be accommodations for two at this place."

"Yes, I told you that." Babrek flung his bag onto the floor. "But I never said we would have two separate rooms."

"But . . . there's only one bed here."

"Don't worry, *yaar*, this bed is big enough for both of us."

Babrek stripped off his clothes and threw them on the floor, unabashedly revealing his fully naked body. He sauntered over to the bed, took Goha's face in his hands, and brushed his lips against his cheeks. The stench of alcohol and cigarette smoke radiated from his every pore. Babrek jumped onto the bed, pinning Goha down by the shoulders, and kissed him on the mouth, hard.

"The moment I saw you, I wanted you," he murmured in Goha's ear. "Oh my God, *yaar*, you are so sexy."

Goha reeled back. Barbed wire entangled his throat, pinching and strangling the words desperately trying to get out.

Babrek reached down to fondle Goha's groin.

Oh my God. What the hell is he doing? Goha squirmed and cried out, struggling to push Babrek away. But he couldn't—he was a deer caught in a lion's den.

"Goha." Babrek ran his fingers through Goha's hair. "You are nineteen. You are definitely old enough for this sort of thing. I'm sure you know people younger than you who are doing it. So why can't the two of us have some fun?"

He pulled down Goha's *shalwar*. "It won't hurt. I knew I wanted you tonight, so I've already put on the very best English lubricant cream."

Then, without warning, he flipped Goha over and entered him from behind. Goha closed his eyes. The room blackened, and he nearly passed out. He started sobbing.

Babrek continued thrusting and stroking him. "One of these days, I'll let you do the same to me," he breathed. "You can dominate over me and show me how manly you are. I promise you'll enjoy it so much you'll never want to stop."

When Babrek finished, Goha mustered a minuscule bit of energy and attempted to break free. But Babrek pulled him back and cornered him.

"You have no idea how long I've hungered for a lover like you. The other recruits have been a far cry from you. So immature, uneducated, and unattractive. You're a *maharaja* compared to them. Come on, *yaar*, let's have another round."

Goha pressed his eyes shut as he was violated again. His world became a gigantic ball of nothingness.

When it was finally over, Goha rolled out of the bed—limp, tear-streaked, and ashamed. He crawled to the bathroom, gagged, and threw up in the toilet. Then he shut the door, locked it, and sat with his back against it, heaving. Blood smeared the floor, and only after a few minutes passed did he comprehend that it came from a far-reaching place inside him. He dragged himself to the shower and turned the knob all the way. The jet sprayed out forcefully, and he cared nothing about the ongoing water scarcity Pakistanis always complained about.

I hate Babrek. I hate it here. I want to go back to Karachi.

He scoured his body until his skin was red, finally registering the throbbing pain surging through his bottom.

When he cracked open the bathroom door, Babrek was fast asleep on the bed, still nude and snoring loudly.

Wincing from the pain, Goha limped to the closet and put on fresh clothes, then gingerly lay down on the recliner in the corner. He pulled a blanket over his body and head. *Could I have prevented this? Is this how sex is supposed to feel?*

Goha had never been sexually attracted to another man, and in the enveloped darkness, he longed for actresses and models he had seen in movies and on TV. Their luscious, full red lips. Their gleaming white teeth and perfect smiles. Their demure expressions. Their fleshy, curvy breasts and hips. Their slender fingers ending in long, seductive, brightly painted fingernails. The way they evocatively cocked their heads back to reveal graceful, sensual necks. Their voluminous hair cascading down their backs. Their delicate features that came together in countless, bewitching ways. He covered his face with his hands, lamenting—he had envisioned his first sexual experience to be starkly different.

There are guns in the closet.

Goha lay motionless, barely breathing. The blanket slipped off his head, and he focused on a shadow on the wall, his gaze intent and slightly demonic as he imagined what would happen if he shot Babrek in his sleep. Could he walk away without punishment? What consequences would he endure in this world and, just as importantly, in the hereafter? Anguished, he shook his head vigorously. *I couldn't live with myself if I took another human's life.* He probably wouldn't get away with it either, he reasoned, and even if he did, he might go to hell for murdering someone in cold blood, even if that person had abused and raped him.

He tried to focus on God and the holy Prophet Muhammad, recalling a story he had read in his childhood about an old woman in Mecca who disliked the prophet so much she threw rubbish on him every day as he passed by her house on his way to the mosque for prayers. He never complained and carried on his journey as if nothing had happened.

One day, the prophet passed by the house and no garbage landed on his head. He soon learned the woman was sick in bed, and instead of holding a grudge, the prophet visited her, set about cleaning her house, and made sure she had everything she needed to be comfortable. The woman, humbled and ashamed, never hurled trash on the prophet again.

Goha breathed deeply, each intake slow and long, but it was a futile, distressed attempt to attain peace and forgive Babrek. He managed a few hours of restless sleep, the lingering smoke from Babrek's cigarette swirling all night around him in a cloud of angst, anger, and guilt.

CHAPTER 5

The room was still black when Goha's eyes flitted open. He heard the shower running and shrouded his head with the blanket, cringing at the inevitability of facing Babrek. What words could he possibly utter after the unspeakable experience?

The bathroom door squeaked open, and footsteps entered the bedroom. Through small woven holes, he saw Babrek pull a prayer rug out of the closet. He laid it beside the bed and quietly performed prostrations for *fajr namaz*, morning prayers. The sun was still below the horizon, and moonlight radiated through the window, casting on him an ethereal glow. A cross between a dead person and a saint.

What a two-faced asshole. What a lecherous hypocrite.

When he finished praying, Babrek folded the rug and glanced at Goha, who had moved the blanket off his face and was leering at him angrily.

"You're up early. Why didn't you sleep in the bed? You would've been way more comfortable. Well since we're both awake, why don't you wash up and we'll go out for breakfast? My treat. There's a good restaurant close by that opens its doors right after sunrise."

"No!" Goha's stomach hardened.

"Why not? Come on, *yaar*. I'm starving and I'd love the company."

"I said no!"

"Why are you so mad? Are you okay? It's been a while since you've eaten. You must be famished. Are you angry because you're hungry? *Hangry?* I think that's the term they use in the West." He laughed as the insensitive, out-of-place English word tumbled out of his mouth.

Goha scowled. *I can't spend any more time with him. I just can't.* His intestines knotted, and they complained just then by letting out a loud, long grumble. He had no idea where he might find a decent meal, and while he wanted desperately to ignore his hunger, his body told him he needed to eat soon or he might faint.

"Fine. But after breakfast you and I need to have a serious talk. I mean it."

"Of course, we can talk. I really like you, and I want to get to know you better."

Goha grimaced as he strode past Babrek to slip on his *chappals* and reluctantly walked out the door.

The restaurant was clean and decorated tastefully with regional handicrafts on the walls, but Goha barely noticed them. After the torrid events the previous night, the strong spices from the kitchen made him nauseous. But when the server placed the fresh-off-the-grill Pakistani omelet and flakey *paratha* in front of him, Goha's ravenous appetite overtook his queasiness.

Meanwhile, Babrek was talking proudly and profusely about local artisans and their skilled craftsmanship in creating pottery, woodwork, prints, and tapestries. As they ate, he commented that the restaurant used the freshest ingredients sourced from local farms. "I'm sure you didn't eat such high-quality and delicious food in Qasba," he said.

"My *ammi* makes the best food in the world," Goha answered stiffly and without hesitation. But in truth, the tastiest meals throughout his childhood had been leftovers, dishes prepared by kitchen servants for Naseebo's matrons and their families, particularly when they hosted *dawats*, indulgent dinner parties. His mother was a good cook, but she generally prepared basic meals consisting of the cheapest *daal* and *subzis*, lentils and vegetables, available at the market. Sometimes she cooked low-quality cuts of chicken or mutton, but those dishes were usually reserved for special occasions.

Goha ate a few bites of omelet and *paratha* and sat back in his chair, picking silently at his plate. Babrek, however, appeared unsatiated. He perpetually tore off pieces of his flatbread and combined them with his egg to make large *niwalas*, bites, which he scooped into his mouth and chewed noisily.

"I can take time off work today. Let's go back to the room so we can talk in private," Babrek said finally, wiping his plate clean with the last morsel of *paratha* and slapping a wad of cash on the table.

The awkwardness pervading the space between them as they walked back to the rooming house wasn't enough for Goha to break the silence with Babrek. He stayed a few feet behind him, tight-faced and aloof, kicking at rocks on the road.

"What's on your mind?" Babrek said as he closed the door to their room. "Something is obviously bothering you."

Goha felt air get caught in his lungs. He glared at Babrek. "What's on my mind? You abused me last night."

Babrek's face contorted. "Abused you? *Kya tum pagal ho?*" What are you, crazy? "I know I was a bit intoxicated and not totally in my senses, but I don't think you objected to anything. You're an adult, Goha. I thought you were enjoying it. Or at least that you didn't mind it."

Heat rose to Goha's face, and it twitched unintentionally. "What are you trying to say?"

"I'm not trying to say anything. Honestly, that's what I thought. A lot of Pashtun men prefer other men—it might be because they're a lot more available for sex than women. I'm sure you've noticed that a lot of women wear burkas or niqabs around here. A friend said to me once, 'How can I fall in love with a girl if I can't see her face?' Anyway, I'm sorry if I offended you or hurt your feelings."

"Offended me? Hurt my feelings? What you did went way beyond offending me and hurting my feelings. Not only did you physically abuse me but what you did was illegal and immoral." Goha was shouting. "You committed a *gunah-e-azeem*!" A big sin!

The warmth that had started in Goha's face started traveling throughout his body, coursing through his veins. At that moment he didn't care that he was hurling insults at his superior and only companion up north—and potentially jeopardizing his lucrative work prospects.

"You call yourself a Muslim. Really? Give me a break. Don't you know that sexual relationships between the same sexes are forbidden in Islam?"

"Wait a minute. Back up. *Gunah-e-azeem?* Where are you getting that from? People here think that as long as men are only using other males for sexual gratification and there's no love involved, there's nothing wrong with it."

Goha's head practically burst. "That's outrageous. Haven't you ever studied the Qur'an? Oh wait, let me guess. You learned it in Arabic—a language you don't speak or understand—and repeat it like a parrot. You never bothered to translate it, right?"

"I read it in Arabic because that's the language it was revealed to our holy Prophet Muhammad," Babrek said coolly, like he was placating an irrational toddler. "I'm not sure what you fancy Karachiites do, but around here, we rely on our learned scholars to shed light on the holy scripture for us."

"Learned scholars? Are those the same people who condone your lewd behavior, even though it's illegal in this country and not allowed in Islam?"

"Calm down. Our scholars are our mullahs and imams, probably similar to the ones at your *madrasa*. They know a few things about interpreting the Qur'an. And I'm not a total *gadha*. I've done a lot of research and reached conclusions that are similar to theirs."

"So you must know what it says about Prophet Lot's followers. They left their wives to be with other men, and they went beyond the limits of indecency and shamelessness. If you don't believe me, I'll show you." Goha grabbed the Qur'an from the shelf, praying he was clean enough to touch it. He found the same passage he had located the day before and pushed it in front of Babrek's face.

"It's right here. Look. '*Then we destroyed them. We rained upon them a rain and evil was the rain for those who were warned. Punishment seized them at sunrise. We moved their abodes upside down and rained upon them stones.*' And here's another one. God says He told Prophet Lot to tell his people they were '*guilty of an abomination which none of the nations had done before.*' It's here in black and white. So what do you have to say?"

Babrek was quiet as Goha crossed his arms at him reproachfully.

"Okay. I've heard Muslims talk about homosexuals in the Qur'an being punished with stones before," he finally said. "But all religious books are full of those types of stories, and I don't think we're supposed to take them literally. Allah said He made some verses in the Qur'an clear and revealed others in symbolic or figurative language that needs to be . . . *decoded*, I guess you could say. I've read a lot about this, and I'm happy to talk about it. But right now, I'll be honest, I'm kind of preoccupied with something else. Do you like cricket? Dumb question. All Pakistanis do, right?" He let out a forced, too-loud chuckle.

"The Multan Sultans are about to play the Peshawar Zalmis in the Pakistan Super League. I can't wait to see the Zalmis crush the Sultans. This is going to be great." Babrek went to the kitchen, took two boxes of unopened *naan khatai* biscuits out of the cupboard, tossed one to Goha, grabbed the remote off the shelf, and plopped into the recliner.

Goha was flabbergasted by Babrek's cavalier attitude about the previous night. Was this a regular occurrence for him and no big deal? Was sexual abuse some kind of twisted initiation rite into the organization? Was Babrek intentionally acting nonchalant so he could avoid justifying his behavior?

Babrek turned on the TV, opened the box of biscuits, and turned up the volume on the sportscasters' pregame commentary.

Goha decided it was prudent to be patient. Although he ordinarily loved cricket and could spend hours glued to a set with a group of fans in the *katchi abadis*, that day he was indifferent. He lowered himself onto the sofa unenthusiastically, Babrek's comments about Qur'anic interpretation floating around in his head like unsettled dust. By the game's first break, his package of Pakistani cookies was left untouched and his head was pounding.

Four hours later, the cricket match ended with the Multan Sultans triumphing over the Peshawar Zalmis. "Oh man, they lost," moaned Babrek. "Oh well, *inshallah*, next time they'll do better. Everyone around here knows the Zalmis are a way better team than the Sultans." When Goha didn't respond, Babrek turned off the TV.

"Okay, Goha. Let's talk. I'll start. Have you heard of Ibn Hazm? He was a theologian, ethicist, and social critic who lived in Spain about a thousand years ago."

"No." *Great. I think I'm about to get a lesson on Islamic history.*

Hazm was around during Islam's classical age, and his ideas were remarkably progressive for his time, Babrek said. He was one of the few theologians sensitive to gender and sexuality issues, and even though he lived in a patriarchal society, he challenged the biased and orthodox interpretations of the Qur'an that were common back then. "Hazm translated early verses about Prophet Lot as saying the people in his tribe were destroyed because they rejected Lot as a prophet, not because they were homosexuals. He pointed out that women and children in the tribe were punished, too, so it didn't make sense they were attacked solely because of their sexuality.

"The Qur'an does say how men in Lot's tribe left their wives to be with men who were the prophet's guests," Babrek went on. "But people tend to focus on the homosexual part of this story and overlook everything else. They see it through a patriarchal lens. I think the moral of that story is less about same-sex acts and more about how Lot's followers forced themselves on their guests."

After the events from the previous night, Goha's jaw tightened at the palpable irony in how Babrek interpreted assault as the main wrongdoing in the Lot story. But he knew he'd already overstepped his bounds by shouting at Babrek before the cricket match, so he said nothing.

A lot of Pakistanis think gays need to be "converted" into being heterosexual, Babrek said. "They point to the Prophet Lot story and say homosexuality isn't allowed in Islam. But progressive thinkers suggest it isn't so clear cut. I personally think it's up to us to examine the Qur'an's larger themes and figure out what's right or wrong. Good or bad. Sinful or virtuous. The book is filled with symbolic language that isn't meant to be taken literally."

He picked up the Qur'an. "So you know about prophets besides Lot, right?"

Goha snorted. "Of course I know about other prophets, Babrek. I've gone to *madrasa* since before I could talk. And unlike you, I learned teachings from the Qur'an in Urdu, not just Arabic." It gave Goha a tiny bit of satisfaction to hold a small but significant piece of his religious upbringing, courtesy of Sheikh Samir, over Babrek.

"Good. Hold on—I want to show you a passage." Babrek flipped through the pages.

"*And certainly we gave Moses nine clear signs to ask the children of Israel. When he came to them Pharaoh said to him, 'Surely I deem them to be one of the wicked. He, Moses, said truly thou knows that none but the Lord of the heavens and earth has sent thee the clear proofs; and surely I believe thee O Pharaoh, to be lost.'*"

Babrek paused. "Do you know what the clear signs were that God gave to Moses?"

Goha shrugged.

"This passage refers to when the magicians in Moses's court cast down their cords, which appeared to be running like serpents. Moses saw the serpents, and God told him not to be afraid. Then Moses put down his staff, and like a big serpent, the staff ate the serpents the magicians created. Anyway, do you really think the staff ate the serpents?" He didn't wait for Goha's answer.

"Of course not. The story is symbolic, just like the passages you quoted about Lot. The point is that God saved Moses because he had unwavering faith."

In spite of himself, Goha admired Babrek for being well-versed in Islam's nuances and ambiguities. While he wasn't sure what to make of Babrek's unorthodox Qur'anic interpretations, they reflected a level of thinking he had never encountered, not by Sheikh Samir or any of his other religious teachers.

"And you must know the story of how Jonah was engulfed by a fish. He got stuck inside it and came out good as new. So tell me, do you really think Jonah was inside a fish's belly? And now that you've had time to ponder it, let me ask you this—do you actually think God rained stones down upon Lot's followers?"

Babrek again went on before Goha had a chance to respond. "The verses in the Holy Qur'an are full of obscurities and metaphors. Few things are black and white; everything's a shade of gray. Why else would we have so many divisions within Islam? If everything were clear as day, we'd all be living happily and without strife as one big, united *ummah*. All the Sunnis, Shias, Ahmadis, Ismailis, Sufis, Hanafis—even the hardline Wahhabis. Everyone." He took a packet of cigarettes out of his pocket.

Babrek had made a point that Goha hadn't bothered to think about too deeply. The ideas held by mainstream Sunni Muslims, like himself, his parents, and Sheikh Samir, about what was permissible and obligatory in Islam differed—often vastly—from people in other sects.

Babrek tapped the box of cigarettes on the arm of the chair to loosen one from the pack. He lit up and inhaled.

"Getting back to the culture around here—in case you haven't noticed, females are seen as receptacles of family honor to be safeguarded at home. There's a popular saying around here that women are for children and boys are for pleasure. That's why there's a lot of homosexual activity going on around here, even though Pashtun men don't generally consider themselves gay."

Goha winced and pressed his eyes shut as he absorbed Babrek's words, but Babrek kept going.

"Speaking of which, there's lots going on in Karachi, too, I hear." He flicked his ashes onto a plate. "I heard the city is called a 'gay man's paradise' because even men who claim they're straight are doing it at underground parties. I even heard about group sex happening in sacred shrines. And it involves men from all levels of society. The shrine thing always seemed sacrilegious to me, but maybe I'm missing something." He shrugged, smiling, and took another long drag of his cigarette.

Goha couldn't believe what he was hearing. He envisioned himself living inside a bubble his whole life, guileless and unsuspecting, drifting above the surface of the earth. *The guy hitting on me on the train. The men and boys on the streets of Peshawar. And now, groups of gay men having sex at holy shrines in Karachi, my hometown, of all places.* In the foggy haze of cigarette smoke, his face flushed at his naivety. It seemed he had spent his entire childhood simply trying to stay afloat and please his parents.

Despite his discomfort, he wanted more, and Babrek appeared more than happy to oblige. It reminded him of the Karachi beggars who were crippled or had exposed severed limbs—his unbridled curiosity made him gawk and avoid turning away.

"It's hard for gay men—and by that, I mean men like me who prefer males and aren't just having sex with them because there aren't enough women around—to have relationships that are out in the open," Babrek continued. "It's easier for people from educated, upper-class families, I think. But I've known a lot of gay men who marry women so they don't have to deal with bullshit from their conservative families. They treat their wives well, but they secretly keep having sex with other men after they get married."

Goha cringed again at Babrek's last comment, but when he sought confirmation of his reaction from Babrek, he got nothing.

"On a related note, *hijras* have been around for hundreds of years. You must have seen them around Karachi."

Yes, I have. My old school friend, Arif.

At fifteen, Arif had started dressing effeminately, even painting his fingernails in vibrant shades and occasionally wearing lipstick. Goha distinctly recalled his horror and shame when other boys in his class called Arif *gandu* and bullied him. "*Tumhara naam Arif nahi hei, Arifa hei.*" Your name isn't Arif, it's Arifa, they taunted.

In one jarring incident in their second year of high school, Goha had been in the washroom with Arif when a group of boys jeered at him and pulled down his pants. Goha wasn't sure what had happened after that. He ardently hoped Arif had escaped, but he truthfully didn't know. Mortified and unsure what to make of the whole thing, he had hurriedly left the scene and kept his distance from Arif in the days that followed. Even after months had passed, he had still agonized over not sticking up for his friend, for abandoning him like a coward. His motivation had been self-centered; he had suffered enough at the hands of bullies and didn't want to be dragged down further in his social standing.

At traffic stops in Karachi's bustling city center, beggars draped in elegant pink, orange, and red saris wore sparkling makeup and had stubble on their upper lips and chins. After he had left high school, he half-expected to see Arif among them, tapping his long fingernails on cars and waiting for drivers to roll down their windows so he could make a few bucks delivering a well-rehearsed, sympathy-evoking pitch.

But Goha never saw Arif, or if he did, he wasn't recognizable. Had Arif changed his name and identity? Did his family disown him? Had he found himself among a community of *hijras*? There was a real possibility he could run into Arif at someone's *shaadi*, wedding, dressed in female clothing, dancing seductively and showering good blessings on the newlyweds as they began their lives together.

Under Mughal rule, *hijras* weren't seen as sexual threats, said Babrek, so they were allowed to work as servants for female royalty and guards of the royal harem. In modern times, some people considered *hijras*—Pakistan's "third sex," comprising transgender, intersex, and eunuch people who lived in communities separate from cisgender society—good luck for newlyweds and newborns. They hired them to perform at weddings and baby showers. But others shunned and condemned them because they assumed *hijras* were addicted to sex and drugs.

Babrek's voice droned on like a never-ending rant, and suddenly, it was all too much. Goha sprang from his chair and went to the closet, opened the safe, and picked up the pistol. His *ammi, abba,* and Sheikh Samir ceased to exist, their supportive voices and words of wisdom eradicated from his memory. His hand trembled.

"Stop. Just stop now. Live your life however you want. I'm not interested in listening to you anymore—I'm done." His voice was hoarse as he pointed the gun to the side of his head.

Babrek grew pale. He rose abruptly, fear flashing across his eyes. "What are you doing? Don't you know that suicide is forbidden in Islam? It's *haram*!"

"Suicide is *haram*? That's ironic coming from you. You're the one who has forced me to do the most *haram* things in the short time I've been here." Goha moved the weapon closer to his temple.

Babrek lunged at Goha, attempting to snatch the gun from his hand. It fell on the floor between them and spun around and around like a dizzying, endless, nauseating ride at an amusement park.

Tension swallowed the room as Goha's heaves gave way to quiet sniffles. Neither Babrek nor Goha spoke for a full, excruciating minute.

"Why don't we go get dinner?" Babrek said finally.

Silence.

"Please, Goha, for God's sake."

Goha's face twisted into a look of disgust mixed with pity. "Fine. I'll go out with you. But do you see what you are doing to me? You are abusing me, confusing me, and taking advantage of me. *Tum mujhe pagal kar rahe ho, Babrek.*" You're driving me crazy, Babrek.

"How are you doing?" Babrek asked when they had been seated at the restaurant. His brow was creased, and the intense gaze of his hazel eyes made them appear a shade of smoky charcoal.

"I'm fine."

"Do you mean that?"

Goha didn't respond.

Babrek tried another approach. "Hey, *yaar*, have you heard of Maulana Jalaluddin Rumi?"

A minuscule spark flitted across Goha's eyes. "Rumi was a Sufi, the greatest one who ever lived. He wrote incredible poetry in Persian. I read some of it in school. The *mevlana* was a brilliant man, but in my opinion, the Sufi community has strayed away from true Islam." Goha uttered the last statement defiantly, unwilling to let Babrek's unconventional viewpoints dominate the conversation yet again.

"I disagree." Babrek took a cigarette out of his pocket and started twisting it nervously between his thumb and forefinger. "Sufis follow the same teachings as other Muslims. They just practice the religion in a more philosophical and mystical way."

Goha wasn't sure what Babrek meant by that, but he did know he wasn't up for another long, drawn-out explanation, this time about how Sufis interpreted Islam.

"Do you know about Shams Tabriz?" Babrek asked.

Goha let out a long, drawn-out sigh.

"Shams was a strange wandering dervish and Rumi's mentor. Some scholars think the two of them had a sexual relationship."

"Oh boy, here we go again."

"There's no need for you to get upset again." Babrek fumbled for his lighter in his *kameez* pocket, emitting a low, relieved whistle when he found it. "Of course, no one can confirm it since they died a long time ago. But here's my point. If two great saintly Sufis were lovers and spent their entire existence searching for the truth of divine love, who are we to condemn homosexuality as impure or un-Islamic?"

The food arrived, and Goha was grateful for a few precious minutes of peace as they dished spoonfuls of saffron-colored rice and braised chicken onto their plates.

"Have you heard of Sheikh Sarmad?"

"I'm not sure, Babrek." Goha couldn't hide his exasperation.

"Sheikh Sarmad was a Jew who converted to Islam and became a mystic. He lived about five hundred years ago, during the reigns of Emperors Shahjahan and Aurangzeb. They called him 'the naked *faqir*' because he barely wore any clothes. Anyway, the story goes that Sarmad and one of his disciples, a Hindu boy named Abhay Chand who also became a Muslim, were lovers."

At that point, Goha stopped eating. "Babrek, I think you're making up stories about allegedly gay Muslims to prove homosexuality is allowed in Islam. I honestly don't care, and I really don't want to talk about this anymore." He avoided eye contact with Babrek for the rest of the meal.

As Babrek snored on the bed beside him, Goha mulled over the deluge of information his supervisor had bombarded him with that day. Guilt and shame from the previous night still gripped him like a scorpion's claw, but after hearing Babrek's Qur'anic interpretations, his perceptions about Muslims who didn't conform to conventional gender and sexual roles were becoming blurrier. In particular, homosexuality, in his mind, was no longer a simple good-versus-sinful issue.

On top of that, while he knew he was attracted to women, the power gap between him and Babrek—combined with Babrek's steadfast views—led Goha to conclude that an intimate physical relationship between them was probably inevitable. *Since sex between men seems commonplace in this part of the country, maybe what Babrek wants from me is okay? I'm an adult now, so I guess I'll tolerate it.* If that meant giving in to Babrek's sexual desires—and even acting like he was enjoying it—Goha reasoned that's what he would have to do to be accommodating during his time up north.

His *ammi* and *abba* were counting on him, he surmised, and they didn't need to know what was going on. *It's a white lie. There's no harm in them holding on to their happy, fabricated dream about my innocence.*

It was a huge step, but one Goha felt he needed to take to survive in an environment he was coming to see as boorish, ungodly territory in his native country.

CHAPTER 6

When they finished dinner one evening a few days later, Babrek, as usual, made *kahwa* for them in the kitchen. Goha eagerly waited for the fragrant, golden drink, which Babrek masterfully prepared by stirring whole cardamom pods or freshly crushed seeds into a boiling pot of dried jasmine tea leaves, at times making it extra rich by adding a dollop of honey or ground nuts. He would hand Goha a cup of the steaming liquid, take his own to the recliner, and turn on the TV. Babrek consistently made it a point to keep up with the latest government and military affairs, as well as national, regional, and local news. He also took a keen interest—one that sometimes seemed to border on obsession—in Pakistan's standing and reputation in the rest of the world.

Pakistan Television Corporation (PTV)—the nation's state-owned channel—was reporting on a 7.5 magnitude earthquake that had hit the Hindu Kush mountain range in neighboring Afghanistan. Although the quake's epicenter was a low-density area, hundreds of people had died and thousands more were injured, most of them in Pakistan. Tremors were felt as far away as Kabul, Afghanistan; New Delhi, India; Kathmandu, Nepal; and even parts of China.

Goha and Babrek sat in horrified silence as devastating images flashed across the screen. For Goha, it was a geography lesson coming to life: He had learned that parts of Pakistan, particularly in the north and west, were in some of the most active earthquake zones in the world. In 2005, when he was ten, he had heard about the Kashmir earthquake, the worst ever experienced in South Asia, that killed as many as a hundred thousand and injured tens of thousands more. Back then, he was just a kid and thousands of miles away in Karachi, personally unaffected by the disaster. This time, the proximity of the calamity and his understanding of its potential ramifications crushed him.

"We need to help with rescue efforts," Babrek said, switching off the TV. "I'll contact our organization's high command. It's likely they've already started sending supplies and workers. We can't rely on the government—it's organizations like ours that get things done at times like this."

Goha nodded. Those types of sentiments had surfaced before. In school, he had picked up a copy of the book *I Am Malala* by the young female Pakistani activist Malala Yousafzai, who had been shot by a Taliban gunman in the Swat Valley. Malala recounted how most rescue and relief volunteers came from Islamic charities or organizations—not the government—when the deadly earthquake had hit nearly a decade prior. She narrated how it was a Saturday, a normal school day in the region during the holy month of Ramadan, when the ground had started shaking. In one Khyber-Pakhtunkhwa district, three hundred and fifty students perished when a school collapsed, and an additional fifty died at a nearby school. People napping after their predawn *suhoor* meal—eaten just before the day of fasting started—were trapped inside their homes. Entire towns and villages had disintegrated throughout Northern Pakistan, and surrounding areas were severely damaged.

Although images of Pakistani army aircraft laden with supplies and tents flooded the news, Malala said they failed to land in the region's smaller valleys. Many aid packages that were dropped from helicopters rolled into rivers and couldn't be salvaged, much to the chagrin of desperate victims. Meanwhile, dedicated local volunteer activists trudged through mountains and decimated valleys, lugging supplies and medical help to obscure areas. They led prayers, organized burials, and rebuilt shattered villages.

"Absolutely," Goha responded. "Those poor victims need all the support they can get." His parents, even with their few possessions, always assisted others, especially those less fortunate. They said there were a lot of *sawab*, rewards, that came with helping people. Sheikh Samir had cemented that idea into Goha's head, telling him he would receive *barkat*, abundant blessings, by being pious and carrying out good deeds.

With his natural ability to absorb information, Goha's altruism had shone when he taught younger kids living in nearby shacks in the settlement. Many of those families kept their kids out of school so they could earn paltry incomes by begging or selling tchotchkes on the sides of the roads. He knew he was helping their future prospects by equipping them with at least basic reading, writing, and math skills.

He was particularly fond of little girls—their bright eyes, feisty spirits, and insatiable thirst for knowledge. He loved how they giggled often and unexpectedly, scrambled up his legs like he was a mountain to be conquered, and poked and teased him endlessly. He often wondered what heights they would reach if only they had been born in different circumstances. He considered himself their older brother, since he'd never had younger siblings. He treasured bonding with them over books that transported them to incredible, faraway places vivid in their collective imaginations.

Babrek had taken out his phone and exchanged a few words in Pashto with the person on the other end. "My supervisor said we can help deliver emergency supplies at a food distribution center in Mingora," he told Goha. "The organization's charity wing kicks into high gear when a natural disaster hits Pakistan. It's part of our mission to help our countrymen—plus, it's a good opportunity to raise awareness and enlist new members."

Goha was relieved to finally be able to help in a meaningful way and gain insight into the organization's inner workings. *This must have been one of the changes Lala Dabir talked about—bringing help quickly to those who needed it.*

"Pack your bag—we may be there for a few days," Babrek said. "We'll leave first thing in the morning."

The rain was hard and swift when they left for Mingora, a city situated on the river outside the Swat Valley, but even through the water-splotched windshield, Goha could make out the picturesque scenery: majestic mountains surrounded by alpine forests and gushing azure streams. He now understood why it was famously called the "Switzerland of Asia."

From history class, Goha knew Buddhism and Hinduism had flourished in the area at different points in time. His giddiness at first learning about unearthed Buddhist remains and carvings prompted a promise he made to himself to visit those sites when he got older, *inshallah*, to acquire more knowledge about the belief systems and cultures of those fascinating ancient peoples. He had been distraught to learn that militant activity and suicide bombs threatened their existence. The national army had supposedly regained control from extremists over the past few months, and he fervently hoped the rumor was true.

He followed Babrek's gaze to the houses along the road that had been reduced to rubble. "The houses here aren't built with reinforcements, so whenever an earthquake strikes, they shatter like glass," Babrek said. "This is so much worse than how it looked on TV."

Goha's parents' ramshackle house was constantly in need of repairs, and if an earthquake of similar severity hit Qasba, he knew it could easily have destroyed him and his parents within seconds.

They parked in front of a large warehouse. A gaunt man with a thin beard and a white *topee* was assembling cardboard boxes and lining them up against the wall. He wore a serious expression, and he eyed their SUV suspiciously, but his face relaxed when Babrek exited the car.

"*Assalam-o-alaikum*, Haroon *sahib*," said Babrek. "Goha, Haroon *sahib* is one of the hardest-working leaders of our organization. He's spearheading the local rescue efforts."

The most pressing need was getting food to the victims, Haroon told them in Urdu. He pointed to a pile of burlap sacks in a corner and instructed them to load them into the truck outside.

The temperature had dropped, and it was still raining, but Goha was thankful to be working in cooler weather rather than in the stifling heat of Karachi.

Haroon switched from Urdu to his native Pashto as they efficiently heaved bags of flour from the warehouse to the truck. "What's he saying?" Goha asked Babrek as he hoisted a sack over his shoulder.

"He said it's good we've come to help. At least three hundred people are dead, including twelve girls in Afghanistan who were trying to flee from their school. A lot of people are injured, and many have lost their homes."

"Oh my God." The little girls Goha taught in Qasba had plump cheeks and sweet, mischievous smiles. He revulsed when he imagined them panic-stricken and running for their lives.

"Haroon said the organization's members understand this harsh climate." Babrek wiped sweat off his brow. "Even if boulders and landslides block roads, they know how to get supplies to isolated areas. That's what happened during the big earthquake nine years ago. Our workers arrived first because they were already inside the villages that were hit.

"People who lost their homes will call on the government, but they won't do much," Babrek said. "They talk big and have fancy, expensive military aircraft and equipment, but they're sluggish and inefficient. On the news they'll make lofty claims about how much they're doing, but it's mostly to gain support so they can maintain power when the next election rolls around. Haroon said he's seen foreign aid groups try to help, but they're ineffective in this environment too. In the end, organizations like ours do most of the work."

Babrek laid an oversized bag of flour onto the truck bed. "We'll be staying here overnight. The temperature is expected to hit freezing, but the organization will provide military tents and blankets to keep us warm."

Goha woke the next morning to the muffled sound of deep voices. When he peeked out the flappy tent doors, Babrek and Haroon sat in a corner a few feet away, drinking *kahwa* and talking quietly in Pashto. He was amazed he had managed to sleep so peacefully in the cold, strange environment. His muscles ached, and his hands were blistered from the hard labor the day before, but the dark interior of the tent, thick wool blankets, and steady rain had helped him fall immediately into an undisturbed slumber.

Babrek caught his eye. *"Pakistani hukoomat aaj fauji helicopter ke zariye imdadi saman bhej rahi hay."* We just got word that the Pakistani government is sending a military helicopter with supplies today, he said.

Goha appreciated Babrek's clear intention to speak in Urdu for his benefit.

"We'll go to the landing site to help unload the supplies," Babrek told him. "A few villages lost power and cell service, so we'll help those areas first."

Goha couldn't help but be impressed. Despite their seeming animosity toward and distrust of the national government and international aid groups, the organization was willing to overlook differences when lives and livelihoods were at stake. When a crisis hit, they strategically and immediately collaborated and mobilized.

The hair on Goha's arms stood up, and he shivered. It was still near freezing, and the rain hadn't let up. "It was so cold and wet last night. What happened to the people who lost their homes?"

"Some stayed with relatives or friends," Babrek replied. "A few children became orphans, but the organization worked with leaders of local *madrasas* to make sure they had food and shelter."

Two powerful emotions overtook Goha: profound sadness toward the youngsters who lost their parents without warning and infinite appreciation toward the organization and *madrasas* for caring for those kids right away.

"Here, have a cup of *kahwa*," Babrek said. "It'll warm you up. We'll leave in a few minutes."

On their way to the landing site, the raindrops splattering the windshield were immediately obliterated by the car's relentless, squeaky wipers. Outside, dozens, maybe even hundreds, of identical black-and-white flags with a prominent image of a horizontal sword on the top were erected along the roadside. They flapped away mercilessly in the cold mountain wind. Goha had never seen such flags, and as rows and rows of them swooshed by, there wasn't even one green-and-white Pakistani flag, distinguishable by its hopeful white crescent and star.

"What kind of flags are those?"

"They were put up by members of a religious organization that's active in this area," Babrek replied, his eyes focused on the slick, wet road.

"I don't see any Pakistani flags."

"People in this area aren't very patriotic toward Pakistan," Babrek responded. "They're Pashtun first, and they're vehemently proud of their tribalism. For them, the border separating Afghanistan and Pakistan is symbolic. It really doesn't mean much."

As they drove through the city center, glossy posters decorated the windows of modern shopping malls. Glamorous male and female models with "I couldn't care less" expressions sat or stood in seductive poses, flaunting the latest fashion trends from Western Europe and America. The female models particularly struck him; Goha had barely seen any women on the streets since they had arrived in Mingora, and the few he glimpsed were mostly covered head to toe in black or neutral-colored niqabs or burkas.

When they hit the outskirts of the city, the huge army helicopter loomed into view, its propeller blades extended like a protective shield over the landscape. Several men in army fatigues unloaded boxes. A short man with a mustache and an army cap stood in the center of a group of about twenty men. When he released them to carry out their tasks, Babrek exited the car and waved at him enthusiastically.

"That's my old friend General Zafar," Babrek told Goha happily. "I didn't know he was going to be here. He's a high-level and highly regarded general in the Pakistani army."

The general walked over, grinning widely. "*Assalam-o-alaikum,* sir. Where have you been?" He whacked Babrek playfully, then put his arm around his shoulder in an affable half embrace.

"*Wa 'alaykumu s-salam,* General *sahib,*" Babrek responded, taking the general's hand. "I'm here now, and that's what counts, right? General Zafar, this is my friend Goha from Karachi."

General Zafar nodded warmly at Goha.

"We have a lot of supplies that need to be delivered to victims. Can you and Goha help?"

"Of course. That's why we're here, friend. Put us to work."

Over the next three days, Goha and Babrek packed and delivered supplies, cleared out debris, rebuilt homes, and searched the wreckage for survivors. Despite its unsurpassed natural beauty, the terrain of Northwest Pakistan presented itself to Goha as a savage, unpredictable monster that could swallow entire villages and ruthlessly spit out the remains. He met dozens of people who had lost everything—beloved family members, houses, and their few trivial belongings. It disturbed him to overhear a few local men implying—or sometimes even stating bluntly—that the earthquake was a warning from God caused by women's obscenity and excessive freedom. He found those days more physically exhausting and mentally trying than any he had experienced before.

To his surprise, Babrek appeared equally traumatized by the experience. After a full day of relief and rescue efforts, they would return to the warehouse with additional helpers for a basic dinner, usually consisting of rice and *daal.* A volunteer would prepare the food, and while he knelt on the floor stirring the pots over a small fire, the other men gathered around to keep warm. When the meal was finished, Babrek put on a *topee* and retreated into a corner with his *janamaz*. Long after he performed the ritual bows and prostrations, he sat on the mat with his eyes closed and hands cupped in front of his body, rocking in silent prayer for what seemed like hours.

By the fourth day, the Pakistani military and international aid organizations like Médecins sans Frontières, UNICEF, and Première Urgence Internationale inundated the area. That day had been an exceptionally grueling one; Babrek, Goha, and a few other volunteers from the organization had uncovered several dead bodies amid the rubble, including three youngsters reportedly from the same extended family. Goha had seen firsthand the harrowing image of a child's limbs severed from the rest of his body. A strewn notebook and pencil lay nearby, as well as a tattered Qur'an, its torn, elaborate Arabic-scripted pages fluttering around the debris. So when Babrek told him they had been given permission to return to the rooming house in the morning, a massive weight dissipated off Goha's body.

Babrek's patience and stoicism during their time in Mingora amazed Goha. He had carried himself with an authority that yielded respect from the other volunteers yet had no airs about rolling up his sleeves and diving into the arduous and mentally draining work. He demonstrated immeasurable empathy toward the victims, talking to them kindly while still efficiently getting things done so their lives could return to some level of normalcy.

Goha had been spending inordinate amounts of time with Babrek, more time than he had ever spent with any one person other than his parents. While he often pretended to fall asleep before Babrek came to bed to avoid his sexual overtures, on the handful of occasions Goha had agreed, somewhat reluctantly, to have sex, he found Babrek generally considerate, even if he wasn't exceptionally communicative.

"Babrek, we've been spending a lot of time together, but I don't really know much about you."

Babrek's posture was markedly more relaxed than it had been in

Mingora. It was like he had been carting a heavy burlap flour sack from the relief efforts on his shoulders, and someone had finally lifted it off.

"Hmmm. I detect a question in that statement. So you want to know where I come from, my favorite color, the games I played as a kid, and the name of my best friend when I was ten?"

"Sure, all that and more." Goha couldn't help but smile. Babrek appeared in an amiable mood, and Goha was glad to have something to talk about other than the grueling aftermath of the earthquake. "It would be nice to know more about you. After all, you seem to know a lot about me."

"True. I guess now's as good a time as any to tell you my story. I should warn you, though—it's not all sunshine and roses." He had finished unpacking and now leaned back in the recliner and pulled a cigarette out of his pocket.

Babrek's dad was a well-known landowner and farmer in a village outside of Peshawar. Like most of the women in their village, his mother stayed at home to care for the kids. When Babrek was born, everyone said he looked like her, and as he grew up, they said he had her personality and temperament too. "She was always calm, always smiling. She rarely got agitated about anything. And she was so smart."

Babrek's mother wasn't formally educated, but she loved learning. She would read whatever easy books she could get her hands on and share them with Babrek and his sister. No subjects were off limits, even ones considered too liberal or blasphemous in their conservative circles. She was a sponge, absorbing information and opening her mind to different points of view. "There was no one else like her in our village. Most of her friends and neighbors didn't know or care to learn much about the outside world," Babrek said.

Babrek's *ammi* always wanted more children, but she struggled to stay healthy during her pregnancies. He found out later she had conceived a few times before and after he was born, but she only gave birth to two babies—Babrek and his sister Amina, who was six years older.

"My *ammi* got sick too. That's why I'm an only child." When he was born, Bala had asked a midwife in the *katchi abadis* to help out when Naseebo went into labor, but she wasn't properly trained. Naseebo ended up with a serious pelvic infection and couldn't conceive more children.

Babrek exhaled a long stream of smoke. "I became one too." When Amina was in high school, she fell in love with her teacher. She was seventeen and he was twenty-five. She snuck out of the house after school and on weekends when she was supposed to be studying or helping their *ammi* in the kitchen. "She would tell us she was going to meet her friends," Babrek said. "She didn't confide in me, probably because she thought I was too young to understand or that I might tell on her. But I knew she was hiding something."

Even though there was an age gap, Babrek and his sister were close. "She was like a second mom to me. Amina *baji* brushed my hair, helped me get dressed, and made sure I ate breakfast before school. She sat on my bed while I said my prayers at night. She took care of me whenever my mom wasn't well." She loved going to school, and because Babrek wanted to be like her, he learned to love it too.

After a few months, Amina and the teacher married in another village. They didn't tell anyone. But Babrek's father found out, and he was furious. Their secret romance was bad enough, but when he found out her husband was from outside their tribe, it made it even worse. His father couldn't forgive Amina for marrying someone he didn't know, and without his permission on top of it.

The affair was a huge scandal and the gossip of the town. Babrek's father said it would bring down their family's reputation and community standing. He was a traditional and controlling Pashtun who was strict about following *Pashtunwali*, the Pashtun code of conduct that emphasized manhood, bravery, honor, and respect.

"He thought the world should hold him in high esteem, even if he didn't deserve it. He would always say, '*Daulat khonay pur kuch naheen khota, sihat khonay pur kuch kho jaata hai, ghairat khonay pur sub kuch kho jaata hai.*' It's a folk saying that means when wealth is lost, nothing is lost; when health is lost, something is lost; when honor is lost, everything is lost." One day Babrek's dad got so mad that he took his handgun and went to their house and shot Amina and her husband dead. Then he came home and shot his wife too.

Goha's body went numb. Losing his mother at the hands of his father—the two people who meant the most in the world to him—was unfathomable.

People who knew Babrek's story asked why his father shot his mother. "I think he believed she knew about my sister's affair and helped Amina secretly get married. I don't know if that's true. I was eleven, and I didn't dare challenge my dad. It all happened in the blink of an eye."

Babrek's dad was arrested. He pleaded not guilty and defended his actions as honor killings. He said he did it because his daughter disgraced their family, but he was eventually found guilty of three murders and sentenced to prison for life. Babrek said he thought his dad became a little remorseful over time. "But he really never wavered from his belief that he did it to uphold our family's reputation," he said.

Goha hesitated for a second, but he wanted to know. "Did you ever feel your father was justified in what he did, Babrek?"

"No, absolutely not," Babrek responded. "He killed the two people I loved the most—the two women in my life who doted over me and cared for me—for no good reason. He didn't have to go to that extreme. He could've reprimanded my sister or even disowned her. He could've sent her to another village—at least she would've had a chance to create a life for herself independent of him and our family.

"But the thing was, my father had a huge anger problem. He would lose control and blow up unexpectedly. Most of the time he would cool down, and sometimes he would even apologize. But he was always a ticking time bomb. What Amina *baji* did was unforgivable in his mind. But from my perspective, what he did was unforgivable—he destroyed my family."

In that last sentence Babrek's voice cracked, but there was also a stony resoluteness Goha had never heard from him. Goha didn't have a sister, but his mother, Naseebo, was the most important woman—the most important person—in his life. His *ammi* was incredibly strong and loving. She worked hard and stood up for herself. She yearned for a better life, but Goha was certain she would willingly give away all her money and possessions if it meant keeping her son and husband safe and healthy.

One time when Goha was little, his *ammi* had to give up her daily wages to care for him when he came down with an illness no one in the *katchi abadis* could diagnose. The memories of her crying next to his bed, reciting *duas*, prayers, rubbing his legs, and blowing over him feverishly for days until he recovered were still as vivid as if they had happened yesterday. His *abba*, too, cared immensely for Goha and his mother, working tirelessly to give them the best life he could. And he had seen over and over again how his father treated children, particularly girls, with tenderness.

Sometimes, after a long day at work, Bala would bring home paper bags from a local *dukandar*, shopkeeper, and give small candies in shiny wrappers to children playing in the alleyways. They would squeal with joy, their dirty, grubby hands outstretched until, laughing, he would hold the bags upside down to prove there were no more sweets left. He would come home grinning, telling Goha and his mother how happy he was to give kids something they loved so much, even though he possessed so little. Goha couldn't imagine Bala doing something so horrific.

"No one deserves what you went through, Babrek."

"I know. It's awful, and it's something I'll never get over. I feel like a piece of me is missing. Since my mom and sister died, I've supported NGOs that empower women and girls to honor their memory."

After Babrek's dad went to prison, his life changed a lot. He became the ward of his dad's distant cousin. They moved to Islamabad for a couple of years, where Babrek was enrolled in an international school for kids of wealthy diplomats and foreign expats. His uncle raised him through his adolescence. He wanted to make sure Babrek had a good start in life and even secured him U.K. citizenship in case he ever wanted to move abroad as an adult.

"He gave me everything I needed," Babrek said. "But soon after I was in his custody, I found out my uncle had a dark side."

"What do you mean?"

Babrek sighed. "He liked boys. He was the first person to convince me there was nothing wrong with same-sex relationships. He assured me it was all normal and natural, even if it was between men and boys. He knew how to rationalize it from every angle—social, political, historical, religious—you name it."

Goha's eyes turned soft. "It sounds like your uncle had a big influence on your sexuality."

"He probably did, but honestly, I've never been attracted to women. I've read that homosexuality is genetic or a combination of genes and the environment you grow up in. It's interesting that some Qur'anic verses point to human differences and diversity being part of God's creative will. Here, I'll show you." He pulled the Qur'an off the bookshelf, appearing relieved at the chance to steer the conversation away from his tumultuous past.

"Look at this verse. '*O People, We created you all from a male and a female and made you into different communities and different tribes, so that you should come to know one another, acknowledging that the most noble among you is the one most aware of God.*'" He turned a few pages. "And here's another one: '*If God had willed, God would have made you one single community, but rather God brings whomever God wills within divine compassion.*'"

"Anyway," he said, closing the book, "now you know my history. I had a traumatic childhood, but it's in the past. And about my sexuality, all I know for sure is that it's part of who I am. I'm good with that, even though lots of people don't want to talk about it or are convinced being Muslim and homosexual are two things that don't go together."

Goha nodded. He got up and walked to the kitchen and took a pot out of the cupboard to make them both a cup of chai.

CHAPTER 7

The following morning Goha was thumbing through a magazine when Babrek told him about a camp where he would soon receive training directly from top leadership.

"They'll also demonstrate how to use your weapons," Babrek told him casually, taking a cigarette out of the box, lighting up, and releasing smoke into the air between them.

Goha waved the fumes away from his face, frowning. "You already showed me. What more do I need to know? Also, didn't you say I wouldn't need to use them? And by the way, you should really cut down on your smoking."

Babrek eyed Goha. "Relax. A few cigarettes here and there and a little chewing tobacco aren't going to kill me. Not right away, anyway. I find it funny how everyone wants to go to *jannah*, but no one wants to die." He shrugged and tapped his cigarette on a saucer to release the ashes. "There might be times you need to use your weapons to protect yourself. That's how it goes around here. Trust me, a little extra training won't hurt. It's best if you know what you're doing."

He told Goha that most recruits were piled onto a bus that took them to the camp, but he had a driver available to take Goha there. "You're lucky—those buses can be crowded, dirty, and uncomfortable. You're getting special treatment. Also, I know I've said it a thousand times, but please don't tell anyone about the camp or the training."

Since arriving up north, Goha hadn't been in contact with his parents or anyone else from Karachi, so he wasn't sure who exactly Babrek was concerned about him telling. Babrek's tone reminded him of the stern warnings from Lala Dabir days before his life-changing train ride. He found all the secrecy intriguing and, at the same time, disconcerting.

Why wouldn't the organization want the public to know they helped victims after the earthquake? Or was it okay to mention that, since it was noble service work they carried out for poor people who needed it most? Did the organization have a public relations wing that touted their humanitarian efforts? If so, why weren't members allowed to help spread the information? Goha assumed the time he spent in Mingora had been one of the organization's "missions," but he didn't know for sure—it was all cloaked in mystery.

Other than their time in Mingora, Goha spent a lot of time idling around while Babrek waited to hear from the organization's higher-ups or attended some meeting or other without providing him details. That gave him plenty of time to reflect on his former life, and—despite all the hardships he'd faced back home—there was a dull, aching pain in his chest.

"Babrek, can I please call my *ammi* and *abba*? It's been a few weeks, and I haven't talked to them. I'm sure they're worried sick."

"Of course. I'll call them from my cell. And I'll reach out to the organization's high command for your phone. Most kids don't get one, but I'll secure one for you before you leave. But remember, you're only allowed to call your parents, and there's no reception inside the camps."

Goha didn't know why he was being treated so well compared to other recruits, but he didn't take it for granted. He appreciated how Babrek joked around but also confided in him about his personal life; how, despite being his superior, Babrek rarely took offense when Goha talked back or hurled accusations. He even seemed to be heeding Goha's nagging about his smoking.

One of Goha's friends, Nasir, had consumed a full packet of cigarettes every day. When Nasir's father fell ill a few years ago and could no longer support the family, his mother was compelled to care for him in addition to five of Nasir's younger siblings. The entire family shared two cramped rooms constructed of cardboard and corrugated iron sheets, which made the Hadis' accommodations look luxurious in comparison. Given his friend's situation at home, Goha was dismayed at how Nasir spent his family's scant savings on something so useless and indulgent. He told Babrek about Nasir, how his frivolous, costly habit compromised the family's food and necessities, made Nasir wheeze, and gave him an annoying, persistent cough.

Although he was still unclear about the specifics of his role and found himself questioning the organization's real purpose, Goha saw himself as one of those sparkling, impossible-to-extinguish birthday candles. Every so often, he had to remind himself it wasn't a dream: Goha Hadi, a boy born in a shantytown in Karachi and sheltered by his doting parents throughout his childhood, had been given a golden ticket to an adventure that other kids in the slums would die for. His resentment toward Babrek had lost its intensity to the point where he felt it slowly diminishing like layers of dead skin.

Babrek dialed the Hadis' number, put the phone on speaker, and turned up the volume. Naseebo picked up on the first ring.

"Hello, Naseebo *begum*. I work with your son, Goha. I'm calling from the human resources department at our company."

"*Ya Allah!* I've been so worried. Please tell me how my *baita* is doing." Though she was hundreds of miles away, Goha sensed Naseebo's anxiety through the phone as if she were right there in the room.

"He is fine, Mrs. Hadi. Don't worry. Goha is here; you can talk to him yourself."

At the sound of her son's voice, Naseebo started wailing so hard she couldn't speak. Thirty seconds passed before she caught her breath.

"Goha, my *baita*, where are you? We heard about a devastating earthquake up north. Are you okay?"

"I'm fine, *ammi*." Goha's heart inflated at the sound of his mother's concern and love.

"What kind of work are you doing? How is everything going? Who are you working with? Are you eating enough? What are they feeding you?"

Goha eyed Babrek cautiously as he attempted to navigate around his mother's barrage of questions. He said he was busier than he ever could have imagined as an office manager trainee.

"My job is complicated, *ammi*. It's too much to explain right now. But I want you to know my boss is happy with my work. I'm eating way more than I ever did in Karachi, and I have a comfortable lifestyle. The next time we see each other, you might not recognize me. My clothes are a couple of sizes bigger than when I left, and my face is so round it looks like the moon." Goha forced a little laugh, hoping it would ease his mother's worry.

"When will you call again? Your father said we aren't allowed to call you from our phone. He isn't here right now, and he really misses you."

"I miss you both too. I don't have my own phone yet, but I'll be getting one soon."

"Okay. Well, since your *abba* isn't here, I'll share some wonderful news. Lala Dabir found a home for us on the other side of Karachi. I know he was the one who secured your job. We haven't seen it yet, but he said it's far from Qasba. Your *abba* and I are so excited. Dabir *sahib* said we can pick our own furniture and decorations. *Baita*, we never could have imagined this in our wildest dreams, and we owe it all to you." She started weeping again.

"I'm happy to hear that, *ammi*." Goha exhaled slowly and gave Babrek a sideways glance. "I can't wait to see the new house. Give my love and *salams* to *abba*. Talk to you soon, *inshallah*."

Goha hung up and reluctantly handed the phone back to Babrek, his throat tight and his eyes moist.

One day, after Goha and Babrek returned from dinner on a cool, windy evening, there was a knock at the door. A middle-aged man with a slight frame and crooked nose, his hair parted neatly to the side, was standing on the threshold.

"Ah *Maulvi* Saber, *assalam-o-alaikum*!" Babrek opened the door wide and ushered the man inside. "It's been awhile. Are you coming back from the *masjid*?"

"*Wa 'alaykumu s-salam*. Yes, I just finished leading *maghrib* prayers," the man replied. "And who is this handsome young man?" He bowed toward Goha.

"This is Gohar Hadi, who is known as Goha. He's visiting from Karachi. Goha, *Maulvi* Saber is the imam of the local mosque. He's well known around these parts, especially for his love of desserts. I always make sure to have something sweet available when the *maulvi* is around. If I didn't, I could get into big trouble." He grinned as he supported Saber's arm and helped him settle into the sofa. "I'll make us chai, and I'll be sure to add extra sugar to yours, *Maulvi* Saber."

Despite Babrek's congeniality toward the *maulvi*, Goha sat beside him in strained silence while Babrek clanged around in the kitchen. He shifted around, tapping his fingers on the armrest and crossing and uncrossing his legs repeatedly, and was relieved when Babrek came out carrying a tray with filled mugs and a plate of biscuits.

"Chai is ready," Babrek said cheerfully.

Maulvi Saber moaned as he got up, holding the armrest for support, and hobbled to the dining table. "My hip always seems to act up in this kind of weather," he said. He lowered himself into the chair Babrek had pulled out for him. "Anyway, in my opinion, not enough men showed up for prayers, as usual. I don't know what's the matter with people these days." He blew on his chai with short, repeated puffs and took a prolonged sip. "But I suppose if they aren't interested in coming to a house of worship to remember our Creator, there isn't much I can do about it."

It occurred to Goha that people could have perfectly legitimate reasons for not coming to the mosque to pray, such as work, school, illness, or caring for loved ones. Plus, wasn't the imam supposed to play a significant role in encouraging the congregation to attend?

Sheikh Samir always provided a warm and inclusive environment at the *masjid*, particularly to newcomers, and was genuinely concerned when regulars didn't show up. The contrast between the two religious leaders seemed chasmic, but he said nothing since he had just met Saber; from the day he was born, Goha had been taught to be respectful toward his elders.

"Speaking of people not showing up at the *masjid*, where have you been, Babrek? I remembered you were staying here, so I stopped by to make sure everything was okay."

"Thanks for checking on me, *Maulvi* Saber," replied Babrek. "Everything is fine. I've just been busy."

"Doing what?"

"Well, Goha and I were in Mingora for a few days helping victims of the recent earthquake."

"I see. Good for you. Although you didn't get paid anything for it, did you? Not sure I would have spent my time helping people who likely won't remember or appreciate it. But to each his own. There's always some kind of disaster or other happening around here, so I suppose that's one way to keep yourself busy."

How could a religious man have such a cavalier attitude toward the victims of a natural calamity? Goha shuddered. The *maulvi* reminded him of snakes who shed their skin; the *maulvi* had discarded his empathy toward other humans.

"I'm heading out of town early tomorrow for business," Babrek told them.

"Where are you going?" Saber asked.

"*Maulvi* Saber, I can't tell you. You know the work I do is confidential. That's why I'm always moving around from one rooming house to the next."

"Right. Well, I'm glad to see your education has paid off and you're working hard. Safe travels to you. On that note, I better get going. It looks like it's about to rain." Goha followed Saber's gaze out the window. Ominous clouds had started crisscrossing the sky.

"Do you know there's a vicious storm headed our way? The downpour tonight will be a trickle compared to what's coming next week. The weather people on TV said it's going to last for several days, and the whole town will be flooded. They said it will feel like the end of the world."

"I'm sure they're exaggerating, *Maulvi* Saber," Babrek said. "I've never understood how forecasters can predict the weather so far ahead—they aren't mystics, for God's sake. But I suppose they need to say things like that to keep people's attention. Anyway, even if it happens, it will be good for the crops."

"Well, you've been here long enough to know this area is prone to floods, and we've had bad ones before. We'll see what happens this time. Anyway, it's almost time for *isha namaz*, so *khuda hafiz* to you both."

"Take care of yourself, *Maulvi* Saber." Babrek's phone buzzed, and he stepped into the kitchen to answer it. Saber rose from the chair with a groan, rubbing his hip.

"Since Babrek will be out, you must come and visit me, young man," he said, turning to Goha as he limped toward the door. "My place is up the hill—it's the brown house beside the *masjid* that resembles a cottage."

Goha was put off by the *maulvi's* offhand and insensitive remarks, but it did seem he could use support with his hip troubles. Plus, it would be nice to have a proper home to visit and more people to converse with besides Babrek.

"Thank you, *Maulvi* Saber," Goha replied. "I will take you up on that and come by soon, *inshallah*."

Early the next morning, before Babrek left, a lanky boy in dirt-stained clothes, riding a rusty bicycle, dropped off Goha's new flip phone at the rooming house. Despite all its restrictions and conditions, Goha considered the device his most valuable possession. The ability to finally communicate with the outside world lifted his mood exponentially.

"This should be enough for your meals and other expenses,"

Babrek said, putting a wad of rupees in Goha's pocket. He hugged him tightly.

Goha surrendered to Babrek's embrace. "How long will you be gone?"

"I really don't know." Babrek ran his hands through Goha's hair. "I'm not sure how much I'll be in touch. Leadership gave us strict warnings about staying attentive during meetings. And there probably won't be cell phone service where I'm going anyway."

Goha's eyes stung. How was he going to survive without Babrek, his only companion up north? Their relationship was complicated and it certainly had a rocky, exploitative start. But it had improved over time, and as Babrek drove away, Goha experienced the same despondency as when he had left his parents behind in Karachi. He stood at the main door of the building and waved at Babrek forlornly until the black SUV turned the corner.

From the moment Babrek left, Goha moped around the room, picking up a random book or magazine every few minutes but unable to escape his encapsulating loneliness. So when *Maulvi* Saber stopped by that afternoon to invite him for dinner that evening, he gratefully accepted the invitation.

As the evening sky swallowed the final glow of sunset, Goha took a shower, changed into a sharp new turquoise *shalwar kameez* Babrek had bought him at the *bazaar*, quickly said his *maghrib namaz*, and left the rooming house. Set on a hill, Saber's house was a sturdy, single-level building constructed of solid wood and bricks, and a dim yellow hue through the window made the interior appear warm and cozy. He knocked at the door.

A woman about ten years younger than Saber answered. Goha gasped at her deep aqua eyes, long blonde hair, smooth porcelain skin, and slender neck. She wore a long black robe adorned with shiny white cowrie shells and delicately stitched embroidery that encompassed all colors of the rainbow.

"Hello, you must be Goha," she said, the warmth in her eyes matching the kindness in her voice. "*Maulvi Saber ne mujhe bataya thha ke tum pahari ke niche walay ghar mein reh rahay ho.*" Maulvi Saber told me you're staying at the rooming house down the hill.

Goha couldn't pinpoint the origin of her accent, but he thought it rendered her Urdu utterly adorable.

"It's nice to meet you. I'm Kajal."

"Hello, Kajal," he replied, convinced she could witness blood rushing to his ears.

A door closed, and a minute later, Saber entered, wearing a walnut brown *shalwar kameez* and a matching *topee*. "Thanks for coming on such short notice, Goha. I just finished saying *maghrib namaz*."

"Thanks for inviting me, *Maulvi* Saber."

"I see you've met Kajal," Saber continued. "In case you were wondering, she's Kalash—that's why she looks like a complete foreigner. She stands out like a giraffe in a herd of monkeys. Her people worship many gods, just like those ignorant Meccans in Arabia before Islam came around." He snickered. "They think rocks are alive. Can you believe how ludicrous that is?"

Is Kajal Saber's wife? She must be, Goha reasoned, *if she is staying in the same house as him. But how can he talk so disparagingly about her in the third person, like she isn't even in the room?* Kajal was objectively one of the most gorgeous women Goha had ever seen up close, and by some unexplained miracle, this woman who could have easily stepped off a Hollywood movie set was standing barely two feet away.

"I've tried to teach Kajal *namaz*, but for some reason, she doesn't get it," the *maulvi* droned on. "She's always messing up prostrations and forgetting how many *rakats* are in each *salat*. I'm not sure why it's so hard for her—Muslims all around the world have figured it out. All I can say is it's a good thing I was named *Saber*, which in case you didn't know means *one who has patience*. God knows how much I've had to endure with her."

Kajal pursed her lips.

"Kajal told me she was going to cook a special Kalash dinner for you, but she woke up this morning and said she wasn't feeling well. I know people like her—I wasn't born yesterday, you know. Look at her now. She's doing just fine."

Goha was astounded at how someone could be reasonably cordial, then a few hours later, become so obnoxious and rude. Saber reminded him of *kheeras*, cucumbers, his mother would bring home from the market—they looked delicious with their smooth green skin but required rubbing and salting to eliminate the unpleasant bitter taste on the inside.

"Don't worry, I won't let you leave here hungry," Saber was saying. "I'll run out to the restaurant and pick up dinner. It will probably taste better than Kajal's cooking anyway, which has been hit or miss these days, and to be honest, mostly miss. I have no problem with the two of you getting to know each other when I'm gone."

Then, before either of them could respond, Saber left the house, banging the door behind him.

Goha's mouth hung open. He turned to Kajal, who appeared equally flabbergasted by Saber's bizarre, hasty departure. She gave him an anxious smile.

"Can I get you something to drink? Water, juice, or maybe a soft drink?"

Goha's throat had been parched the moment he laid eyes on Kajal. "A glass of water would be great. Thank you."

He followed her apprehensively into the sitting room and sat on the sofa, astonished at how the *maulvi* seemed to have no problem with Kajal being left alone with a *na-mahram*, a man with whom marriage was permissible.

Kajal went to the kitchen and returned with two silver goblets. She set them on the coffee table in the middle of the room and perched herself beside him.

"Saber told me you're from Karachi," Kajal said finally, breaking the silence. "I've never been there before, but I know it's a huge city down south, on the coast. The biggest city I've been to is Peshawar. Do you like it here? It must be so different from the city life you're used to."

"It is different, and I do like it. It's a breathtaking part of our country. There's a lot more nature and fewer people. It's less polluted and more peaceful than where I grew up. I'm so glad I had the opportunity to come here." *Especially now that I've met you.* Goha couldn't remember the words he had just spoken or if they made sense. He was staring at Kajal, but he couldn't help himself. His hands became clammy, and sweat formed around his brow.

"The area I come from is north of here and even more beautiful," Kajal said. "Have you heard of Bumburet?"

"Hmmm, not sure," Goha admitted, suddenly conscious she might write him off as a *gadha.* "I love history, but I was never very good at geography. Don't laugh, but is it near Turkey? You have an accent, and I'm probably not the first to tell you that you look more European than Pakistani."

"Nope, not nearly as far away as Turkey. But I would love to visit there one day." Kajal laughed, and to Goha, the sound was as delightful as a flock of seagulls chattering on the waterfront where he had hung out with friends during school holidays. "And you're right—you aren't the first to tell me I look European. Saber says I stick out like an albino around here." A bemused smile emerged on her face.

The Bumburet Valley was actually in Pakistan, not far from the Afghanistan border, she told him. The Hindu Kush mountains were to the north, Chitral was to the northeast, Kunar Valley was to the south, and the Alishang River was to the west. Bumburet was about a seven-hour drive from Mingora.

Goha was already awed by her appearance and was now becoming equally smitten with her precise geographical knowledge of the area.

"Did you experience the earthquake a few days ago? It struck really close to my village. I feel so useless being here. I wish there was something I could do to help."

"I went to Mingora with my supervisor, Babrek, after the earthquake hit. We worked with the government to give food and supplies to the victims." Goha stifled a gasp. *Oh shoot, I wasn't supposed to tell anyone. Or is it okay to talk about the relief effort since Babrek mentioned it to Maulvi Saber?* Goha decided it wasn't worth dwelling over—the only thing he wanted in that moment was to impress the woman in front of him.

"I'm so happy you were able to do that."

"The members of the organization I work for were the first ones on-site," he continued, encouraged by her admiration and grateful to talk about the experience in a way that didn't appear braggy. "They really know how to reach remote villages. Other groups weren't nearly as effective as ours. We saw the destruction up close and even pulled bodies out of the wreckage. It was terrible, but I'm so glad I was there to help."

"I'm glad you were too." Her eyelashes fluttered, and she took a sip of water.

Goha tilted forward. He didn't want to talk about the earthquake anymore—all he wanted was to intimately get to know the beauty in front of him that fate had so kindly bestowed upon him. "So tell me about Bumburet. What's it like there?"

"Our valley is the most gorgeous place in the world." Kajal's voice was dreamy. "It's lush green with natural streams and rivers surrounded by majestic mountains. It's like paradise."

Their land had come to be known as Kafiristan—the land of disbelievers—because Kalash people didn't follow Islam. Throughout history, Muslims had come into the valley to try to save the souls of the people in her community. "They consider us infidels," she said. "Sometimes people come to help us after natural disasters hit, but then they try to convince us to join a cause we don't believe in or do things against our peaceful nature."

Goha shook his head. One of Sheikh Samir's first teachings was that there was no compulsion in religion, and it saddened him how people misrepresented and exploited Islam. While he had always believed his faith was the true path to God, his compassion overflowed toward this woman, who, along with the rest of her tribe, had clearly been berated for being blasphemous and heretical. Once again, *kheeras*, the outwardly appealing but bitter cucumbers, came to mind, but out loud he said, "I'm sorry to hear that."

The total Kalash community was only about four thousand people now, and that number had steadily declined for years. Everything about them—their appearance, culture, customs, language, clothing, what they ate—was starkly at odds with other native groups in Pakistan. "It's like we dropped out of the sky like aliens and randomly landed on the Indian subcontinent, and now we're in a country that's almost one hundred percent Muslim. It's pretty hilarious if you think about it." Her words until then had a serious overtone, but with her last statement, her face spontaneously broke into a grin, and she giggled.

"I actually do recall learning about the Kalash, and it was fascinating." Goha was irritated how, at that exact moment, the details from the lesson on indigenous tribes of Pakistan seemed to vanish from his memory. "I honestly didn't think I'd have the opportunity to meet a Kalash person, and I certainly never imagined it would be someone as lovely as you." He wasn't used to talking like that to a woman, let alone someone as drop-dead gorgeous as Kajal, and he averted his gaze to his feet as soon as he said it.

"I guess the Kalash people represent the white part in the Pakistani flag," he added, looking up and attempting to shift the conversation into a more scholarly, neutral tone. In school, he had learned the large green block on the right side was a traditional Islamic color representing Muslims in the country, and the smaller white strip on the left was meant to recognize non-Muslim, minority religious groups. The white crescent indicated progress, and the white star symbolized knowledge and light.

"I wish Kalash customs and traditions were given more respect," he told Kajal. "Your community deserves it. Minority groups are an invaluable part of our nation's fabric and history."

A dispiritedness came over Goha; the symbolism behind the Pakistani flag was at odds with how society had moved forward since the country's inception. In the aftermath of British colonial rule, India had become Pakistan's long-standing enemy from the moment it had emerged as a fledgling nation of its own in 1947. Progress in Pakistan had focused on building nuclear stockpiles and military might to ward off real or perceived advances from India, at the great expense of social services to help the country's impoverished masses. Ironically, all this was counter to what Muhammad Ali Jinnah, the revered, secular founder of the nation, had envisioned.

Kajal smiled wistfully, and Goha had to turn away. *How did someone as amazing as Kajal end up with someone as uncouth and ill-mannered as Maulvi Saber?*

He gulped down his water. "Kajal, I hope you don't mind me asking, but how did you meet Saber?"

"Randomly in a store when I first moved to Peshawar to find work. We started talking, and he seemed . . . well, friendly, I guess. He helped me find things I was looking for. He kept in touch and seemed genuinely concerned about my well-being. We went out a few times and got along well. At the time, I think he was attracted to my feistiness and free spirit."

Most boys she had met in college considered her stunningly attractive but beyond their reach. Some harassed her; others hadn't been interested in becoming serious with a girl so independent and opinionated. Saber had presented himself as open-minded and accepting, and that pleasantly surprised her. She never thought a Muslim leader would want to be with a woman from a different faith.

"Within a few weeks, we talked about getting married, and he told me as his wife I would have . . . what did he say? A comfortable life. That I'd never have to work for a living if I didn't want to." She thought he had said that because he respected the work women do at home without pay—and realized too late he wanted control over her and their finances.

She told Saber she wanted to work, and he promised that after they married, she could teach kids about her tribe and minority rights in Pakistan at a school beside the *masjid* where he served as the imam. Kajal couldn't wait to meet new people, make friends, use her degree, and earn her own income. She accepted Saber's marriage proposal in good faith, thinking it might help her feel less insecure and more rooted in her new environment. The Kalash as a whole were honest and trustworthy, and they truly believed others were, too, until proven wrong, she said.

She halted. "Oh my goodness. I'm telling you so much, and I've only just met you."

"No, it's okay. Really. I'm flattered that you're confiding in me." *Don't stop. Don't ever stop.* He cleared his throat. "Your story is so fascinating. And it sounds like you need someone to talk to. You can feel free to tell me anything. Anytime." *Always. For the rest of my life.*

"Thanks. I don't have many friends around here. People are intimidated by my looks and unusual background. They really have no idea what to make of me. Anyway—where was I? Oh yes. Saber asked me to become Muslim, and I was fine with that, even though I didn't know much about Islam."

Saber had said it would be better for his standing as an imam if he had a Muslim wife. He told Kajal the basic tenets and asked her to repeat phrases in Arabic. She didn't understand them, and he didn't bother to translate. When she asked what they meant, he said it wasn't important. Then, on the day they married, Saber read the *nikah*. It was just the two of them present. "But since then, I found out that at least two witnesses are necessary for a *nikah* to be valid. Isn't that right?"

Before Goha could answer, she edged forward and kissed him on the lips.

"Sorry, I couldn't help myself. You're so handsome." Her face was inches away from his, so close he could see her pores and the exact shape of an asymmetrical small brown mole on her neck. "I know where Saber went to get dinner, and it will be at least an hour before he returns. Why don't we take Saber's advice and get to know each other better in the meantime?"

Kajal opened the top button of her shirt to reveal her ample cleavage. She turned an inviting gaze over to him.

Words evaporated from Goha's mouth. Most of the girls at his school and *madrasa* were shy and modest around boys. He had never encountered a woman so sensual, confident, and forward. A story across Abrahamic faiths about a woman called Zulekha flashed through his mind. Married to a rich and famous resident of the town, she became consumed by her desire for the Prophet Yusuf. The Qur'an related the story of how she brazenly seduced him to satisfy her lust, even as Yusuf tried to resist her advances.

"But we're Muslims and not married. What about . . . *Maulvi* Saber . . . I can't do this . . . wait . . . this isn't allowed . . ."

"I'm not Muslim; I'm Kalash," Kajal reminded him. "I may be wrong about this, but I'm pretty sure reciting Arabic phrases I don't understand doesn't make me a Muslim. And like I said, there were no witnesses at the *nikah*, so evidently I'm not married either."

Goha was awestruck. How could she be so calm when his hormones were racing rampantly around the room?

Kajal tilted her head and let her long hair cascade down her back, and something smoldering inside Goha unleashed. *Even if this is forbidden, I've already crossed the line with Babrek.* He began kissing Kajal's neck and running his hands over her shapely body as she writhed and moaned.

"That horrid Saber hasn't touched me for months," Kajal breathed in Goha's ear. "Don't stop. I love what you're doing."

She ran her hands down Goha's chest and started tugging at his *shalwar*, and Goha sat up swiftly. "Wait—what if you get pregnant?" he stammered. It had happened to a few unmarried teens in the *katchi abadis*, and he had witnessed firsthand how the community shamed and ostracized them. When Goha was younger, he had overheard Zaida, the busybody neighborhood gossip, tell other women he was conceived before Bala and Naseebo were married, an idea so scandalous he fervently made every effort to erase all hints of it from his mind. His face drained, and his passion began to subside.

"I have a cream we can use so that doesn't happen. Let's go to the bedroom," she pleaded, holding up her arms and pointing to an adjacent door.

Goha lifted Kajal and gingerly carried her into the bedroom, placing her in the middle of the bed. His libido again took over as he took in her alluring body and delicately removed her clothing.

He attempted to make love to her but went limp. He caressed her body over and over, unsuccessfully trying a few more times. He finally sat up, dejected, and covered his face with his hands.

Kajal pulled the sheet over them both. "Don't be upset, Goha," she said gently, stroking his cheek with her index finger. "You're young and so handsome, but I can see you're inexperienced."

As Kajal rose to dress, Goha locked himself in the bathroom, turned the knob, and stared at the water dripping out of the faucet. *I'm so humiliated. I can't even look at her.* He finally washed his face and returned to the room, avoiding her gaze as he helped her tidy the bed in silence.

A few minutes later, Saber arrived with vegetable *pakoras, bhuna gosht,* chicken *tikka, khamiri* naans, and spicy yogurt. The food looked delicious, but Goha was too discombobulated to enjoy it. He sheepishly made banal small talk and tepidly took a few bites from the plate in front of him in a vain effort to act as normal as possible.

CHAPTER 8

A hard copy of *Sufism: An Introduction to the Mystical Tradition of Islam* was face down on Goha's lap as he lay back on the recliner. Two days ago, he had left Saber's house jumbled and guilt-ridden, and although he tried his hardest, since then it had become nearly impossible for him to concentrate on the book or much of anything other than his intimacy with Kajal. Sometimes he became so aroused that he spontaneously had to jump into the shower to cool himself off. There was, however, one section of the book he found himself fixating on: Jalaluddin Rumi's love poetry, and one quote in particular that consistently ran though his brain: *Your task is not to seek for love, but merely to seek and find all the barriers within yourself that you have built against it.*

A jarring knock blasted through the stillness of the room like a gunshot. It couldn't be Babrek; he wouldn't bother knocking. Goha got up cautiously and cracked open the door. *Maulvi* Saber stood outside, tapping his foot.

"*Assalam-o-alaikum.*" He pushed the door open and brushed past Goha to let himself inside.

Goha's mind raced like an overwound electric toy. *Oh God, I've been caught. Maulvi Saber found out what happened. She must have told him. It was all a setup—and I'm such a bewakoof gadha I fell right into the trap. Oh my God, I'm such a fool . . .*

He eyed *Maulvi* Saber's *kameez* pockets for the bulge of a weapon.

Maybe I can outwit Saber and get my gun from the safe. Maybe I can distract him by pointing at something outside the window . . .

"Goha, if you're not busy, I'd like to have a cup of *kahwa* with you." He pulled out a chair at the dining room table.

Goha recoiled at his affable tone. *Who is this strange, contradictory man?*

"So, did you have fun at my place the other night?"

Goha flinched. "Yes, I . . . I really enjoyed the visit," he sputtered. "Your wife . . . I mean Kajal is . . . really hospitable. And the food you brought was delicious."

"That Kalash woman? Hmmph. She is not my wife—she is my ex-wife."

"Wait . . . your ex-wife?"

"Correct. I divorced her, and I have absolutely no interest in her anymore."

Goha let the *maulvi's* words sink in, shock and relief hitting him all at once like colliding waves. But there were still gaping pieces of the Kajal and *Maulvi* Saber puzzle missing in his brain.

"*Maulvi* Saber, Kajal told me you performed a *nikah* ceremony to make your marriage official, but there were no witnesses present. I'm no expert, but aren't two witnesses required according to *sharia* law? And even if you were married to Kajal, isn't divorce considered a last resort? My *madrasa* teacher said married couples should try their best to get past differences. And if they do decide to separate, they need to pronounce it on three separate occasions—at least a month apart—so they don't make a rash decision. Did you do that?" Even as he said it, Goha registered that the last thing he wanted was for Kajal to stay tied to the *maulvi*.

Saber glared at Goha, his eyes narrowing. He grunted.

"I should know what makes a *nikah* and divorce valid or invalid in Islam—I'm an imam! What's more, I really don't have the time or interest to talk about these kinds of petty topics with you or anyone else." He sat back in his chair and crossed his arms on his chest, scowling.

"But let me make two things clear: I don't agree with you or your so-called *madrasa* teacher, and as I already said, I don't consider Kajal my wife. She and her people are *kafirs*. They worship a wild goat, for God's sake! So you are free to have her and enjoy her as you like!"

Maulvi Saber sat motionless, his eyes riveted on the wall. And then, without warning, he got up, opened the door, and left the room.

Goha spent most of the next day pacing, ruminating over the *maulvi's* bizarre declarations and becoming more and more confused.

When evening set in and his rumbling stomach reminded him he hadn't eaten anything since morning, he heard a soft tap on his door. He tiptoed, barely breathing and hypervigilant. He finally opened the door just a smidge, prepared to slam it shut and drop to the floor if needed. He fully expected Saber to show up again with a change of heart, ready to take him out with a loaded gun.

He jerked back when Kajal appeared through the slit, holding a large paper bag. Her hair was tied back in braids, accentuating her high cheekbones, and a meticulously threaded headband crowned her golden hair. *She's even more radiant than I remembered.*

For a second, he heard voices. It was his mother, then father, then Sheikh Samir, all conveying the same gentle but firm message: *Be careful, baita. Watch out for danger and look out for yourself.* But Kajal's nervous yet earnest expression suggested she was a genuinely sweet person who'd had the misfortune of inadvertently getting stuck in Saber's malicious web.

He opened the door wider.

"Kajal! What a lovely surprise. Please come in."

"Thank you, Goha."

"I see you've brought something. Here, let me take it."

"Oh, it's nothing, really. I made some meatball curry, *chapatis*, and *daal*. Are you hungry? I was hoping we could eat dinner together."

"I'm always hungry. In fact, I was just about to make myself something, so your timing is perfect. This food smells incredible."

For another fleeting second, his rational brain took over. *Did Saber send her to spy on me, hurt me, or worse? Did she poison the food?* His *ammi*, *abba*, and even Sheikh Samir would be devastated, downright shattered, if they learned about his doomed fate in the very place he was positioned to jump-start his family's prosperous new life.

"Do you know where *Maulvi* Saber is?"

She said he had left for Peshawar for an interview to be an imam at a much larger mosque and would be gone for a few days. "They're offering twice the salary he's getting now, and he thinks he deserves it. Saber's always had a healthy ego." She smiled wryly.

With that, Goha's intuition took over. He'd spent the past few days absorbing Rumi's poetic reflections, mulling over whether it was appropriate to see Kajal again and, if so, how he could make it happen. And now, here she was like a technicolor mirage in the middle of a bleak, arid desert, standing right in front of him. This was meant to be. Rumi's profound words once again echoed: *Lovers don't finally meet somewhere. They're in each other all along.*

Kajal took off her *chadar*, shawl, and pulled out a chair. She was wearing another striking black dress, this one accented in mint green with ruby red flowers. "To be honest, I don't really want to talk about Saber." She said she was glad she had remembered where Goha was staying so she could come see him. "I had a great time the other night, and I'd like to get to know you better."

Goha's heart melted onto the floor.

"What was your life like before you came here?"

Goha faltered. The time he had spent watching Pakistani TV shows in the slums taught him that coming from a poor family was a turnoff as far as serious romantic interests and marriage prospects went. *Should I tell her about my impoverished upbringing?* Kajal had told him he was handsome, but he wasn't *bewakoof*, idiotic, enough to think that good looks were enough. He was certainly well-compensated by the organization, but sometimes, all his experiences up north—all the secrecy, all the unanswered questions—felt as slippery as mercury.

Goha heard Sheikh Samir, wise and patient, telling his students that being forthright was one of the most important and powerful aspects of Islam. Kajal had opened up to him without reservation about Saber, personally demonstrating the Kalash attributes she said she admired: genuineness, honesty, and trustworthiness. He took a deep breath. *Please let my truthfulness pay off. Please let this irresistible woman with the most soulful eyes in the world understand me.*

"I was born in a poor area of Karachi," Goha started. "My parents wanted more kids, but I turned out to be their only child. I guess it was our family's *kismat.* For my whole life and even before I was born, my *abba* has worked as a day laborer. My *ammi* is a domestic helper. She cleans big houses in affluent areas of Karachi, and for years, she's seen how rich people live. She's always wanted that kind of life for our family, where we don't have to constantly worry about money and we can easily afford necessities, where we are able to travel and buy nice things. But it always seemed far beyond our world, so far that there was no way we could possibly reach it."

He glanced at Kajal, who was listening to him with the intense adoration of a fangirl. It was exactly what he yearned for, and it gave him the courage to go on.

"I went to a government school close to where we lived. The school was understaffed, underfunded, and overcrowded. A lot of times, the power went out and teachers didn't show up. But I love learning, and I always scored at the top of my class." Many families kept their kids out of school to make money, he told her, but Goha's parents always prioritized education, saying it was the ticket to a better future.

Goha's school was Urdu-medium, which meant classes were taught mostly in Urdu. That was common in government schools for the lower strata; wealthy kids in private schools were instructed in English. But Goha knew it was important to learn the language of the elites. "I used to watch American and British sitcoms after school to learn basic English words and phrases. Like 'How's it goin', y'all?' and

'Mind the gap, ol' chap.'" Goha delivered the sentences in exaggerated American South and British accents, and Kajal laughed out loud.

At both his secular government school and *madrasa*, Goha had encountered a mishmash of students, some like him, many from even poorer families than his, others from more middle-class backgrounds. Some were friendly and inclusive, others outright bullies. One group of boys, led by a chunky, cheeky boy named Hamid who regularly boasted about his rich entrepreneurial *mamoo*, poked fun at him, calling him *"ghareeb larka* Goha" or "poor boy Goha." While supportive classmates encouraged him, tormentors like Hamid often got the upper hand. Hamid envied and resented Goha's natural intellect and exceptional scholastic accomplishments, and his ongoing harassment made Goha even more determined to pursue higher education so he could leave behind the dingy conditions of his upbringing and achieve something big in his life. But the time wasn't right to reveal any of this to Kajal. Not yet.

"My parents are the most hardworking, caring, and generous people," he said instead. "They've done everything possible to keep me safe, healthy, and happy. They didn't want to send me so far away, but since we couldn't afford college, this work seemed like a great opportunity for me to help make our country better." He considered mentioning the large sum of money Lala Dabir had unreservedly laid out in front of him and Bala but decided it would sound too boastful.

"Your parents sound amazing. You are lucky to have them. And they're lucky to have a son like you."

Goha smiled wistfully. "Okay, your turn. Tell me about you."

"Oh, you are so wonderful." Kajal threw her arms around his neck in an unexpected, affectionate hug. "Saber was so condescending and superior when I talked about my family and culture. You're not like that at all."

"Kajal." Goha pushed her away slightly. "You are an incredible woman, but . . . well, I guess I'm just having a hard time justifying what we did the other night." Even as he uttered the words, he questioned their truthfulness. He wanted her—badly. But he also wanted to be a good Muslim. His intimacy with Babrek made his words taste bitter and ironic.

Kajal turned away and started to pick the plates off the table.

"No, wait." His voice was desperate as he took her hand. He pulled her gently down beside him and brushed a stray hair from her face. "I'm really attracted to you. You honestly remind me of a Hollywood actress—you're so beautiful. I haven't been able to stop thinking about you. I guess . . . well, I guess I'm just overwhelmed. I've never been in this kind of situation before."

"When we met the other night, I'm sure you thought I was a promiscuous and maybe even crazy person. After all, who on earth would seduce someone they just met, especially when they're living in the house of an imam?" Kajal's laughter filled the room, echoing off the walls and seeping into Goha's skin.

In Kajal's family, she said, they bragged about their sixth sense, what their gut instinct told them about people they had just met, and it was almost always right. "I knew you were genuine and caring when I met you. I just knew it. With Saber, it was different—he changed after we got married. I got distracted when he said I could teach kids about Kalash culture. But now that I know him, I think . . . well, I think he's just a really clever man who's a master at fooling others."

In Pakistani dramas, Goha viewed the poor, love-stricken boy with a mixture of pity and envy, always rooting for him wholeheartedly from the outside, never knowing if he truly had what it took to triumph over the villain and attain the woman of his dreams. Now he was the boy—this was his drama.

Kajal said her parents were farmers who grew fruit and raised goats. They made cheese, butter, and *ghee*, and sold it in Bumburet and the local area. The natural world was the center of everything they did. Kalash people believed the mountains surrounding their valley protected them and that changing seasons brought different food sources to nourish and sustain them.

Her parents were in their seventies but still in great health. Kajal believed their longevity was in large part because their lives centered around nature and community, the things that really mattered. A lot of the grapes, apricots, apples, and pears available in Pakistan came from the Bumburet Valley, she told him. "So make sure you think about us the next time you bite into sweet, flavorful grapes or a fragrant, juicy apricot. Okay?"

"You're already on my mind constantly. I won't need to bite into an apricot to think about you." Goha wondered how he had suddenly become so bold, if Kajal's openness had brought out his vulnerability.

"Hey, question for you: Are Kalash people descendants of the Greeks? I remember hearing that one time. Do you know if it's true?"

"Yeah, that theory has been circulating around our village for as long as I can remember. I honestly don't know." Researchers from around the globe came to the valley to study the Kalash, and many believed they were descendants of Alexander the Great's invading army. But others said there was no real evidence. "What I do know is we're indigenous to the land, and we've been around for centuries." She rubbed her cheek thoughtfully. "I suppose it doesn't really matter where we came from originally. We definitely look different than other Pakistanis, but what's on the inside counts more."

"You're beautiful inside and out." Goha coughed, suddenly self-conscious. "Your talk of all the fruits from your valley and the smell of your cooking is making my mouth water. I'm starving. Can we eat?"

"Of course. But now that we've established we're each other's biggest fans, can you please tell me the meal is delicious even if the meatballs are raw, the *daal* is undercooked, or there isn't enough salt?"

Goha nodded solemnly. "You got it, Chef Kajal." He took the food out of the bag. "And while we eat, you can tell me more about Kalash culture. Before I met you, I was arrogant enough to think I knew everything about the people and history of Pakistan."

"I could go on about it all day long. Tell you what, I'll start at the beginning and only stop if I hear you snoring."

As they dug into the food, Kajal told him she was born in Bumburet, in the largest of the three valleys in Kafiristan. Her two older brothers, Timuk and Yansing, were married with kids. They lived in the valley and helped her parents out a lot. Kajal was a lot younger than her brothers but had never felt lonely because there were dozens of kids her age in the village to play with.

"My parents were over the moon when I came along—they said they always wanted a girl," she said.

In Bumburet, one person's roof was somebody else's veranda. Little staircases connected one house to another. "When I was little, climbing those stairs with my friends was magical, like we were ascending into a tree house in the clouds. Our valley is secluded, and when I peeked through the wooden window frames and ladders of the houses, there were massive, jagged stones and dense green mountains. It was like living in a fairyland." Kajal's voice was far away.

Most people in Bumburet lived in poverty, and many only spoke the tribal language, Kalasha. The things they held most dear were not material possessions but their unique culture and traditions. Kalash people had a strong work ethic—they believed all work was dignified and no job was below them. After all, Kajal asked rhetorically, how could a community function if there weren't people with different talents and skills doing various kinds of work?

Growing up, Kajal said she had everything that mattered—love, family, community, food, and spirituality. "It was a simple and happy environment where we made our own food and sewed our own clothes. I still prefer wearing handmade dresses. They're so much more special and interesting than factory-made ones."

As a kid, she hadn't experienced anything other than the Kalash way of life. It was only when she moved away that she learned how insulated her community was from the modern world. "Honestly, we're the kind of people anthropologists dream about. Flocks of them visit during our festivals."

Suri Jagek, the traditional Kalash meteorological and astronomical knowledge system, predicted the best times for sowing seeds, managing livestock, and preparing for natural disasters. It also determined dates for social events, festivals, feasts, and religious ceremonies. Kajal had heard a rumor that *Suri Jagek* would soon be protected by UNESCO, and if that happened, they would, in all likelihood, get more support from the global community. "Maybe then our numbers will stop declining so rapidly," she said, her voice hopeful and ruminative.

With so many people going out of their way to learn about the unique Kalash community, it reminded Goha of Pakistan's rare blind Indus River dolphins he had studied in school. "Did having outsiders wandering around your valley asking questions ever bother you?" he asked.

Kajal said she didn't mind it, nor did most people from her tribe. Kalash people received money from tourism, and most visitors were genuinely interested in getting to know them and learning about their culture. "We feel proud when our guests say we're special. They're worried we'll become extinct, which would be a national tragedy and an international embarrassment for Pakistan." The Kalash were the last surviving animist community in the country, so advocates stood up for them and used the media to share their plight, she said.

In the past, people from neighboring tribes had taken advantage of their trusting nature and unassuming habits by stealing herds of sheep and goats, running businesses on their land, and robbing the Kalash of profits. However, on a positive note, the government put initiatives in place to make sure the community got fresh water during the winter, and safeguards ensured money from crops went directly to Kalash farmers like Kajal's parents instead of unscrupulous middlemen. Plus, a new generation of young Pakistanis was emerging who adamantly spoke out in favor of different cultures coexisting, and Kajal was encouraged to see more Kalash youngsters attending school.

The Kalash had no real power or influence because they were such a tiny minority. Most were intimidated by the modern world and spoke only minimal Urdu or Pashto. Kajal said she was worried about her people, especially the older generation. "They just want to live uncomplicated lives connected to each other and the earth as they have for centuries, and that's put their entire existence in jeopardy," she said sadly.

"I'm so sorry about everything you've had to deal with. Why did you leave initially?"

"I wanted to explore life outside the valley. When I was little, I always had my nose in a book, and I was exposed to fascinating worlds, worlds that were so different from Bumburet it was almost impossible for me to believe they were real."

She ended up graduating from high school with distinction and received a four-year scholarship from an international NGO to study at a brand-new university, the University of Chitral. It was hard for her parents to send her away, but they supported her decision. It was a big deal for a Kalash kid to go to university, she said, and the community had thrown a big farewell party in her honor before she left.

Her love for children and learning about human behavior led her to pursue a joint degree in education and psychology. She said she hadn't had a chance to use it since she met Saber, but she hoped to soon. "It could be a challenge, though, since extremists around here seem intent on destroying schools. I don't get it," she said, shaking her head.

When Kajal had moved to Chitral, she saw how widespread technology had become, how it connected people and ideas and made the world smaller. Many of her friends were happy to stay in the valley, get married, and keep Kalash traditions alive—sewing clothes, farming, cooking, preparing for the festivals, and raising children. She respected that but yearned for more. "I wanted independence, at least for a little while, before I settled down. I thought getting married too early would stifle my free spirit."

Kajal was thankful she could make decisions for herself; many girls from nearby villages were forced into arranged marriages. Kalash women could marry whomever they wanted, and if it didn't work out, they had the freedom to leave their husbands and marry someone else, she told Goha.

"That sounds really progressive for these parts," Goha said. As he reflected on Kajal's story, he lamented the area's dismal state of education and, at the same time, marveled that his and Kajal's paths had converged. After her terrible experience with Saber, he wondered if she would risk marrying again, and if by some divine luck she had considered him as the person she would choose to marry next.

"Would you like some *kahwa*? I always assumed women should be the ones in the kitchen, but now that I think about it, there's no reason why I shouldn't make it. I've really acquired a taste for it since I've come here."

Kajal grinned. "Sure. You can make me *kahwa* or cook for me any time of the day or night. You don't need to ask."

They sat together on the sofa, drinking the sweet, fragrant tea, their arms and legs intertwined like tangled seaweed. Goha tousled Kajal's hair. "I'm reading a book by Rumi, and I came across a quote I think you'd like. He said, 'Your task is not to seek for love, but merely to seek and find all the barriers within yourself that you have built against it.'"

Kajal tilted her head back and laughed, a joyful, uninhibited expression of delight. "Sounds to me like Rumi's describing you."

She glanced out the window. "It's late, and the sky's turning dark," she said. "Kalash women are known for being strong and brave, but this one is pretty scared right now. Thunderous nights and I don't get along so well."

"Turns out that's something you and I have in common." As a child Goha had been petrified when rain pelted their makeshift roof like mirrors smashing into millions of pieces. He put his arm around her, burying his nose into her hair, and she nestled into his chest.

"Why don't you spend the night here? I could walk you back home, but I really wouldn't feel comfortable leaving you alone in Saber's empty house."

"Are you trying to get me in bed with you?" She pulled away slightly and poked him playfully in the ribs. "Of course I want to stay here. I've been trying to seduce you from the beginning. You're the one who's been resisting my advances."

In bed that night, they shared stories about their respective upbringings: times they spent with their families and friends, their school experiences, their frustrations, and their dreams. Goha confided the traumatic details of Hamid's constant bullying; Kajal relayed how conservative men in the area considered Kafiristan a haven of prostitution filled with mixed-gender dancing and drinking. When Goha said he hoped to marry and have children one day, Kajal's eyes glistened. He fully expected her to seduce him again, and after the first failed attempt at sex, his stomach constricted in apprehension. But as the evening went on, to his relief, Kajal appeared content to snuggle and grateful to be in his company as the barrage of water from above the earth drummed down like a band of marching elephants.

CHAPTER 9

Goha woke before Kajal and lay flat on his back, his eyes wide open. He kept thinking about their conversation the day before and how badly Kalash people fared in Pakistan simply because of their unorthodox beliefs and customs. He was concerned about their extinction and ashamed he wasn't more clued in about their mistreatment despite his ongoing quest for knowledge.

Kajal's head rested on his arm, and though his muscles were growing numb, he feared that moving even the tiniest bit would disturb her sleep. He glanced at the angel beside him, deep in slumber, lying in the same place Babrek had occupied just days before. *I'm a feigned gentleman, a dirty two-timer.* Outside the window, a cacophony of chirping birds compounded the discord in his head. He knew he was playing a dangerous game by inviting Kajal to spend the night, and he hoped in earnest that Babrek wouldn't walk in on his rendezvous with his new girlfriend without warning. Goha hadn't heard a word from him since he left, and it unnerved him to have no idea where Babrek was or when he would return. At the same time, he was becoming obsessed with wanting to satisfy Kajal physically, since he hoped beyond hope he would be spending the rest of his life with her.

✦ ✦ ✦

"Sweetheart, you seem strong and healthy," Kajal said as she poured him a cup of chai. Even first thing in the morning, with her eyes slightly puffy and her hair unkempt, she exhibited an otherworldly beauty. "I'm not an expert in this, but maybe you should see a doctor? You know, just to make sure everything is okay."

Goha was taken aback. Kajal hadn't initiated sex the previous night, but she clearly hadn't forgotten his impotence during their intimate evening at Saber's. His face burned. "Thank you for your concern. I'm sure I'll be fine."

Kajal's face twisted, but not unkindly. She told him about an amazing doctor, Dr. Rustam Khan, who had opened a clinic down the road a few years ago after seeing a dearth of physicians in the area. He was a general practitioner as well as a psychiatrist who had studied at Khyber Medical University in Peshawar and also trained for several years in New York City.

"Everyone who knows him thinks he's outstanding," she said.

"How do you know him?"

"When I first came here, I missed the valley a lot. Then Saber and I supposedly got married, and his negative attitude toward me made things worse. Maybe he wanted to play the savior, like he was saving me from the heathen Kalash people? Or maybe he thought of me as his showpiece, kind of like a trophy wife."

Soon after they had gotten together, Saber often ignored her, and when he wasn't shrugging her off, he seemed to take pleasure in manipulating her, she said. Occasionally he treated her well, complimenting her appearance or cooking, so she tolerated his erratic behavior for a long time. "I barely see him now, and I'm surprised he hasn't thrown me out of the house. Maybe he thought word would get around and it would ruin his reputation? Anyway, I got off topic. I was trying to say that if it wasn't for Dr. Khan, I think I would have ended up in a mental hospital."

Kajal's testimony about Saber was consistent with how Goha witnessed him malign and insult her. The *maulvi*'s strange proclamation—that Kajal was his to "enjoy as he liked"—ran through his mind constantly.

Kajal said Dr. Khan was open-minded, nonjudgmental, and one of the nicest people she had met. "I wouldn't suggest you see him unless I trusted him completely."

"Okay, *jaan*, if you really think he's that good, I'll make an appointment."

Goha had just hoisted himself onto the examining table when a burly man with bushy eyebrows and a Captain Hook–style mustache entered the room carrying a chart.

"It's nice to meet you, Goha!" Dr. Khan's deep voice bounced off the walls. He sat on a rolling stool and pulled out a small laptop computer from his desk drawer. "Let's begin so I can get to know you better."

Dr. Khan wasted no time delving into Goha's background, upbringing, physical condition, and mental health. Each time Goha answered a question, Dr. Khan banged his thick, hairy fingers on the keyboard.

"Given the reason for your visit here, I want to ask you something personal. This is a taboo subject in our culture, but please be honest so I can help you as best as I can. Have you ever been in a sexual relationship with another male? It's common in our society, even though the people involved usually aren't comfortable talking about it and often don't consider themselves gay."

"Yes," Goha mumbled. *Is Dr. Khan a mind reader, or is there something obvious about me? Does my skin look different? The texture of my hair? How does he know?*

"Did you initiate that activity?"

Goha pushed his shoulders back indignantly. "No, sir," he said. "I've never initiated it. It has only happened a few times, and I haven't been doing it for very long. I don't think I'm gay. But given everything that's happened recently, I'm not entirely sure."

"Are you in a relationship now?"

"Yes. Well two, actually. But I don't want to be in one of them. It just sort of started before I knew what was happening." *Goddamn Babrek.* His anger toward Babrek billowed up, resurfacing at the memory of their first nonconsensual, barbaric time together.

"Tell me more."

Goha fell silent. Even if he opened up, he certainly wasn't going to name names, even though Dr. Khan appeared professional and trustworthy. He looked into the doctor's empathetic eyes, and before he could help himself, Goha was revealing graphic details about his eventful past few weeks, starting from the fateful night when Lala Dabir knocked on his family's door in the *katchi abadis*. When he reached the part where he had been intimate with Kajal in the same room where he was cohabiting with Babrek, Dr. Khan raised his eyebrow and twisted the end of his mustache with his thumb and index finger.

"I think I'm in love, Dr. Khan."

"With the imam's ex-wife?"

"Yes."

"And what about your supervisor?"

"It's complicated. He's taken me under his wing and treated me well overall. I sympathize with all he's gone through. But he forced me into a physical relationship without my consent, so I also resent him."

"Are you attracted to him?"

"No, I don't think so. Since I became a teenager, I've always fantasized about girls. It wasn't my choice to be with him. Not in that way. But I didn't feel like I had a choice."

Dr. Khan stopped taking notes, put his laptop down, and rolled his stool over to Goha.

"I see. Goha, even though you occasionally consent to having sex with your supervisor, it seems to me you're doing it out of fear and obligation. It's concerning because of the power dynamic between you. He is calling the shots, and you have no choice but to comply. I suggest you talk to him and tell him you no longer want to be in that kind of relationship. He is educated, so hopefully he will understand and respect your choice. You told me he was abused as a child, and it appears he is unwittingly continuing the cycle as an adult. Unfortunately, I see this pattern a lot in my clinic."

Goha nodded glumly.

"Does any part of your body hurt or feel unusual?"

"I bled the first time. But not since then."

Dr. Khan got up and conducted a quick physical exam.

"From what I can tell, you are fine physically," he said. "You're healthy and in good shape for someone your age who didn't grow up with much. You appear to be a young, straight man who inadvertently got involved in a homosexual relationship without your full awareness or consent. If that's the case, being with a loving, understanding, and committed female partner will go far in helping you get over your impotence. The good news is, it sounds like you've already found that partner."

Dr. Khan suggested Goha try yoga, meditation, and relaxation techniques whenever anxiety crept up. "And since you're a practicing Muslim, praying to God for His guidance and forgiveness will help give you peace of mind," he said.

The doctor walked toward the door to leave, and Goha slid off the examining table.

Kajal was right. Dr. Khan is phenomenal. His words make everything so much clearer.

"Dr. Khan, you are wise and very kind. Thank you so much."

While Goha met with Dr. Khan, Kajal had been busy in the kitchen preparing *bilili*, walnut bread, *jā'gai*, walnut butter, and *sat'uk*, a sauce made from fresh ground apples.

"Wow, this looks scrumptious, Kajal," Goha said as he entered the room and saw the effort she had put into laying out the table.

"I wanted to treat you to some special Kalash dishes from the valley. How did it go with Dr. Khan?"

"He's amazing."

"I know. I'm so glad you saw him."

"I told him everything."

"What's *everything*?"

Goha wavered. Should he tell her about his situation with Babrek? It was a big deal, but he had been honest with Kajal about his life so far, with no apparent ramifications. Sheikh Samir always said being truthful was emphasized in Islam so much that it was one of God's divine attributes—*Al-Haqq*, the truth.

"Babrek and I have been in a sexual relationship," he said finally. "It wasn't something I wanted. He abused me, and then I felt indebted to him for all he's done for me. But I'm not gay, and you and Dr. Khan helped me see that more clearly. As soon as Babrek returns, I'm going to tell him I don't want to be involved with him in that way anymore."

"I'm sorry that happened to you. Unfortunately, I think it's pretty common around here." Kajal twisted a strand of hair around her finger. "Hey, I wanted to tell you I'm thinking about going back to Bumburet. I know it's not the greatest timing, but one of the big Kalash festivals is coming up soon, and I want to help prepare for it. It's a huge event in the valley."

The rhythm of Goha's heart faltered, like an ocean current disturbed by a massive cargo ship. *Is Kajal having second thoughts about me? Did she make a split-second decision to leave for the valley just now, right after I told her about Babrek? Is this going to change things between us?* Now he knew what poets meant when they said they were drunk on love. Kajal had braided her hair the night before, and when she undid it, it flowed down her back like luminescent waves of gold. If there were fairies walking on earth, he was sure Kajal was one of them. His throat constricted. *How will I survive being away from her?*

A cage closed in around Goha's heart. But he put on a brave face, nodded feebly, handed her a stack of rupees, and told her he would help arrange travel back to her village.

CHAPTER 10

Kajal's unforeseen departure the next morning left Goha empty. He had expected a more charged and negative reaction out of her—anger, bitterness, jealousy, confusion, or some combination of those emotions—when he told her about his situation with Babrek. He yearned for something, anything he could hold on to that indicated her possessiveness toward him. She seemed apologetic about leaving, but the timing of her plans to go home seemed a little too sudden and coincidental to Goha.

Kajal didn't own a cell phone, and even if she did, there was no wireless service in the valley. When it dawned on Goha that he was in the dark about how long she would be gone and communicating with her would be impossible, he sank into a deep, cavernous hole. He tried to distract himself by reading or watching TV, and sometimes he ventured outside and wandered around, but he always returned to the rooming house forlorn and pensive, his head hung low. Kajal was a seed that had taken root in his heart and had started sprouting tiny, fragile leaves. What was she doing? Was the distance between them making her feelings toward him stronger, or—God forbid—was she swiftly losing interest in him since he wasn't in her immediate presence?

He deliberated calling his parents and telling them he'd met the love of his life and couldn't wait for them to meet her. Maybe sharing the news would shake him out of his rut and manifest his long-term future with Kajal into reality. He anticipated his *ammi* and *abba* would have questions—lots of questions—about her Kalash background, and they might even try to dissuade him from seeing her. He was ready to face their resistance, to convince them about her through his charm and reassurances.

But with all the warnings he had received about misusing his cell phone, he honestly couldn't recall if he was allowed to call his parents or not, and he decided to be safe and get permission from Babrek first. Through all the difficulties, he had managed to stick out his time up north, and he would regret unwittingly doing something that was forbidden, a misstep that risked soiling his reputation or jeopardizing his future. Plus, he reasoned it was probably better to tell them about her in person anyway, when he was at a point where he felt more confident about the status of their relationship.

Compounding his loneliness was uneasiness from not hearing from Babrek. While he always felt slightly on edge with his supervisor, he missed their camaraderie, and he was also anxious to tell him about Kajal so they could start fresh. He hoped to rebuild their relationship into a platonic, mutually beneficial one that didn't involve sex.

Goha was about to go to bed the following evening when he heard a knock. He peered through the crack in the door and saw the profile of a man with a side part and a bent nose—the unmistakable silhouette of *Maulvi* Saber. Despite his mystifying latest encounter with the imam and his contemptible character traits, Goha opened the door. It was a distraction from his preoccupation with Kajal, plus he couldn't help himself. Being *tameez-daar* was part of Pakistani culture and ingrained in his DNA. His mother always told him politeness and good manners were never wasted—they were a positive reflection of his upbringing and would help him go far in life.

"*Assalam-o-alaikum, Maulvi* Saber. Welcome back. How was Peshawar?"

"Fine, fine. Peshawar was fine. Kajal must have told you I was there. She hasn't been at the house, from what I can tell. My best guess is she's been spending time with you here."

Words lodged in Goha's throat. He coughed.

"Regardless, what you two are doing is none of my business. I'll be moving to Peshawar soon to become the imam of a much bigger mosque and the head of a *madrasa*. I had planned to lead the school beside my *masjid*, but it was smashed to pieces. Anyway, I'm done with this place. It has nothing to offer me anymore. I'm ready to move on to bigger and better things."

To Goha, this proclamation was like a burst of celebratory fireworks.

"That sounds like the right move for you. *Inshallah*, things will work out for you in Peshawar."

"I will make sure they do. Anyway, in case you hadn't heard, I came by to tell you the major storm forecasted last week is coming our way. The weather people said it will push through this area tomorrow. It's supposed to last several days and cause major damage."

"*Ya Allah*, I didn't know it was going to be that bad."

"Haven't you been watching the news?"

"Not really. I've been so absorbed in a book on Sufism that I've barely looked up the past few days."

"Oh, I see. Well, I'm not sure why you're so consumed with the heretic Sufis. They're not much better than the infidel Kalash. You'd be wise to get your nose out of the book and prepare for the storm before it hits. This house is in a low-lying area, so it will probably get flooded.

"Since Babrek hasn't come back yet, you can stay at my place. Kajal is gone, so there's plenty of space. It's on higher elevation, so we'll have a better chance of staying dry. The downpour is expected to start tomorrow evening, so come over in the late afternoon, and we'll have dinner together."

Maulvi Saber was just about the last person Goha wanted to be stuck with during an unpredictable storm. But when he pondered an alternative, he came up with nothing.

"Thank you, *Maulvi* Saber," he said. "I'll take you up on that."

"You're welcome. I went to the store and bought enough food to last a few days. *Khuda hafiz* for now, and see you tomorrow."

As the local news had predicted, the rain started late the next morning, sprinkles at first and then large, plump drops carried by air currents that hit the walls of the rooming house with ear-piercing force. Goha hoped desperately the crux of the storm would bypass the town and give him a valid reason to circumvent *Maulvi* Saber, but as the day progressed, the dark, low-hanging clouds only turned blacker and angrier.

That afternoon, as he packed his clothes and toiletries, he decided he would bring his pistol. Until then, Goha had been negligent about heeding Babrek's advice to take it along whenever he left the house, seeing it as an unnecessary burden that would only cause him undue tension and stress. But since the next few days with *Maulvi* Saber were uncertain, he took it out of the safe and put it into his pocket, then grabbed his phone and slid it into the other side. At the last minute, he spotted Babrek's long, sleeveless wool vest in the closet. He slipped his arms through the holes, smoothing the creases with the palms of his hands, glad to see it mostly hid the bulges. He slung his bag over his shoulder, left the building, and walked up the hill to *Maulvi* Saber's place, holding a magazine over his head as the cold, wet wind struck his face.

"Come in, come in; you're going to get sick," *Maulvi* Saber chided as he opened the door. "I was just about to say *maghrib namaz*. We can pray together and then eat."

Goha took his feet out of his soggy sandals and left them at the door. As he followed *Maulvi* Saber down the hall through the dining area, he caught sight of three beige candles on a polished silver stand, a vase overflowing with flowers, and two table settings with white plates, crystal glassware, and cloth napkins. A heaping platter of *biryani*, saffron-colored and white rice layered with savory chicken, was centered on the table. It was surrounded by yogurt *raita*, mango pickle *achar*, and a small dish of *kachumer*—chopped-up tomatoes, onions, cilantro, and green chilis.

"The table looks lovely, and the *biryani* smells delicious, *Maulvi* Saber."

"Well, hopefully it tastes as good as it smells. I always knew I was a better cook than Kajal, but she never let me step foot in the kitchen."

A kink formed in Goha's neck as Saber led the way into the bedroom.

"We can say *namaz* in here," he said. "There's a pile of *janamazes* right there—help yourself." He pointed to a stack of folded prayer mats inside the wardrobe.

Goha grabbed a thick royal blue rug with a white fringe and an elaborately stitched image of the *Kaaba*.

"The *qibla* is this way," *Maulvi* Saber said, pointing toward the bed. "Not sure you'll be able to focus on your prayers, though, given what's directly in front of you." He smirked.

Mortified, Goha laid his rug as far away as he could from Saber's without hitting the wall and kept his eyes fixed on the *Kaaba*.

Saber started mumbling the prayers out loud. Each time he stood up and bowed down, he grunted and groaned so loudly Goha found it impossible to concentrate. More than once, Saber mispronounced the Arabic scripture so badly it sounded like a nonsensical, made-up language.

Saber finally ended his *namaz*. "I'm done," he proclaimed, pulling his *janamaz* off the floor. "Come to the dining room when you're ready." He left the room, pulling the door closed behind him.

Ya Allah, please give me strength to endure this time with Saber. Goha finished his prayers and quickly said two more voluntary *nafl salah*, solemnly asking God to let him leave the imam's house unscathed.

As they sat down to eat, the pelting rain turned into coin-sized hail that smashed the windowpanes so violently that Goha was convinced they would shatter, and they would end up being assailed by shards of watery glass.

"It's not safe here," *Maulvi* Saber said. "Even though we're on a hill and this house is sturdy, water could seep in. We could become stranded. But as you probably know by now, I'm always thinking ahead." He tapped his index finger on the side of his head. "I built a room on the roof of the mosque a couple of years ago; we can go there."

Goha glanced outside. The sky was coated in black. The increasing ferocity of the wind alarmed him, and at that point, he was willing to do anything to ease his nerves. He quickly finished his meal and helped Saber clear the table, then put on his waterlogged shoes and waited for the imam at the door. As Saber strode into the entryway carrying his overnight bag, his gait was steady. *Wow,* Goha thought. *His hip trouble seems to have miraculously disappeared. I wonder if he was faking it.*

Although the mosque was only about two hundred yards away, they reached the main entrance soaked and bedraggled. As Saber fumbled for his key, Goha made out the battered remnants of a nearby building he suspected was the decimated school where Kajal had once dreamed of teaching local kids about Kalash culture.

Maulvi Saber shepherded Goha inside, securing the lock behind them. They climbed up a narrow stairwell, dripping trails of water, until they reached a solid wooden door. When Saber pushed the door open and turned on the light, a modern, fully furnished suite emerged like a magical illusion: a bedroom with a queen-size bed covered with tasseled, tube-shaped throw pillows; an attached bathroom with a stone-tiled bathtub and massage shower head; a kitchenette with a stainless steel stove, full-size fridge, and glass-top dining table; and a separate TV room with a wood-grained desk and swivel office chair. A deep horizontal bookshelf housed a diverse selection of books and board games, and on the walls hung scenic, artistic photos of Northern Pakistan. It reminded Goha of glossy magazine photos of deluxe hotel rooms in the country's finest luxury resorts.

"There's food in the fridge and snacks in the cupboard," *Maulvi* Saber said. "Help yourself. I even have a flashlight with new batteries in the kitchen drawer in case we need it. Like I said, I'm always thinking ahead."

Goha unzipped his bag, eager to change out of his sticky, wet *shalwar kameez*. Meanwhile, the *maulvi* had opened the closet and taken out a rolled-up foam mattress.

"Goha, the bed is for you. I will sleep on the floor."

"No, please. You sleep on the bed, *Maulvi* Saber."

"No, you are my guest. You will have the bed," insisted Saber.

Thunder clapped and lightning blazed across the sky as the wind gained momentum. The hail had engorged into golf ball–sized pellets that slammed onto the roof. The lights flickered for a few minutes, and seconds later, the room went black. Goha peered out the window: Power from nearby houses had vanished, with only a few lampposts casting a dim, unsteady glow onto the quickly flooding streets.

Goha shivered as he tentatively lowered himself onto the bed. He was too skittish to fumble around in the dark in an endeavor to change his clothes and brush his teeth—it wasn't worth the trouble. His *shalwar kameez* clung to his skin, and that, combined with the stiff metal of his gun and phone, made it nearly impossible for him to get comfortable, despite the luxurious bedding. However, he was so terrified that he kept the objects securely in his pockets, just in case. Saber had unrolled the mattress and was lying on the floor beside the bed, breathing heavily.

Goha lay still, attempting to focus on Kajal, then on every single good time he'd had with his parents and friends in Karachi—anything to relax his mind and body. He tried desperately to recall prayers meant for times of adversity.

And then, just as the drumbeat of the rain was helping him drift off to sleep, *Maulvi* Saber climbed into the bed. Saber's probing hand started on his thigh, then shifted swiftly toward his groin, his fingers crawling upward like a big, hairy spider.

Goha's eyes shot open. "What the hell are you doing?" He shoved Saber's hand away. "Get away from me, you pervert."

"Come on, *yaar*. Let's have fun on this miserable night. You're not a child, Goha. Don't be coy and act like you've never done this before."

"Get away from me. I mean it. Get away from me now, or I'll strangle you."

In the faint light, Goha saw him smirking.

"You think you're so smart, don't you, Goha Hadi? Well, let me tell you something: I know all about you and Kajal. My ex-wife. She's a looker, isn't she?"

Goha's nostrils flared.

"Cooperate with me now, boy. If you do what I say, everything will be fine. But if you resist me, I will make your life a living hell. I will make sure everyone in town knows about you. You will be a spectacle around here, and news of your immoral behavior will reach your parents and friends back home in Karachi. Your life will be ruined. Mark my words."

Goha struggled out of the bed. His hand quivered as he pulled the gun out of his pocket.

But Saber lurched forward and grabbed Goha's arm, yanking him back and pushing him down.

In the commotion, the weapon slipped from Goha's grasp. He thrust his leg out and kicked it so hard it went sailing to the far corner of the room, out of Saber's reach. Goha's skin was still slippery from the rain, and he pried himself loose from Saber's grip. He seized the *maulvi's* throat with both hands and dug his nails in, a leopard pouncing on its prey.

"Stop . . . wait . . . please . . . don't," cried Saber. But he was no match for the younger, stronger Goha.

"You were about to rape me, you despicable *haramzada*. And you would have had no remorse. How many times have you done this to others? WHAT KIND OF A MONSTER ARE YOU?"

Lightning flashed, and for a second, Goha saw Saber's lucid skin, blue veins bulging from his neck—an inflated toad ready to burst.

"You pretend to be a pious and religious man, but you're a hypocrite. You are an evil person. Do you understand me? Do you?" Goha yelled. Blood vessels protruded from his face.

"Bastards like you don't deserve to live. YOU BELONG IN *JAHANNAM*, TO BURN IN HELLFIRE!"

And then, before Goha could stop himself, he pressed down with all his force, hard and relentless.

Saber's face twisted. He gurgled and gasped.

But Goha's rage was maniacal. He was out of his senses. He couldn't stop—he didn't want to stop. And after a few minutes, Saber stopped moving.

Oh my God. He's dead.

Goha stood up, stunned. Time was meaningless as he fixated on Saber's pallid body. He walked to the window in a trance, realizing even in his traumatic state that he needed to get rid of the evidence immediately. The windowpane was thick and heavy, the latch broken. As Goha strained to keep it open, powerful gales kept slamming it shut.

Stay open, damn it.

On the fourth attempt, Goha propped a large, heavy book into the pane to keep the window ajar. Torrents of water gushed into the room, saturating the carpet and bedding. Goha hoisted the corpse over his shoulder and heaved it to the opening. For several agonizing minutes, he bent and turned Saber in a desperate effort to fit him through the frame. Then, with one final push, the figure slid down the roof and landed with a dull thud.

I'm a murderer, and I've just disposed of the body.

The storm had turned the street into a fast-flowing, muddy river. In the hazy light, with clouds still unleashing buckets of rain, currents carried Saber downstream. The dead body floated toward the rooming house, then turned the corner and disappeared.

Goha slumped into the chair, drenched in rainwater and sweat. He closed his eyes and tried unsuccessfully to erase the haunting image of Saber's limp, lifeless figure from his mind.

Minutes passed like hours. Goha eventually pulled himself out of the chair and stumbled to the kitchen. He eventually found the flashlight and switched it on, disoriented from the shadows created by its narrow, dusky hue. He peered through the blurry, water-streaked window and gasped: Saber's bloated body was right there, floating on the surface of the river below. But then he blinked hard several times in succession, and the image was gone.

Goha shuffled to the bathroom, stripped off his clothes, and turned the knob of the shower faucet. He stepped in and closed his eyes, barely feeling the cool water running over his body. When he dried himself, he glimpsed his image in the bathroom mirror—mussed-up hair, bloodshot eyes, grayish-brown skin, and stubble. The face of a killer.

He summoned all his energy to take dry clothes out of his bag and change into them. Then he slumped onto the bed and shut his eyes. The events from the evening replayed in his mind in a continuous, nightmarish loop.

Could I have done anything to stop Saber? Goha didn't think so, but in his lightheaded and confused state, he wasn't quite sure. *Did Sheikh Samir ever talk about what justified killing someone?* As he pondered the question in earnest, all he heard was his teacher's steady, calming voice quoting a passage from the Qur'an: *Whoever kills an innocent life, it is as if he had killed all of humanity. And whoever gives life to one, it is as if he had saved all of humanity.*

At first light, Goha dragged himself out of bed to the window. The storm's fury was unrelenting. He plodded to the door, opened it cautiously, and slowly descended the stairs. Two feet of water blanketed the main floor. Cracks had begun settling into the foundation. Furniture, decorations, and trinkets floated amid dirt and debris like desolate miniature islands.

Goha headed back up the stairs despondently; he wouldn't be able to leave anytime soon. He found a prayer mat in the bedroom closet and laid it down for his *fajr* prayers. When he bowed in *sajda*, he started sobbing uncontrollably. *Please, Allah, have mercy on me and forgive me for the atrocious crime I committed. Ya Allah, protect me and make this storm end.*

When he was done, his throat ached and his stomach churned. In the fridge, he found two store-bought *naans* and a container of plain yogurt. He fixed himself a plate, sat at the dining table, and, oblivious to the taste, instinctively put *niwala* after *niwala* into his mouth.

Over the next two days, wailing winds and obstinate rains continued to rise and fall in a turbulent cadence. The town was eventually submerged in several feet of water.

The electricity stayed out, and Goha was relieved that the storm's wrath prevented anyone from coming to the mosque for prayers or to visit the imam. The most activity Goha witnessed was animal carcasses swept downstream, along with countless pieces of broken furniture; empty cardboard boxes; and sad, rotting wooden planks from destroyed houses.

CHAPTER 11

By day three, Goha had managed to clear out some water on the main floor using a jug from the kitchen and a plastic bucket he discovered under the bathroom sink. He had gone through nearly all the food—a loaf of white bread, a packet of raw almonds, a box of fennel seed cookies, a bag of masala potato chips, two bananas, a bottle of shelf-stable mango juice, and four cans of Pakola he had found in the cupboard. The power failure had caused the yogurt in the fridge to spoil, and its sour, fermented odor permeated the room and made him feel nauseous. Though the streets were still deluged, the rain had finally let up to a point where heading back to the rooming house seemed possible.

He had just exited the bathroom when muffled voices and a rap at the mosque's main door downstairs made him start. He stayed as quiet as he could, hoping whoever was outside wouldn't look upward and decipher his shadow. The banging continued. *Maybe I should answer the door. I haven't seen another human in so long.* He rolled up his *shalwar* past his knees and climbed down the stairs barefoot, praying the caller would take pity on a stranded stranger and not ask too many questions.

He waded through the dirty water and carefully navigated his steps around the buoyant wreckage until he reached the entrance. He fiddled with the latch and unlocked the door, finding himself face-to-face with five wet, hostile-looking men who appeared to be in their mid- to late twenties.

"*Assalam-o-alaikum*. Can I help you?" He acted as if a stranger answering the door of the *masjid* in the middle of a ruthless storm like it were his own residence was the most normal thing in the world.

A tall and skinny man came forward. His eyes were narrow, and his pointy hair protruded from his scalp like tiny spears. "We're part of *Maulvi* Saber's congregation," he said. "I am Dastagir Ahsan. Who are you, and what are you doing here?"

"My name is Gohar Hadi. I'm visiting from Karachi. I've been staying at the rooming house down the hill. *Maulvi* Saber suggested I come here for a few days until the storm passed." As he spoke, Goha cursed inwardly for being such a *gadha*. He was so gullible and trusting that it hadn't even occurred to him to disguise his identity and manufacture a story that explained his bizarre circumstances.

Dastagir gave him an icy stare. "Where is *Maulvi* Saber?"

Goha sucked in his breath. "I'm not sure. We were upstairs, and he came down to make sure everything was okay on the main floor. I haven't seen him since."

The men exchanged looks. "How could he just disappear?" Dastagir demanded. "Did you call the police?"

"My phone has been dead for the past two days," Goha said truthfully. "And the storm has been so bad that I haven't been able to go outside to look for him."

"This all sounds very strange," Dastagir said. "How long have you been here? Anyone who stays at the *masjid* needs to pay a nightly fee." The wingmen surrounding their ringleader nodded dutifully.

Goha bristled at Dastagir's performative air of authority. He knew many people who had benefited from free accommodations and meals at places of worship—and not even one who had been charged even a minimal amount for staying there.

Dastagir gave his companions a sideways glance, and his tone suddenly changed. "Listen, we can help you. You'll need to pay us for our services. But we have connections. Just tell us what you need."

Ah, so this is what it is about. These guys take me for a fool. They see I'm in trouble, so they're trying to scare me out of my wits and swindle me.

"I don't need anything," Goha replied coolly. He paused. "Actually, wait, I do need something."

I might be able to use these guys to get the hell out of here.

"The storm has been so bad that I was forced to stay here a couple of nights. I want to leave, but I don't have a key to the *masjid* and I didn't want to leave the door unlocked."

"We have a spare key. Just give us a few hundred rupees and we can lock the door behind you," Dastagir replied.

Goha hesitated. Money wasn't an issue; he had brought with him the wad of cash Babrek had given him before he left town. His heart palpitated as he deliberated whether to leave the strangers at the door while he collected his belongings. *I had better risk it—this might be my only chance to leave the crime scene.*

"Okay. I'll be right back." He waded to the stairwell, climbing the stairs two at a time. When he reached the roof, he turned around, half expecting the sketchy characters to be at his heels, pointing their guns at his head. But thankfully, no one had followed him. He entered the room and locked the door, panting.

As he packed, a glimpse of shiny black metal in the corner caught his eye. *Ya Allah, I almost forgot the gun.* He picked up the weapon like it was a rare fossil, put it in his pocket, grabbed his bag, and bolted back downstairs in two minutes flat, reciting the *ayat-al kursi* under his breath to ward off any evil intentions the strangers might have toward him.

The men had stepped inside to get out of the rain. Goha pushed several one-hundred-rupee notes into Dastagir's face, then strode past the group through the main door without speaking. They followed him out one by one, and Goha didn't turn back when the door latch clicked behind him.

Goha headed down the hill toward the rooming house, his eyes fixed straight ahead like a laser beam, barely perceiving the destruction all around him. The men walked in the opposite direction, the sound of their footsteps diminished in the pattering rain, talking in hushed tones in a language Goha couldn't understand.

Back at the rooming house, Goha threw his bag on the floor and flopped onto the sofa. Now that he was in a familiar setting again, the fog lifted from his brain. He inspected the room, astounded that, unlike the mosque, the damage was minimal. *How on earth did this building survive the storm?* Then it came to him. Early on, Babrek had mentioned it was owned by a savvy businessman who kept up with maintenance and made sure the property was fitted with high-quality water extractor pumps, foundation vents, sealants, and backup power generators to keep it profitable during inclement weather. He pounded his head with his fist. *Damn it. If only I had remembered that before, I could have avoided this whole crazy predicament.*

Goha draped the wet clothes from his bag over the furniture and changed into a dry *shalwar kameez* from the closet. He ventured outside again, carefully treading onto the street, his muddy sandals squeaking and squishing with each step. Water accumulated on massive open surfaces, and the roads were full of gaping potholes. Uprooted trees and bushes had landed like fallen soldiers, making it impossible for traffic to pass on either side. Homes had been wiped away or ruined beyond repair. Rubble and garbage littered the landscape. The whole town appeared drenched in a sea of dead, brownish-gray sludge. There were few cars and fewer people. He took in the scene for a few minutes, then headed back when he simply couldn't take it anymore.

Goha plugged in his phone in his room. The green charging light on the device lit up. *Thank God the power is on and my phone still works.* He sat on the bed and turned on the TV.

On the national news, a young female broadcaster solemnly proclaimed that many districts in and around Mingora were still without electricity. Around a dozen individuals were presumed dead, and huge numbers of livestock in the adjoining hilly areas had perished. Scenes of residents and rescue workers sifting through homes submerged in several feet of dirty water inundated the screen. They were trying desperately to salvage whatever few pieces of furniture and possessions they had left.

Was the flooding God's punishment toward people in the area who exhibited rampant promiscuity? The Qur'an relayed how Prophet Noah's tribe drowned in a massive flood when they disobeyed God's commands. Goha let the thought settle in his brain for a minute, then chastised himself for being judgmental. He was hardly a saint, and in his heart, he knew a seismic catastrophe could have just as easily impacted Karachi and the people he loved.

Over the next couple of days, Goha slumped into despair. He attempted to envision Sheikh Samir telling his students how water was a venerated gift from Allah, how the rain He sent down from the heavens gave life to the earth after its death. He forced himself to skim through magazines on the shelf instead of watching the news. At one point, he left the room to wander outside again and was grateful to be able to support a local grocer who had opened his doors to sell nonperishable foods.

He wondered when—or if—he would see Babrek and Kajal, his two lifelines up north, ever again.

Much to his relief, no one came knocking. Dastagir Ahsan and his cronies seemed to have vanished, and Goha concluded it was just fine if he never saw them again.

Then, one afternoon a few days later, his phone unexpectedly buzzed. It was Babrek.

"Are you safe, Goha? I heard about the brutal storm."

"I am fine, but the town is ravaged." Goha's voice trembled. "Where are you? You've been gone for so long." He had agonized for days over Babrek's safety and well-being, but now there was an unmistakable impatience in his tone. "Are you finally coming back?"

"I know. I'm sorry. I'll be back in the morning. In the meantime, take care and don't talk to anyone. There were unexpected developments in the organization that we need to keep to ourselves. I'll fill you in when I see you tomorrow."

CHAPTER 12

Babrek did not show up the next morning as promised. Instead, Goha received a call from him while he was eating breakfast, and Babrek spoke so faintly that Goha had to stop chewing to turn up the volume.

Goha dreaded dropping the bombshell of Saber's death on Babrek, but he felt a pressing need to at least hint at the news so he could avoid an extreme reaction when he told him in person. But Babrek's words came out like a gushing stream, and Goha could barely insert two words into the conversation.

Goha eventually made out that a driver in a black SUV similar to Babrek's would pick him up that evening and take him to a private residence in Peshawar, where he would attend an *ijtema*, congregation, the next day.

"You will be traveling at night because it's less conspicuous," Babrek whispered.

"Is this where I'll get the training you talked about before?"

"Sorry, Goha, I don't have time to chat. I'm really busy. You'll be staying there overnight, so remember to pack your bag." He hung up.

In his nervous anticipation of the *ijtema*, Goha was able to block out the trauma of the storm and *Maulvi* Saber. The favorable treatment he had received from the onset—staying in comfortable lodging and riding in nice vehicles rather than dangerously jam-packed buses like the other recruits—had made him a VIP lone wolf, excluded from the pack. He yearned to experience the adventure with a throng of other young men with similar backgrounds and aspirations, and hoped the upcoming congregation would give him that chance.

The car arrived just after the sun went down, and when the driver pulled onto the main highway to Peshawar, Goha had to shield his eyes from the glaring street and vehicle lights. However, as soon as the driver turned into the residential neighborhood where the *ijtema* was being held, darkness took over. Goha strained his eyes to make out a high boundary wall topped with barbed wire. The shadow of an armed sentry stood at the gate.

When the driver rolled down his window and showed the guard his ID, the doors swung open to reveal a massive house with a circular driveway. Goha saw the shape of a camouflaged bus parked at the entrance, where a stream of young men were disembarking. They were ushered inside by security guards with long, sleek Kalashnikovs strapped to their waists. The driver pulled up behind the bus, and a watchman with a stoic face opened the rear door. He took Goha's bag without a word and led him into the house.

The guard walked alongside Goha down a long, narrow hallway. Goha stopped abruptly when he saw a vibrant mural on the wall, contrasting starkly with the otherwise bleak surroundings. The painting depicted young, sprightly, half-clothed women who resembled fairies. They encircled a river of milk flowing through a lush green valley. "Where is this?" he asked.

"Paradise," the guard responded in a monotone voice.

He stopped at a room at the far end of the hall. "You will sleep here tonight," he said without expression. "Someone will come by in the morning with breakfast." He shut the door behind him.

The room was barely furnished: Two sets of bunk beds with minimal bedding lined the corners, and there was an adjoining bathroom with a toilet, sink, tiny shower stall, and *wudhu* area with a low faucet and plastic step stool for performing ablutions. Goha figured three men from the bus would be dropped off at the room to occupy the additional beds, but after waiting about thirty minutes, no one else came. So he washed up, took a clean towel from the bathroom, set it down on the floor, and quickly said his *isha namaz* before turning out the lights.

The next morning, Goha was already awake when he heard a knock. He opened the door an inch, surprised to find a hearty breakfast of fresh fruit, buttered toast, fried eggs, and chai set on a tray in the hallway. His body ached from fatigue, and after several days of scant eating during the storm, he ogled the wholesome and filling meal gratefully. He brought the food inside his room, perched himself on a lower bunk, and voraciously devoured it all.

He got dressed, dropped his phone into his pocket, and minutes later heard another rap. It was the same robotic guard from the previous night, who contemptuously eyed his dirty dishes, reluctantly picked up the tray, and escorted him down the hall into an expansive, windowless room.

About thirty chairs were neatly arranged in rows, and they were steadily being filled by men who generally appeared to be in their late teens and early 20s. Most were dressed in *shalwar kameezes*; some were in Western clothes: jeans, sweatshirts, and T-shirts. A few wore Pashtun-style turbans or flat, earth-toned, rolled-up caps called *pakols*; others had on forward- or backward-facing baseball caps emblazoned with company logos or American sports teams. Some sported beards of various lengths and shapes; others were clean-shaven. Several appeared hesitant about the upcoming day's events; others carried a look of exuberant anticipation. There were no female faces in the crowd.

Goha made himself comfortable in the front row, close to the podium and screen. He leaned forward, eager to take in all the details. Despite all the time he had spent with Babrek before he left, he still felt clueless about the organization's inner workings and his duties. Babrek hadn't shared much information, and whenever he did, it was always with a caveat that it was top secret and not to be discussed with anyone.

He hoped that, like the earthquake relief efforts, the upcoming missions he participated in would help Pakistanis who needed it most. He imagined that at the *ijtema*, the work might be framed as

Robin Hoodesque, where the organization and its members stood up for common men in the face of adversity and tyranny. He pictured coming back to Karachi and being lauded as a hero, a philanthropist intent on spreading wealth and resources more evenly among disparate classes, taking from the bloated, impetuous rich and giving to the meek, suffering poor.

Maybe we'll be trained on how to transport sick people to hospitals so they can get the care they need. Or maybe they'll teach us the best way to distribute food and medical supplies to impoverished communities. Goha envisioned being in a position similar to General Zafar, the army general who had greeted Babrek so warmly at the military helicopter site in Mingora. Ten years down the line, Gohar Hadi, whose mother had given him an auspicious name meaning *gemstone*, would be the one developing strategies and commanding teams beneath him during desperate times. His *ammi's* prayer would come true: His name would predict his successful and benevolent future.

Decades ago, the revered, saintly Abdul Sattar Edhi had launched the Edhi Foundation in Karachi. It offered twenty-four-hour emergency assistance to anyone who needed it, especially those on the fringes of society, and had grown to include orphanages, health-care services, food distribution, and educational centers. Goha had personally seen its impact on a few families in the *katchi abadis*—their lives had improved dramatically thanks to the group's tireless, selfless volunteers and generous donors. Did this organization have similar plans? The country could certainly use more groups like Edhi. In addition to helping people, the foundation built up national pride and made Pakistan less dependent on international aid and all the strings that seemed to come attached with it.

When everyone was seated, a middle-aged man dressed in a black *shalwar kameez* walked to the front and stood behind the podium. He was fair-skinned with light brown eyes, a sharp nose, and round wire-rimmed glasses. He cleared his throat and tapped the microphone.

"*Assalam-o-alaikum!*" He greeted the audience in an authoritative tone, his voice reverberating through the room. "Please rise for the *shahada* and our organization's pledge of allegiance. Repeat after me: *La ilaha Illallah Muhammadur Rasulullah.*" There is no God but Allah, and Muhammad is the Messenger of Allah. He scanned the room like a cougar surveying a herd of deer. The men recited the *shahada.*

"Good. Now please raise your right hand to your heart and say this: 'I swear to be loyal to this organization and its officers.'"

There were sideways glances.

"I can't hear you. Please repeat it."

Several men muttered the pledge; others declared it emphatically.

"Now say this: 'I swear to keep information I receive at this *ijtema* sacred.'"

Several men shifted uncomfortably.

"I want to hear this last one loud and clear from everyone in the audience. 'I vow to never divulge information about the mission and goals of this organization to anyone.'"

A few men in the back shouted the words back passionately.

"That was very good. Now, please be seated." He rapped the microphone with his finger again as the men took their seats.

"It's good to see so many of you dedicated to bringing about social and political changes," he started. "This organization aims to give our Pakistani countrymen the rights and privileges they deserve while preserving our society's rich culture and heritage. Some of you have come from far away and left your families to be here. Our work is invaluable, and we wouldn't be able to do it without you."

Goha was pleased the speaker had started by recognizing the sacrifice of the men in the room but was a little disconcerted that the speaker hadn't introduced himself. *Who is he in the organization? Is the omission of his name and title intentional?* Goha didn't even know if the organization had an official, legitimate name—as far as he could remember, Lala Dabir and Babrek had only ever referred to it as "the organization."

"Pakistan's decrepit sociopolitical situation is the fault of corrupt officials who have unjustly seized hold of power," the man continued. "They have failed to live up to their oath of office and care only about themselves. They have no regard for the people of our country. That is why our organization and our mission became inevitable. It is time for us to TAKE BACK CONTROL OF PAKISTAN!" With the last declaration, his voice crescendoed to a bellow. Some of the men clapped, and a couple in the back whistled and cheered.

"*Takbir*!" a man in the back shouted. Goha turned and saw it came from an older man with a full, chest-length beard, raising his fist ardently above his head.

"*Allahu Akbar*!" the men in the audience responded in unison.

The speaker banged on the microphone head until the men settled down. His posture had loosened at their newly acquired energy.

"Until now, we've mainly impacted northern parts of Pakistan where our movement began," he said. "I'm proud to report we've reinvigorated and strengthened some of those areas tremendously. Now, please listen closely, as there's one thing I want to make very clear. If you hear rumors that our organization is associated with terrorist activities, don't believe them! People thrive on gossip, innuendos, and propaganda. We're not terrorists; we're the keepers of our country's Islamic state. We're the ones upholding Pakistan's righteous morals and values. We're the ones who have been divinely chosen to save our countrymen from the infidels."

He stopped to take a sip of water, and a couple of men stood to ask questions.

"Please sit down," the man ordered. "The Holy Qur'an says patience is a virtue. I will answer your questions when I'm done speaking."

He pulled out a laptop from the podium and gestured to a guard in the corner to dim the lights. A video of commercials and scenes of youthful men and women partying and drinking permeated the space. When it was over, he pressed a button to start another clip. This one depicted Pashtun children wearing traditional clothes, playing in picturesque mountains, and praying obediently in *madrasas*. It featured patriotic images of iconic mosques and mausoleums, with melodic recitations of the Qur'an in the background. Goha glanced at the presenter, who had pushed his glasses to the tip of his nose and was scrupulously peering out at the crowd.

Over the next two hours, the speaker rambled on about the deteriorating state of Pakistan: how outside involvement and influence had caused Pakistani culture to wane, how materialism and capitalism were the root causes of evil, how the Westernized media corrupted young minds and fostered immoral behavior, how true Islam was being diluted by leaders preoccupied with secularism.

Around noon, a man from the front row approached the podium and whispered into the lecturer's ear.

"It is time for a lunch break," the presenter announced. "Please follow the guards in an orderly fashion, single file, into the dining area."

Prerecorded military band music started blasting as Goha and the other attendees obeyed the speaker's orders and followed the armed, uniformed men out of the room.

As Goha stood in the queue for the buffet in the kitchen, two men in front of him spoke in low tones in Urdu. He tilted his head forward, pretending to take great interest in the contents of the lentil curry. "I hear drug money—opium—is keeping this organization afloat," one of them said, glancing around nervously.

"Yeah," the other whispered back. "I heard that too. I also heard there's been a lot of infighting among the top brass."

Goha's eyebrows raised inadvertently as he filled his plate. *Maybe I should join them for lunch—I might get more of the inside scoop.* But as they drifted off to sit at one of the large communal-style tables, he decided he wasn't in the mood to socialize. He ambled to the back of the room, finding a spot in the corner where he could eat alone.

He finished his meal, put his tray near the sink, and unenthusiastically returned to the meeting room. He was misaligned with the *ijtema's* messages so far, and he wondered if his facial expressions or the way he carried himself made it obvious to the presenters and other attendees.

Only a handful of men had returned from lunch, including a man with a trimmed goatee and a gold hoop in his ear, sitting in the back row. He was slouched in his chair with a bored expression, picking at invisible lint on his shirt. When Goha approached, he glanced up and gestured to the empty seat beside him. Goha sank into the chair, thankful to be far from the podium and out of the presenters' line of sight.

A few minutes later, another speaker strode to the lectern, dressed head to toe in white. He wore a Pashtun turban, had a dark scar across his right cheek, and appeared about twenty years younger than the morning presenter. As the men filtered in from the cafeteria, his eyes followed them with an intense, stony expression that seemed to bore straight through their skulls.

When the second speaker addressed the crowd, his voice was steady and modulated. He instructed the participants to again state the *shahada* and the organization's pledge, but this time, he added a torrent of long, difficult-to-pronounce Arabic words that Goha didn't recognize. Since he had arrived at the *ijtema*, Goha had only heard people speaking Urdu, Pashto, and a few short, broken English phrases, and when the group repeated after the presenter, they jumbled the Arabic together incoherently. He guessed most of them, like him, had no idea what they were reciting.

From what Goha could piece together, the organization had a hierarchical, military-style structure, where the top echelon made decisions about the missions, and a gang of young foot soldiers obediently carried them out. Since he had no doubt he was one of the soldiers, he was anxious for clarity around his work and hopeful he would receive at least a basic level of training. Instead, the second speaker merely regurgitated the majority of the first presenter's rhetoric.

"The failing state of our country has led to the development of our conservative ideology," he said. "Officials in our highest government offices have allowed corrupt and immoral ideas to infiltrate our large cities, and now our smaller towns and villages are also at risk. Our organization does whatever it takes to bring communities back to their righteous moral state. We take inspiration from the great spiritual minds of the Sufi mystics, the legends and heroes of our land, and incorporate them into our work."

Goha leaned back, perplexed. He couldn't begin to imagine how the orthodox, conservative philosophy the organization espoused had even one thing in common with the peace, tolerance, and love for the Divine that Sufism symbolized. A few men shook their heads.

The man with the gold earring nudged him and leaned over. "It's not true," he whispered. "Organizations like this attack historical Sufi shrines and try to abolish holy rituals. I've seen it in real life and on the news. They consider Sufism a threat and believe people who follow it are heretics."

The presenter glared at him, and the man hastily straightened up and stopped talking.

The turbaned man at the podium finished his presentation and announced they would take a short break before congregating for *maghrib* prayers. Then, without warning, the first speaker rushed to the front of the room and grabbed the microphone from its holder. His head flicked about like a mouse stuck in a trap.

"The *ijtema* is over. Our intelligence told us government troops are about to descend on our facility. EVERYONE MUST GET OUT NOW!"

Security guards stationed at the doors began shouting orders, corralling the men together and shepherding them into the front yard. "You will be picked up and taken back to your residences," bellowed one with a bullhorn. "When your transportation arrives, you must leave the premises immediately!"

Goha was swept into a mob of frazzled and disoriented men. When the familiar black SUV approached the entrance, he broke away to wave down the driver. He collapsed in the back seat, flustered and out of breath, as the vehicle pulled out of the complex.

Goha peered out the back window at the horde of men left behind. His belongings were still at the house, but that was the least of his concerns. He was alert, on edge, and unable to stop think-ing about the *ijtema's* oppressive, regimented environment and the presentations filled with contradictions and self-righteous piety.

This whole experience is turning out to be completely different than what I expected.

CHAPTER 13

After riding in the car for a few quiet and uneventful minutes, Goha's eyelids started drooping. His lack of sleep the previous night was catching up with him. Although there had been an influx of bombings in the area, it seemed they had escaped imminent danger, and he allowed himself to rest his head back and close his eyes.

Deafening gunfire jolted him awake. Two bullets hit the SUV on either side, missing Goha's head by inches. The driver swore, gripped the steering wheel, and slammed on the brakes, but he couldn't stay in control. The vehicle swerved, spun around mercilessly, crashed through the guardrail, and landed with a heavy thud into a cratered gorge.

Moments later, Goha's eyes fluttered open. Stunned and confused, he cried out when he finally comprehended what had happened. He was horrified to see his leg stuck under the front seat. He pried open the door and managed to crawl out, dragging his wounded leg behind him and clenching his teeth through the pain.

To his dismay, he saw the driver lying face up on the seat with his eyes open. Blood spurted out of his forehead and neck like molten lava. Terrified, Goha shook his arm manically through the front window. "Mister, are you okay? Are you okay?"

The driver lay motionless and silent. Goha put his hand to the driver's face—no air came from his mouth or nose. He lifted the driver's arm and put his thumb on his wrist—no pulse.

Oh my God, he's dead.

Goha struggled up the hill to the roadway on his hands and knees. His right leg, raw and tender, felt like it was ripped into shreds. Unable to bear weight on it, he desperately clutched onto broken tree branches and rocks for support.

He eventually reached the road and continued limping along in a daze. His head pounded like an incessant hammer, but he kept going, unsteady but determined, until he approached a small village.

The twinkling lights inside a minaret shone like a sanguine lighthouse beacon, and Goha staggered toward it. When he finally arrived at the mosque, he used all his strength to push open the copper-plated door. He entered the prayer hall and fell headfirst onto the carpet.

The unmistakable sound of the *fajr adhan* and people talking over him brought him back to consciousness. His eyes popped open when droplets of cool water landed on his face and trickled down his cheeks. Two middle-aged men were kneeling over him with worried expressions.

"*Yeh larka con hei, aur kya hua is ko?*" Who is this boy, and what happened to him? they asked out loud, patting Goha's face and hands.

Even in his dazed and distressed state, Goha heard Babrek, Lala Dabir, and the *ijtema* presenters threatening grim consequences if he disclosed information about the organization.

"My name is Goha Hadi," he said in a small voice. "I was walking to my village when I stumbled over a fallen tree and fell into a ditch."

"*Ya Allah*, you poor thing," one of the men said. "We will take you to the village elder's house. His family will take care of you."

Goha grimaced and nodded weakly.

The men sitting at the dining table at the village elder's house regarded Goha with a mixture of morbid curiosity and compassion. Seeing his pathetic, injured state, they gave him a clean hand towel and pointed him toward the bathroom. Though the mirror was cracked, Goha could still make out the bruises and gashes on his face, arms, and neck in various shades of purple and blue. He touched one of the welts delicately, smarting from the tenderness. He barely recognized himself. He turned on the sink and gingerly attempted to wipe his sores with his wet towel, but stopped when the pain became too unbearable.

When he floundered out of the bathroom, a steaming plate of rice covered with spicy chicken curry had been set out for him. Ordinarily, he would have savored the pungent, delectable aroma and made an effort to engage in friendly small talk with his hospitable hosts, but Goha was too distressed and uncomfortable to prolong the visit. He managed to eat a few bites out of courtesy, thanked the family profusely, and told them he needed to leave.

"I'm so sorry, but I have an appointment this evening I need to attend," he said, trying to sound convincing.

One of the men from the mosque offered to drive him to the rooming house, but Goha politely refused. His encounter with Dastagir and his unsavory crew had taught him it was critical to be cautious and not disclose too much information. He didn't want anyone in the village to know the location of his lodging, so he assured his hosts he could make it back safely.

Goha hobbled to the main road. The headlights of a small truck behind him shone like the menacing yellow eyes of a Bengal tiger. It came dangerously close to him before screeching to a halt.

Oh God, they've come for me. I've somehow managed to survive until now, but my time has run out. He started praying.

The truck driver rolled down the window, and Goha saw the tranquil, wrinkled face of an older man. "Where are you going? It's getting late, and it's not safe for you to be out alone."

By then, Goha's knee was hurting so severely that he knew it was fruitless to attempt walking all the way back to the village. He told the man where he was headed.

"I'll be passing the road close to where you're staying," he said. "Get in my truck, and I'll drop you off."

Goha pulled the rusted door handle, said a silent *dua* the driver had no malicious intent, and climbed into the front passenger seat as his body yelped silently in pain. He was thankful for the shadows that hid his gashes so he could avoid explaining his feeble state to the kind stranger.

By the time he reached his room, the sky had turned an inky blue and Goha's knee had swollen to twice its original size. He crashed onto his bed, slept through the morning, and barely managed to raise himself to a sitting position when his phone vibrated. It was Babrek.

"I heard the *ijtema* ended early," Babrek said, his words tumbling over each other like falling cards. "You can tell me what happened when I'm back tomorrow." He hung up.

Why was Babrek always in such a rush? And where would he even start to tell him about everything that had happened? It seemed like eons had passed since Goha had seen him. He limped to the bathroom, soaked a towel in cold water, wrapped it tightly around his knee, and at long last felt the throbbing pain subside.

Goha's driver was an unassuming working-class man who had lost his life simply by being in the wrong place at the wrong time. As he poured water into a pot to make himself chai, he heard the voices of the *ijtema* speakers claiming the organization's ideas were championed by religious scholars around the world ringing in his head. The presenters even went so far as to reference sources, none of which Goha recognized, to try to convince attendees that their interpretations of Islam were correct.

The second speaker had emphatically stated that although women were granted certain rights, their physique and limited intellect made them obviously and unequivocally inferior to men. Meanwhile, Naseebo held an inordinate amount of power and influence over their small family, and Kajal spoke proudly about the status and freedom of women in the Kalash community.

Goha was absorbed and broody as he drank his tea. The injustices, power plays, and dichotomies seeped into his every pore like festering bacteria, causing him interminable confusion and distress.

Babrek entered the room the next morning, carrying two large, crinkly black plastic bags filled with takeout from a local restaurant.

"*Assalam-o-alaikum*!" he said boisterously. "I hope you're hungry because I brought a ton of food. I'm starving!"

Goha rose from the recliner and shuffled over to greet Babrek. He acted as normal as possible, taking the bags from his hands and placing them on the dining table.

"There's no need to warm up anything. I just got it a few minutes ago, and it's still hot. Wait—are you limping?"

Babrek flipped on the lights.

"Oh my God, what happened to you?" Babrek's forehead puckered in concern.

"It's nothing serious. Let's eat first, then we can talk."

"We can eat and talk at the same time. You need to tell me what happened."

As Babrek took the food out of the bags, his face contorted as Goha described how the organization's leadership had called off the *ijtema* earlier than expected after learning government troops were about to invade the residence. He told Babrek how the SUV had been targeted by gunmen minutes after they left the property.

"The car spun out of control and landed in a ditch. I checked the driver's pulse, but it had already stopped, and there was nothing I could do for him," Goha said. His voice was trembling. "I'm lucky to be here right now. I left the scene, so I don't know what happened to his body."

Babrek's expression was somber as Goha relayed how he passed out at a mosque in a nearby village, received help from local residents, and eventually found his way back to the rooming house.

"I'm sorry this happened to you while I was away," Babrek said. "But accidents happen, and sometimes people die. It was the driver's time." The car had a tracking device so the organization would be able to retrieve his body, Babrek told him.

"It sounds like the past couple of days have been terrible, but you survived the accident and didn't get seriously hurt. Allah is merciful. *Alhamdulillah.*" He took Goha's hands in his own. "Don't worry, Goha. I'm back now. Everything's going to be okay."

Goha nodded meekly. *Yes, Allah is merciful, but did the driver have to die?* Many of Bala's friends and acquaintances, whom Goha knew well from the *katchi abadis*, worked as full- or part-time drivers and could have easily suffered the same fate. If Goha's driver hadn't been instructed to pick him up from the *ijtema*, it wouldn't have been his time. The driver had been put into a pre-carious situation, and he paid for it with his untimely death. Could Babrek rationalize his mother's and sister's deaths at the hands of his father as being "their time"? He didn't need to ask him—Goha already knew the answer.

"You've sure dealt with some crazy stuff the past couple of weeks," Babrek said as he stacked the breakfast dishes. "How's your knee doing?"

Goha hobbled over to the recliner. "Better. It's not hurting as badly as last night, and the swelling has gone down."

"Good. You had me so worried."

Babrek walked to the window and gazed outside. "It must have been one hell of a storm. Now that it's daylight, I can really see the destruction."

"It was appalling. I've never experienced anything like it." Goha drummed his fingers on the armrest, his stomach tightening at the seared impressions of those recent traumatic days.

"Did you stay here? This is a solid building. *Maulvi* Saber's house is up on a hill, so you could have gone there too, although . . . well, never mind. Anyway, I'm glad you're safe now."

Goha examined Babrek's face to try to decipher the meaning behind his cryptic words.

"Actually, *Maulvi* Saber came by the day before the storm and invited me over."

"So you stayed there? I should have told you that *Maulvi* Saber can be . . . well . . . a little testy at times."

"A little testy at times?" Goha couldn't help his outburst. "The man is a monster, Babrek."

A knowing look crossed Babrek's eyes. "Don't tell me the son of a bitch tried to take advantage of you. Turns out some things never change. Dirty old man."

Goha was incredulous. *Does Babrek know about Saber's sordid history? If he does, why didn't he warn me?* Goha felt like he had been gut-punched. Dr. Khan had talked about a power dynamic, a cycle of abusive behavior . . .

The hypocrisy of Babrek's words and his recollection of their first night together surfaced like gray ashes after a slow burn. It reminded Goha of an idiom he had learned in school: the pot calling the kettle black. However, he wasn't going to bring it up, not now. He folded his hands together until his fingers turned numb. He desperately needed to get the burden of Saber's death off his chest.

"Saber did try to take advantage of me. He jumped into my bed and started molesting me. I lost it, Babrek. I lost control. I was so angry. I . . . I . . ."

"What? What happened?"

"He was saying the most disgusting things. He was so vicious. I shouted at him and told him to stop, but he wouldn't. I couldn't take it anymore, Babrek. I put my hands around his neck. I . . . I . . . I killed the bastard."

"What? *Ya Allah!* You killed *Maulvi* Saber?"

"He came into my bed and tried to rape me. I did it in self-defense. You've got to believe me. Please believe me. Please."

Goha shut his eyes. Despite the *maulvi's* maliciousness, Babrek somehow had an amicable relationship with him, one that curiously appeared to border on being affectionate. He overlooked his off-color remarks and joked about satisfying the *maulvi's* sweet tooth so he wouldn't get into trouble. Goha didn't want to face Babrek, to deal with the guilt and shame of what he had done, to hear his accusations or, even worse, suffer through his frosty silence.

He opened his eyes. Babrek was slouched on the sofa, his face in his hands.

"I jumped out of bed and . . . and the pistol you gave me was . . . it was in my pocket. You told me to keep it with me at all times," Goha stammered on. "*Maulvi* Saber . . . he tried to grab it. We wrestled for a while and . . . and I was able to kick the gun into a corner. Then I . . . I . . . pinned him down. I lost control and . . . and . . . I strangled him." Goha was heaving.

Babrek lifted his head, his hair rumpled and eyes red. He fixated on the wall with a strange and incomprehensible look. "Goha, I need to tell you something about *Maulvi* Saber." Babrek's voice was flat and barely recognizable.

"What is it?

"He was my father's second cousin, the distant relative who raised me. The one I told you about. My *rishtay ka chacha*."

"What?" The floor sank under Goha. "Oh my God. I killed your *chacha*? No! Babrek, please forgive me. Oh Allah!"

"Goha. It's okay. Listen to me."

"I can't. I just . . . oh my God, I can't believe this."

"Listen to me. Saber was my uncle, but our relationship was . . . well, complicated." His words came out heavy and labored.

When Babrek had moved in with Saber after his father went to jail, his *chacha* showered him with attention, Babrek said. His uncle sent him to the best schools, bought him new clothes, and propped him up at *madrasa* to the point where the whole town saw him as the poster boy of the *masjid*. He stood up for Babrek when he was bullied, and after he graduated from high school, he introduced Babrek to the organization. Saber thought it would help him find purpose in life.

"My father didn't think education was important; he said it made people have airs and think they were better than everyone else. But *Maulvi* Saber valued it, even though he didn't always agree with what schools taught. He made learning a priority, and he let me study whatever I wanted." Plus, he was much more lenient and forgiving than Babrek's dad, and Babrek was grateful to him for that. In a lot of ways, Babrek said, his uncle treated him like the son he never had.

As Babrek's words sank in, Goha desperately and unsuccessfully tried to imagine Saber as a father figure.

At the same time, Babrek hated Saber for taking advantage of him and abusing him. "When it first started, I didn't know what the hell was going on. I was just a kid," he said.

Everyone saw *Maulvi* Saber as a hero and a saint because he had taken Babrek in after what went down in his family. "There was no one I could turn to or confide in. So after a point, I figured I had to tolerate it as long as I lived under his roof."

When Babrek had moved out of Saber's house, he hardly associated with him. He couldn't stand the thought of being related to him. Then Saber became the imam of the local mosque, so Babrek started seeing him more often. But he called him *Maulvi* Saber like everyone else so new people in town wouldn't ask questions about their relationship. "I thought it was hypocritical he chose a religious path, but I figured maybe he was trying to redeem his sins and get closer to God," Babrek said.

Obviously, that didn't happen. He kept abusing boys and even built a room on top of the *masjid* so it would be easier to get away with it. Babrek knew now that Saber was mentally ill, but that didn't excuse him from what he did. "I haven't forgiven him, but over the years, I've focused on his good qualities. Even if it's just to give myself some peace."

Babrek ran his fingers through his hair, his thumbs pressing down hard on his temples. He had been talking to the wall, and when he turned his head, it was like he registered Goha's presence in the room for the first time. His tone turned from reflective to matter-of-fact. "Anyway, he's gone now, and his actions are in the past. Allah will be his final judge. It's time to move on. I'm glad you didn't use the gun—that would have made it easier for the cops to find you guilty. What did you do with his body?"

"I threw it out the window. It landed in the floodwaters on the street and floated downstream toward the river."

"People were taking cover from the storm, so hopefully no one saw that. It's been a while since it happened, so it's unlikely the body will be found at this point. Do you still have your gun?"

"Yes, thank God I remembered it." The question reminded Goha of his unpleasant encounter with Dastagir and his crew. "A group of shady guys came to the mosque looking for Saber while I was there," he told Babrek. "I was terrified they would find out what happened. But I haven't seen or heard from them since."

"Hmmm. I think I know who you're talking about. Did you get any of their names?"

"Yeah. One of them did all the talking. He called himself Dastagir."

"I know that guy." Babrek said he was the head of a bunch of hoodlums who got their kicks out of causing trouble and loitering in places where they didn't belong. The group had been tied to numerous petty thefts and drug peddling. "If Dastagir tries to malign you, I really don't think anyone will listen," he said.

Babrek was thoughtful for a minute. "I just remembered someone who may be able to help us."

Inspector Israr Nek, a senior police officer in Babrek's home district in Peshawar, had recently transferred there, and Babrek was well acquainted with him. But Goha was wary. He had heard one too many stories about corrupt officers working in cahoots with criminals—in exchange for handsome kickbacks that puffed up their lifestyles and societal ranks.

Babrek seemed to read his mind. "Even if we do work with Nek, I don't think we'll tell him what really happened," he said. Goha had obviously killed Saber in self-defense, but they should stick with the story that they didn't know how he disappeared. "You never know whose side the police will take. I've personally seen how some of them have no problem throwing their ethics out the door if it means they can live like kings."

The tightness in Goha's shoulders lessened, and he regarded Babrek with newfound respect. Other than his parents and maybe

Sheikh Samir, Goha had never had someone so unconditionally willing to go to bat for him.

"Babrek, I'm truly sorry for any trauma I've caused you," he said. "You've been a loyal friend, and you've done a lot for me during my time here."

"You should know by now that I would do anything for you."

The silence that followed carried an unmistakable tension, and something inside Goha told him he urgently needed to tell Babrek about Kajal.

That evening, Goha panicked. It was likely Babrek knew, or at least knew of, Kajal. He stressed over Babrek's reaction to his romantic relationship with her, and also feared he might reveal something negative or surprising about Kajal that would sabotage his dream of their happy future together.

"Babrek, you said you kept a distance from *Maulvi* Saber after you moved out of his house. Did you know he got married?"

"Yes, to a Kalash woman from Bumburet. Their relationship caused quite a stir because she looked and behaved so unconventionally. I haven't met her, although I hear she's quite beautiful. She's apparently bold and forward-thinking, which offends a lot of traditional men around here. Why do you ask?"

"I met her when *Maulvi* Saber invited me over for dinner the day you left," Goha said, flicking barely visible dust off of his sleeve. "He went out to pick up dinner, and Kajal and I started talking. I . . . well . . . I thought she was really attractive and . . . she told me she thought I was too. And then . . . well . . . things sort of happened between us."

"Wait, what? Things sort of happened? Did you make out with Saber's wife? *Kya tum pagal ho gaye ho?*" Have you gone completely crazy?

Goha met Babrek's eyes. He couldn't hold back. "I'm in love with Kajal, Babrek."

"You're in love with Kajal?" Babrek guffawed. "Give me a break, *yaar*. Do you even know her? Plus, isn't she practically old enough to be your mother?"

"You were gone for a long time. We got to know each other well." Goha's voice came out terse.

"Have you heard of something called infatuation? That's what this is. Trust me, this isn't love. You are infatuated by the beauty and confidence of an older woman."

"This isn't just infatuation. Kajal is older than me, but she certainly isn't old enough to be my mother. Anyway, what's it to you? The age between us is none of your business. She's a few years older than me, but so what? Our holy Prophet Muhammad married Khadija, who was fifteen years older and married twice before, and they reportedly had an amazing life together."

When Babrek spoke next, his voice was more obstinate than condescending. "But what about me and you, Goha?"

"Babrek, you started a sexual relationship with me without my consent. I went along with it because you're my supervisor and the only person I knew here for a long time. I didn't think I had a choice."

Babrek's face fell, his expression turning from defiant to hurt. "When I met you for the first time, I really wanted you. And now I consider you my best friend. I thought it was mutual."

Goha sighed deeply and shook his head.

"I think I proved to you that homosexuality in Islam isn't black and white. We're both grown adults, so I see no problem with us being together."

"I consider you more like an older brother. I'm not gay, Babrek. I went to a doctor when you were away, Dr. Rustam Khan, and he confirmed what I always knew—I'm straight. I've always been attracted to women."

"I know Dr. Khan, he's pretty popular around here," Babrek said. "I saw him once, thinking he might be able to cure me of my 'gayness.' He told me that if I knew for sure I preferred guys, there was nothing to cure." He reached for a cigarette and lit up.

"You know, Goha, lots of people in the world are bisexual. They have physical relationships with both men and women. Maybe you could consider that since I've done so much for you."

The air in the room shifted. *Is Babrek blackmailing me? Is the special treatment I've received from him only because of the sex I never chose or wanted?*

"I know about bisexual people, Babrek, but frankly, I don't think I'm one of them. I've never been attracted to guys. I love Kajal, and one day I want to marry her. I already feel my life won't be complete without her. I really don't want to talk about this anymore." Goha closed his eyes. "I'm really tired, Babrek. I want to go to sleep."

"Me too," said Babrek. Then his tone hardened. "I don't want to sound dramatic, but in the short time I've been back, you've hit me with three spears: your car accident, my uncle's untimely death at your hands, and now your undying love for his ex-wife of all people. This is a lot for me to handle—I hope we can work things out."

And then, without waiting for a response, he got up and turned out the lights.

CHAPTER 14

The next morning, Babrek asked Goha about Kajal's whereabouts with sincere curiosity. Goha hoped it was a positive sign that, after a good night's rest and a chance to see things more objectively, Babrek had come to accept the new state of affairs. He told him Kajal had left for Bumburet a few days earlier.

"When she comes back, I'm sure she won't want to go to *Maulvi* Saber's house," Goha said as he stirred sugar crystals into his chai and watched them merge gracefully into the milky brown liquid. "Can she stay here?"

"Hmmm. I guess I can arrange for her to stay at the rooming house for now." Babrek said he saw a European couple leave with their bags, so there was likely at least one vacant room. "When will she be back?"

"I don't know." Goha was concerned he hadn't heard from Kajal and petrified when the thought crossed his mind—as it had more than once—that she may have left for good. But, he tried to reassure himself, it was difficult—if not impossible—for her to be in touch with him since cell service hadn't yet reached the valley and she didn't own a phone.

"Hey, *yaar*, on another note, do you know how to drive? Since you've been here, you've been driven around like royalty."

"Nope. I never learned to drive because my parents never owned a car." Bala had bought a three-wheel auto-rickshaw once, hoping to start a side hustle by transporting people around Karachi. His goal was to attract wealthy tourists with his pleasant, limited English phrases and charming demeanor; travelers who would willingly or ignorantly accept a higher rate than he offered to locals. But he sold it when the competition became too fierce. "I drove that rickshaw once for fun with my *ammi* and *abba* sitting in the back seat as passengers. But my parents really didn't encourage me after that because I almost slammed into a fence." He grinned wryly, his memories and long explanation leaving him longing for home. "Anyway, my name means *gemstone*, so you treating me like royalty seems appropriate."

"Well, Mr. Gemstone, you have access to a car now—mine. I can teach you how to drive."

"Cool. But doesn't the organization own your car?"

"Yep. I'll make sure you don't crash, now that you reminded me you're a precious commodity and all. Don't worry; I'm getting kind of used to having you around."

Goha wasn't sure why Babrek was in an affable mood after the awkwardness of the previous night, but he decided it might be an opportune time to bring up his concerns about the *ijtema*. He couldn't forget the discomfort he felt listening to the biased declarations of the presenters. Their words had been pulsating through his head like an incessant, annoying alarm clock, keeping him up at night.

"Babrek, before we go out driving, can we talk about the organization?"

"Sure. You must be eager to go out on a mission—you haven't done much since we came back from Mingora. But you really can't complain; you're being paid pretty well for all the sitting around you do."

"I attended the *ijtema* and almost got shot afterward, remember? Plus, I certainly deserve to be compensated for putting up with you."

"Fair point."

"But seriously, how is the organization funded?"

"Most of the money comes from wealthy Pakistani expats and others who are sympathetic to the cause. There are some large and influential international groups that support our mission too."

"I heard something different. I heard opium smuggling is what keeps it going."

A darkness passed over Babrek's face, and he looked at Goha warily. "Where did you hear that?"

"Are the leaders of the organization fighting?"

"Where are you getting this information from?"

"Never mind. Forget I asked."

"You need to tell me where you heard those things. That kind of talk is dangerous and can lead to serious repercussions for both of us."

"I overheard people at the *ijtema* talking about it."

"From what I know, there's unity throughout the organization. A lot of people thrive on gossip. Don't believe everything you hear. And for God's sake, Goha, please don't spread baseless rumors." Babrek picked up a magazine off the shelf and started flipping through it.

Goha sighed, exasperated over yet another muddled, unproductive conversation about the organization. He was disheartened that so many attendees already seemed to be brainwashed by the *ijtema's* unbalanced, contradictory messages. Then there was the incident Babrek called an accident but, to Goha, felt more like a planned attack. Who had shot the vehicle? What was their motive? Was someone trying to kill him, or did they mistake him for someone else, someone more threatening and influential within the organization? The assault had come out of nowhere and had shaken him to his core. He was frustrated with Babrek for erecting barriers that blocked him from lifting the seemingly impermeable veil of secrecy.

But despite it all, Goha knew he shouldn't complain. Most kids in the slums had no feasible way to escape their poverty, and other than the few days he spent with Babrek after the earthquake, Goha had barely worked. Plus, as Babrek often noted, he received far better treatment than other rookies. He decided it wasn't worth continuing the discussion, so he reached for a book instead.

Later that day, Babrek taught Goha basic driving skills, and when he walked to the bazaar afterward, he didn't ask Goha to join him. He returned early in the evening and said he was hungry, and when Goha insisted it was his turn to buy them dinner, Babrek didn't refuse his offer.

Goha was pleased to discover that a new Peshawari restaurant had opened down the road. The regional dishes were less fiery than the Karachi cuisine he had grown up with, and they presented him with an opportunity to fully savor the taste and texture of the fresh, flavorful ingredients like walnuts and dried fruit. He returned with two full bags, excited to sample the *shinwari tikka* made with roasted lamb, Kabuli rice *pulaw* cooked with caramelized carrots and raisins, and Afghani-style *aushak*, vegetable dumplings covered with tomato paste and yogurt.

After dinner, he planned to call his parents with Babrek around so it didn't look like he was hiding anything from him. He knew he couldn't share details about his incredible past few weeks, so instead, he had decided to tell them about his experiences with the local cuisine.

When he opened the rooming house's main door, Kajal stood in the doorway of his room.

"Kajal! Oh my God, is it really you?" The bags fell from his hands.

Kajal was wearing a black dress with an intricate coral and indigo border that he hadn't seen before. A circular headband with brocade flowers in various shades of blue covered her forehead and accentuated the color of her eyes. "Goha! I missed you so much!"

They stood together in the hallway, embracing and wiping tears from each other's eyes, oblivious to their flagrant violation of social mores.

Babrek appeared from the kitchen. He cleared his throat and crouched to examine a scuff on his shoe.

"If you lovebirds are able to break apart from each other, we can have dinner together," he said at last, standing. "Kajal and I just met. I put her bags in the room next door."

Goha nodded at Babrek, sorry he was forced to deal with the

clumsiness of Kajal unexpectedly showing up at their door. He picked up the food and led Kajal inside their room.

At the dining table, Kajal gushed on about her trip, telling them about the extensive preparations for the annual Kalash *Chawmos* winter festival, which involved traditional dances, purification rituals, and prayer chants. It was amazing to be back in the valley and among her people, she said, but having to deal with swarms of visitors meant she couldn't properly catch up with family and friends. "Our guests are so fascinated by us. They make us feel like celebrities," she laughed.

Goha waited nervously for Kajal to inquire about Saber, but as the conversation lingered on Kafiristan and the uniqueness of the Kalash people, Goha could only surmise Kajal was subconsciously trying to wipe her scarring, over-extended experiences with the imam out of her memory.

Goha's eyes flitted open early the next morning when he heard Babrek shuffling around. By the time he was fully awake, Babrek was already out the door. Later he found a note in narrow, slanted handwriting on the dining table:

Gone overnight to attend a meeting. Babrek

It wasn't unusual for Babrek to leave for work without notice, but Goha guessed it was also a handy excuse for him to escape the rooming house after the previous night. The time Kajal had been gone had solidified Goha's feelings for her, and there was a tangible awkwardness when Babrek witnessed firsthand the magnetic attraction between them. *Babrek must have felt like a third wheel, a huddi, bone, in a kebab.* Goha's reconnection with Kajal made him conclude with certainty that he wasn't interested in a homosexual relationship with Babrek or any other man, and it gave him a little peace of mind to envision an easier, conventional life path going forward.

He washed up, wandered down the hall, and knocked on Kajal's door, thinking he would prepare breakfast for them both. He got no response and placed his ear against the door. *Maybe she's so sound asleep that she doesn't even hear my banging.*

Just as he was about to rap again, he heard a rustling and someone unlatching the main door. He turned to see Kajal standing on the threshold. Behind her stood a woman wearing stylish oval sunglasses. An oversized off-white *chadar* was wrapped around her body and loosely covered her hair, which was highlighted with auburn streaks that complimented her two-piece maroon *jora*, outfit.

"Kajal *jaan*, look at you, already up and about," said Goha cheerfully, standing up. "Who's your new friend?"

"Good morning, Goha! She's not a new friend at all. Nargis Durrani is one of my oldest and dearest friends from the University of Chitral." Nargis had taken Kajal under her wing like she was her little sister when they were at school together, Kajal told him. After graduating, Nargis had moved to Karachi to get married, and she and Kajal had lost touch.

But now, she happened to be visiting a cousin in the vicinity to check on her after the storm. "When I went outside this morning, I had to pinch myself. Nargis *baji* is one of my favorite people in the world. The universe brought us back together." Kajal beamed, putting her arm around Nargis and squeezing her shoulder.

"Wow, that's an amazing story. It's a pleasure to meet you, Nargis *baji*," Goha said.

"And it's lovely to meet you. Kajal has been raving about you all morning."

"That's a relief. I thought she forgot all about me when she went to Bumburet. Why don't you both come to my room and I'll make us chai."

"That would be wonderful. Thank you."

Nargis pulled out a chair at the dining table. "Kajal told me there is an age gap between you. But my advice is to not let anyone give you a hard time about that. Your union with each other seems destined. I read a lot of Urdu poetry, and you remind me of a couplet

I came across recently: '*Dono taraf hai aag barabar lagi hui*,' the fire is burning equally on both sides."

"I'm glad you said that," Goha said, setting a pot of water with loose tea leaves on the stove. "I read one time that couples are made in heaven, and now that I've met Kajal, I think I finally understand what it means. The age between us doesn't matter."

Nargis's own late husband, Kasim Zaidi, had been nearly twenty years older than her, but he was her soulmate, she said. She would never have traded him for a younger man. "I carry this around to feel like he's still here with me," Nargis said, reaching into her purse and pulling out a small photo.

Goha set three steaming mugs on the table. He took the picture from Nargis and saw a distinguished man in a uniform. "So he was a police officer?"

Nargis said Kasim was a detective who rose to become an inspector with the Karachi Police. They had met when she was working in the front office, and she fell for him at once. "He was so handsome and intelligent. He was one of the head officers, but Kasim was kind and considerate to everyone, regardless of their position."

Kasim worked a lot, but he was always there for her, she said. When they weren't able to conceive children, he retired early. He worried about her health and well-being, and didn't want her to feel lonely.

After Kasim left the department, there was an outbreak of kidnappings and targeted killings in Karachi. It was dreadful, she said, and it touched them personally when the brother of their close friend, who was a well-known and highly respected university professor, was abducted and taken hostage.

Soon after, an agency approached Kasim and asked him to help with investigations. The lucrative income, plus the moral obligation he felt to help the country restore order and justice, sent him back into the workforce. Kasim was bound to secrecy, but he did tell Nargis that top officials believed the criminals were religious extremists who felt threatened by well-to-do individuals who espoused liberal viewpoints.

"That's horrendous." The conservative propaganda from the *ijtema* bubbled up in Goha's mind, and his face grew hot. His foot tapped uncontrollably as he downed his chai.

That job was what ended up tearing them apart. Just weeks after Kasim was hired, he mysteriously disappeared, and almost a year had passed since that life-changing day. Nargis said the agency had gotten in touch with her recently and told her Kasim likely perished in a suicide bombing. "But they never found his body, so I'm holding on to a little bit of hope. I have been praying day and night for a miracle that my Kasim will return." She pulled a tissue from her purse and dabbed her eyes.

It upset Nargis immensely that most of the crimes from that time were still unresolved while the perpetrators roamed around freely. Every so often the government issued a statement that said they were on the verge of arresting the offenders, but until then, nothing had happened. "It's been so unsettling and frustrating," she said.

"I can only imagine what you've been going through, Nargis *baji*," Goha said, rising to clear the dishes off the table. "May Allah continue to give you *himmat* and strength."

CHAPTER 15

Babrek had barely returned from his trip the next morning when Police Inspector Israr Nek arrived at the rooming house. It was a Saturday, and Kajal and Nargis were at the bazaar. Goha had escorted them there and walked back by himself after they told him they wanted to spend a few hours browsing the stalls. He was washing up when he heard a knock on the door.

Goha emerged from the bathroom, disheveled. He ran his fingers through his hair nervously at the sight of Nek's official badge, holstered gun, and no-nonsense demeanor.

"Inspector *sahib*, it's good to see you again," Babrek said. "I just got back into town. This is my friend Goha."

The inspector nodded at Goha curtly.

"Please have a seat. What can I get you to drink? Water or perhaps a cold bottle of Pakola?"

"The assistant police chief asked me to come here to talk to Goha, so in the interest of time, I'd like to get right to business." Nek took out a small recorder from his leather satchel bag and pushed a red button.

"Gohar Hadi, I'm here to discuss the mysterious disappearance of *Maulvi* Saber," the inspector said.

Goha pulled out a chair across from the inspector at the dining table, drops of sweat forming on his freshly washed face. "Inspector Nek, I'll tell you what I know, although I'm not sure it will help you." Goha cast Babrek a look that attempted desperately to hint at the support he expected. He frantically tried to remember tips for speaking assertively from his time in the debate club.

"From what I understand, you were the last person to see the *maulvi*. What happened that evening?"

"*Maulvi* Saber had gone to Peshawar for a job interview, and he came back right before the big storm hit," Goha began.

"When he returned, he invited me to stay over. He said it would be safer to ride out the storm at his house since it was built on a hill. Babrek was out of town, so I walked there by myself. By the time we finished dinner, the rain had turned to hail, and he thought the main floor could get flooded. He suggested we go to a room he had built on the roof of the mosque."

The crackling sound of static echoed through the device, and Inspector Nek picked it up and turned it around to examine it. Although it appeared to still be recording, he took a notebook and pen out of his bag and began to rapidly scribble down notes. "Please continue. What happened after that?"

"When the storm was at its worst, *Maulvi* Saber went downstairs to see if the rain had seeped inside," Goha said, pressing his hand down hard on his thigh under the table to stop his leg from shaking. "He didn't come back for a long time, so after a few minutes, I went to check on him. I got halfway down the stairs, and saw that the front door was open and the rain was coming inside. There was a lot of water on the floor, but I didn't see *Maulvi* Saber anywhere."

"That's strange. Well, since you were the last person to see him, you'll need to come to the police station tomorrow so I can cut a First Information Report. That will make the investigation official."

A noisy buzz emitted from Inspector Nek's chest pocket. He pulled out his phone, glanced at the screen, and answered immediately, listening intently for several minutes. Then he said, "Yes, I'll be there right away."

"I'm sorry, but I have to go. Something urgent happened that needs my attention. I'll be in touch." He stood quickly, slipped his recording device and journal into his bag, and rushed out the door.

Babrek and Goha exchanged glances.

"Well, that was interesting," said Babrek.

"Did you know he was coming?"

"Nope, he just showed up. I wonder what happened that made him leave so fast?"

Later that evening on TV, Babrek and Goha discovered the reason for Nek's hasty departure. A top news story showed grenades being lobbed at a local girls' school a few miles from their rooming house. Since it was the weekend, the building had been vacant, and no one had been killed or injured. However, the anchor solemnly reported that the attack had left the community anxious and fearful. And, with obvious indignation, he added that funding for repairs and more surveillance would now be needed for the building and surrounding property at the high cost of necessary books and school supplies.

Goha had a fitful night. He woke up even before the wan light of dawn emerged on the horizon, determined to visit the police station early so he could get the FIR over with. He took a quick shower, quickly pulled out a *janamaz*, and said his *fajr namaz*, praying he would soon be able to put the whole unnerving mess behind him. He left quietly so he wouldn't wake up Babrek, who, every night since Kajal had arrived, had opted to sleep on a mattress on the floor.

When Goha arrived at the station, the receptionist told him to take a seat in the lobby. Inspector Nek had gone back to the girls' school to investigate the attack and would return soon, she said.

Goha sat on a chair, his head pressed against the wall, his eyes half closed, recalling the traumatic incident that had landed him there. The more he ruminated over *Maulvi* Saber's despicable behavior, the more justified his actions felt, even despite his *rishtedari*, familial ties, to Babrek. The only thing he truly lamented was how that one critical night might dramatically affect his future with Kajal.

A few minutes turned into a few grueling hours. When Inspector Nek finally returned, he was scruffy and absent-minded. Goha sat up straighter as he walked past him into the lobby, but Nek barely glanced at him. "Oh yes, Goha Hadi," he said, turning around, a look of recognition finally passing over his face. "You're here for the FIR. I already prepared one based on the information you provided. Come with me." He led Goha into his office and shuffled papers on his desk, eventually pulling a stapled document from a pile. "Sign here and you'll be free to go for now. And by the way, I was told a few men showed up at the mosque looking for the imam. We'll be asking them questions too."

Thank God I'm not the only suspect. Babrek had told him Dastagir and his delinquent gang had a bad reputation in the area, which meant they would likely be interrogated harshly about their whereabouts during the storm. But what if they reported seeing Saber's dead body close to the *masjid*? Goha prayed they hadn't, since that would likely keep the case open indefinitely through a whole new series of investigations.

Goha's stomach was growling when he came back to his room and found Kajal standing over the stove in front of two steaming pots.

"Lunch is ready," she announced cheerfully, kissing him on the cheek. "I hope you're hungry. Where were you?"

"I'm starving. How do you always know exactly what I need?" He sat at the table. "Where's Nargis? And do you know if Babrek will be joining us?"

"Nargis *baji* went back to Karachi this morning. I saw Babrek as he was heading out the door. He let me in so I could make lunch. He didn't tell me where he was going or how long he would be gone, but he said we shouldn't wait for him."

"Well, it's not unusual for Babrek to be cagey."

"Someone else is being cagey today too," she teased. "Where were you off to so early this morning?"

"I was at the police station."

"Why?"

"It's a long story."

"I've got plenty of time, my *jaan*."

Goha looked at Kajal remorsefully. Then, before he could help himself, everything that had happened over the past few weeks released like a deluge of water from floodgates, starting with the first night of the storm and ending with the FIR and meeting with Inspector Nek. When he got to the *ijtema*, however, he glossed over details from the presentations, remembering the oath he had half-heartedly recited about never divulging the organization's information to anyone, and he gave her the same version of Saber's disappearance he had given the inspector. He couldn't bear to tell Kajal he had killed *Maulvi* Saber, not right at that moment. When he was done talking, he watched her face ruefully, praying she wouldn't hate him—or worse, decide to leave him.

"I'm so sorry about everything you've gone through. I can't believe you're a suspect in Saber's death—that's so crazy and stressful. It's baffling how he vanished and still hasn't shown up." Kajal put her elbows on the table, cupping her head in her hands. "It sounds like it was a frightful storm, so maybe he got disoriented by the high winds when he went outside? You'd think someone would've seen him, but maybe there just wasn't anyone around."

Goha scrutinized Kajal's expression, trying to discern how she would react to the truth, especially given her torrid history with Saber. With Bala and Naseebo, it seemed that open communication and trust over the years had brought them closer to each other.

"Kajal, my *jaan*."

"Yes?"

"There's something I need to tell you about *Maulvi* Saber."

"What is it?"

"He didn't disappear in the storm. I . . . I . . . I did it, Kajal. I killed him. I strangled him, and I killed him."

"What are you saying? This can't be true." Her head tilted, and her brow furrowed.

"It's true. The night I went to Saber's house, he said we would be safer if we spent the night in the room on the roof of the *masjid*. Then the power went out, and he jumped into bed beside me and started groping me.

"I warned him if he didn't stop, I would kill him. I swear I did. But he wouldn't listen. He was mocking and threatening me, and he was about to rape me. I started thinking about how badly he mistreated you, and I just couldn't take it. I put my hands around his neck, and I strangled him. Then I threw his body out the window into the flooded street. And now I will burn in hell for taking a human life." He slumped forward, unable to meet her eyes.

For Goha, hours seemed to pass before Kajal finally spoke again.

"I don't think you'll burn in hell." Her voice was small but resolute, and she placed her hand on his shoulder, gentle yet firm. "Remember what I told you about Saber? He was an evil man. A monster. I think he built that room so he could molest naive, unsuspecting kids and satisfy his perverted sexual desires. What you did is a horrible thing to live with, but you did it in self-defense. The Kalash believe that when you are a good person with good intentions, divine grace is with you. You were in a dangerous situation, and God protected you. You did what you needed to do to save yourself, to save innocent boys . . . and to save me."

Her words had the effect of enveloping Goha in a soft, cozy blanket. For the first time, he saw multiple divergent paths: some wide, some narrow, some elevated, some low. Some were strewn with jagged, hazardous rocks, and others were smooth and paved, tantalizingly curving around lush, rolling green hills. But all led toward a brilliant, glowing center. Salvation.

Kajal's voice turned pragmatic. "Have you told anyone besides me?"

"I told Babrek. And you won't believe this. Saber was his distant uncle who raised him after his parents died."

"Oh my God—I had no idea. Saber never told me that."

"I'm sure he didn't tell you a lot of things. Anyway, I know

Babrek cares about me. We've had a tumultuous history, but I trust him. He's the only one who knows the truth about that night other than you."

CHAPTER 16

When Babrek came back that evening, he delivered unexpected and surprising news: The organization's leadership had ordered them to vacate the rooming house by the end of the week.

"Why do we need to leave?" Goha had gotten used to the house and the surrounding locale, and he assumed he would stay there for his entire duration up north. Plus, having Kajal in the same building where he could protect her around uncultured, leering strangers put his mind at ease.

"All I know is that I've been told we need to get out of here. I didn't ask why. Unlike some people I know, I make it a point not to question orders from my superiors."

Goha chose to ignore Babrek's pointed attack.

"Would it be possible for me to get a room in the new location too?" Kajal piped. "It's not safe for me to go back to Saber's house alone, and I don't really have anywhere else to go."

"I'm sorry, but I can't help you," Babrek said firmly, appearing to have anticipated the request. "I already bent the rules to get a room for you here. You aren't part of the organization, so I can't do that for you anymore."

"The organization is completely dominated by males. As a female, Kajal probably wouldn't have been able to join even if she wanted to," Goha pointed out, putting his arm around his girlfriend possessively. His mind raced as he tried to think of an alternative solution that would keep Kajal close to him. *Maybe she could camp out in my room at the new boarding house?* But Babrek's funny reaction when Goha had confessed their relationship gave him pause, and it compelled him to drop the idea altogether.

In the conservative tribal environment, rooming with Kajal when they weren't married could mean trouble. He found it interesting and ironic that premarital sexual relations between men and women were considered more taboo than sex between males.

"If I can't come with you, I'll probably just go back to Bumburet for a while. It's not the end of the world." Kajal smiled, but the sentiment didn't quite reach her eyes. "I love it there, and I'll get to hang out with my family more. Maybe I'll make a trip to Chitral and visit some of my old college friends too."

Goha didn't like the way things were unfolding, but he couldn't argue that her suggestion made sense.

"Hey guys, cheer up," Babrek said, looking at their fallen expressions. "I have some good news. Goha, your phone restrictions have been eased, so you two can stay in touch when you're apart. Since there's no service in the valley, maybe you can talk when Kajal is in Chitral." He had told the organization that Kajal was a relative who would appreciate hearing from Goha occasionally. "They've been known to tap into conversations, though, so make sure you keep your calls lighthearted and brief."

"Thanks, Babrek," Goha said.

The next day, Goha took Kajal out to buy her a new cell phone, and the day after, they all packed up and left in opposite directions—Kajal for Bumburet, and Babrek and Goha for a new bunkhouse in a desolated, obscure area somewhere between Mingora and Peshawar. As Goha embraced Kajal goodbye, he took a mental image of her, luminous in a full-length dress accented with beaded turquoise and yellow geometric designs, and wearing a matching circular head cap with a narrow fabric embellishment that flowed all the way down her back.

❖ ❖ ❖

On the drive to their new location, Goha passed the time taking in the arresting mountain landscape of colossal trees and aquamarine streams that twisted and turned as they gurgled lazily over moss-covered rocks. At some point he would return to the sprawling urban jungle of Karachi, and he didn't know when—if ever—he would make it back to that part of Pakistan when his time with the organization ended.

On the side of the road, groups of men wearing hard hats climbed the steep terrain with hammers, chisels, and pickaxes. Goha rolled down his window. The muffled clang of tools tapped and ground against the hard rock. "What are they doing?" he asked Babrek.

"Mining for gemstones," Babrek answered. "This area is full of them. Precious and semiprecious ones like emeralds, rubies, garnets, and pink topaz."

Pakistan had a thriving jewelry industry where artisans labored in workshops, painstakingly crafting intricate pieces with machines or their bare hands. The elegant gold and silver rings, bracelets, and necklaces inlaid with rich-colored gemstones found their way into boutiques in the country's cosmopolitan cities, where they were scrutinized, ogled, and tried on by elite, mostly female, customers and often purchased by their doting husbands, fathers, sons, boyfriends, or secret lovers. His mother would talk wistfully about her female clients' treasured jewelry collections that she had seen while she was cleaning houses in the poshest areas of Karachi.

Babrek told him the mountains were filled with quartz, a strong and versatile material used to make clocks, countertops, medical devices, electronics, and even jewelry. It was a big business in the area, and Pakistan exported massive quantities of it to countries all around the world.

"Quartz," Goha repeated. He had never heard of it before, and he liked the way the strange English word made his tongue press against the roof of his mouth. He said it a few more times out loud, extending the last syllable and blowing air out of his mouth, and Babrek laughed.

"You should try your hand at mining for quartz and other gemstones. You might have a knack for it. You have the right name for it, after all."

At the new accommodations, Goha was relieved to find his room was too small to fit more than one person. "This room is tiny," he said, feigning disappointment.

"Yeah. These rooms aren't big enough for both of us. I'll be staying in the next bunk next door," Babrek replied casually, tossing him a room key and turning toward the door. "Oh, and you're finally assigned on a mission. I know it's taken forever."

"But I haven't even been trained," Goha countered. It was unlikely to happen, but at that point, all Goha wanted was to fall off the organization's radar. He didn't want to carry out the assignment or to be on any list for any mission, now or ever. The elusive training Babrek mentioned hadn't happened at the *ijtema*, and he didn't even care. He was more than ready to abandon the organization and start a fresh, unburdened life with Kajal.

"There might be some training when you get there. You're smart—I'm sure you'll figure it out," Babrek responded.

Babrek would drop Goha off at the remote camp the next evening, where he would receive bedding, food, and clothes. "I'm not sure how long you'll be there—sometimes plans change or things go awry. Kind of like what happened at the *ijtema*. Anyway, as far as I know, there won't be fighting involved, but take your weapons just in case. You may have to fire at buildings or defend yourself if the enemy comes after you."

"Wait. Who exactly is 'the enemy,' Babrek? No one has ever told me directly."

"I think you know the answer to that, Goha." His patronizing tone was unmistakable. "The enemy is an individual or group who opposes or obstructs the organization's goals. Anyone who stands in the way of our progress and changes. And in case you haven't realized it, they aren't just the enemies of the organization but of Pakistan as a whole."

"But why are we calling people 'the enemy' as if we're waging a war? Can't we bring about positive changes peacefully? We weren't fighting anyone when we went to Mingora to help the earthquake victims. So why do I need to take my weapons this time?"

"Goha." The word came out of Babrek's mouth like he was speaking to a toddler. "Don't you remember from school that revolutions require force? Throughout history, weapons have been used to overcome resistance. You should know that by now."

Goha let out a frustrated sigh. *Since when did I become a revolutionary?*

"There's no cell service at the camp, so I suggest you call your parents before we leave. And by the way," Babrek added, "I was told you'll get a nice bonus if you manage to carry out the assignment successfully."

Goha pressed the buttons to call Bala's cell phone slowly and reluctantly, like he had been given the uncomfortable task of handling extremely fragile china. He wasn't in a mood to once again skirt around the nature of his work and act like everything was okay. He had been brooding over the mission since Babrek told him about it, and now he just wanted to get it over with. But since he hadn't talked to his *abba* since arriving up north and didn't know how long he would be on the assignment, he decided he should at least give his parents a quick call.

His father picked up on the first ring. Goha had barely even said *salam* when Bala started gushing effusive praise on him.

"Goha *baita*. Your *himmat* and perseverance have changed my life. I heard a saying recently, and I thought about you. '*Mehnat kamyabi ki kunji hai.*'" Hard work is the key to success. "You've certainly shown that to be true." His voice cracked.

Bala said he went out on work projects only occasionally now. "My health has really improved. I'm not in pain anymore—I feel better than I've ever felt before. Wait until you see me—I look twenty years younger than when you left. I think I could pass for your brother." He chuckled, and it occurred to Goha how rarely he had heard that breezy, carefree sound come from his father.

"Did you know we've moved out of the *katchi abadis* into a better neighborhood? Our new house is like a palace compared to our old shack. Your supervisor must be so pleased with the work you're doing."

They had always wanted more children, Bala told him, but now he and Naseebo understood God's plan. "Allah knows best. You, my son, are more than we could have asked for. You've given us so much, and you make us so proud."

Tension crept into Goha's neck. "I'm so glad your health has improved, *abba*," he said at last. "You've worked so hard all your life to provide for me and *ammi*. You deserve a break."

"When will we see you, *baita*? Didn't the organization say they would pay for your visits back home?"

For the first time, Goha registered how quickly time had passed. "I think so, *abba*. We have so much to catch up on."

A rap on the door gave Goha a welcome excuse to cut the conversation short. His father's exuberance was simply too much.

"I need to go, *abba*. We'll talk again soon, *inshallah*."

Goha hung up, his throat constricted. He wasn't sure how or when it had happened, but a gulf had developed between him and his parents in the short time he had been away. He opened the door to face Babrek.

"I overheard you talking to your parents," he said. "How are they doing?"

"Great," Goha replied glumly.

"Good. Oh hey, *yaar*, before I forget, this is for you." Babrek pulled an envelope out of his pocket. "I was told to make sure you read this before you go on your mission."

The envelope was creased and smudged, and a piece of lined notepaper had been folded clumsily several times and shoved inside. Goha took the paper out, placed it on the table, and smoothed it with his fingers. A familiar name was littered throughout the messy, handwritten Urdu script: Malala Yousafzai.

"It's quotes from Malala that have been pulled from her speeches and writings," Babrek said. "She's from this area, and she's made it her mission to educate kids around the world. It might surprise you to know she also supports our organization."

Babrek peered over Goha's shoulder. "The writing isn't very legible. Someone from the organization probably transcribed it from Pashto into Urdu. Here, let me read it for you." He took the paper from Goha's hand.

"'When the whole world is silent our guns become powerful.'"

"'I raise up my gun—not so I can shout but so those without a gun can be heard.'"

"'Let us pick up our guns—they are the most powerful weapons we have.'"

"'I speak not for myself but for all militant girls and boys.'"

"'If one man can destroy everything—'"

"Wait a minute." Goha grabbed the paper from Babrek and scanned the text. "She's been grossly misquoted," he said disgustedly, throwing the paper on the floor. "Malala advocates for education, not violence. Why in the world would she support guns when she nearly lost her own life from a misogynistic group that shot her in the head?"

"I don't know, Goha," Babrek said sheepishly. "I'm sure you've heard the controversy surrounding Malala. People around here aren't exactly sure what she believes."

But Goha couldn't stop fuming. "Illiterate bastards," he muttered. "They probably transcribed the document incorrectly on purpose."

Members of some ultraconservative groups mocked Malala's appearance after her face had become disfigured from the school bus shooting a couple of years earlier. Their cruelty sickened Goha—he couldn't fathom how they could be so callous. After brooding over it for months, the only explanation he had come up with was that they carried deep-rooted insecurity that manifested into a machismo culture and fostered baseless subjugation of females.

"You know, it's possible someone put this document together to sabotage the organization's mission," Babrek said. "There are rumors that agents have infiltrated our group and write stuff like this to make us look bad."

Goha listened to Babrek's feeble attempt at a conspiracy theory and silently cursed the organization. But he said nothing more—he knew he would achieve little by challenging Babrek about an establishment that he seemed to follow without reservation and commit to wholeheartedly.

Goha lay in bed that night with fragmented thoughts coursing through his brain. How had he landed in such undesirable and treacherous circumstances? *Maybe I've been a bad son. Maybe I haven't been regular enough with my namaz. Maybe I should have stuck up for Arif when I had the chance.* He banged his fist against his forehead, thinking maybe he could have helped others more, even with his paltry upbringing. Or begged for God's mercy and forgiveness for his sins, which, in his mind, had amassed exponentially since he'd left home.

He was still agitated about the paper Babrek had given him that blatantly misrepresented Malala Yousafzai. At school, he had learned about Malala and her peace-oriented work that spanned the globe and earned her the distinguished honor of being the world's youngest Nobel Peace Prize laureate, in addition to being the second winner from Pakistan. In her autobiography, she relayed how some Pakistanis considered her a traitor for fighting against the Taliban and earning accolades and reverence in Western countries. Some even suggested she manufactured the shooting event for global attention and to establish a better life abroad. They were resentful when she accepted invitations from American talk shows and allegedly said disparaging things about her home country's government and the Pashtun society she grew up in.

Pakistan–U.S. relations had always been complicated; scores of Pakistanis considered America a fickle ally that only got involved with their country when it benefited them and didn't hesitate to abandon the friendship when it didn't. They were angry about U.S.-led drone attacks in Northwest Pakistan in the years following 9/11 that were aimed at military targets but also took the lives of hundreds of civilians, including children. In addition, many Pakistanis condemned the killing of al-Qaeda leader Osama Bin Laden in 2011 by two dozen U.S. Navy SEALs, questioning why he wasn't captured alive since he was unarmed at the time of his death. Conspiracy theories abounded when the U.S. government decided not to publish any photos or DNA evidence following the attack.

Goha pondered whether he should try to escape after—or maybe even before—his first real mission. In the best-case scenario, it would cut off financial security and send his family reeling back into a cycle of poverty. It was heartbreaking to envision his parents moving back to Qasba, his father returning to the grueling manual labor that made him sick, and his mother sweeping floors, scrubbing toilets, and yearning for luxuries once within her reach. In the worst-case scenario, leaving would put his life and the lives of people he loved in grave danger. There were no good options other than to stick with it and pray it all ended soon.

The following night, the sky was wrapped in a dense bluish-gray canopy when Babrek and Goha left for the camp. The bumpy forty-minute drive on unpaved roads made Goha queasy, and the atmosphere had turned a murky charcoal black when Babrek stopped the car. Goha opened the door and hesitated before exiting.

"When will you pick me up?"

"As soon as the operation is over. You'll be fine."

In the darkness of night, Goha could only make out vague shadows until a stream of light particles fell on him. It came from a man in military fatigues pointing a flashlight. He nodded at Goha and led him to a small bunkhouse with two stacked beds. Two teenage boys were perched on the top bunk, their legs swinging.

"These are your roommates, Munir and Moustaffa," the man told him. "Tomorrow, they'll go out on a mission while you do your fitness training." He walked to the closet, slid open the door, and pulled out a cardboard box from the top shelf. Inside the box were four rows of neatly packed hand grenades. The day after training, Goha would be expected to use them on a couple of girls' schools. "We don't intend to hurt anyone," the man added quickly. "They're just to create panic. The only time we burn a school to the ground is when we're sure no one's inside."

The boys were silent and expressionless, but Goha wrinkled his nose. "Excuse me, sir, but why are we doing this?"

"You don't know?" the man said, irritated. "The girls are being taught things that are blasphemous and obscene. They are *haram*."

What were the girls learning that was so awful? Why were they being punished when the administration and teachers were responsible for the curriculum? And even if the lessons were haram, weren't the boys absorbing the same information? Goha had so many questions and no answers, but didn't want to expose himself as a troublemaker on his first real mission—or jeopardize the possible bonus Babrek had mentioned. When the man left, he crawled under a blanket on the bottom bunk without a word to his roommates and went to sleep.

The following day, after an early morning congregation of *fajr* prayers and a communal breakfast in an adjoining building, Goha and roughly twenty other young men were led to a field behind the bunkhouses where an expansive military training–style assault course had been set up. Over the next several hours, while group leaders shouted commands through bullhorns, the men obediently crawled under barbed wire and nets, slithered through pipes and tunnels, climbed over walls and beams, balanced on planks, climbed up and down steps, practiced target shooting, negotiated mazes, and threw small grenades and incendiary bombs at piles of dry straw and grass.

By the time they gathered again for the evening meal and *maghrib namaz*, Goha's muscles were like rubber. As he sat cross-legged on the floor with the others in a common room after the prayers, one of the leaders began chanting the Holy Qur'an. Many boys closed their eyes and swayed forward and back and side to side in a trance to the soothing melody. When the recitation was finished, another leader, an older man with a soft, woolen *topee*, stood up.

"You had a hard day, and you all did well," he said sympathetically, stroking his beard as he looked at the tired, young faces. "You're now ready for your missions over the next couple of days. Some of you asked why we are targeting schools, so let me explain.

"Western education was first introduced by missionaries. It dates back to colonialism, the control of our land by foreigners and infidels. Schools, colleges, and universities across Pakistan are leading young people away from pure religious education. They are producing apostates who challenge God's sovereignty. When Western thinking takes over, it leads to Western domination, and that leads us further away from our true culture and heritage."

His words buzzed around Goha's head and soon became indecipherable background noise. He started fading. After the man stopped talking and dismissed the group to their rooms, Goha crashed onto his bed without even washing his face or changing out of his dirty clothes. He was barely conscious when Munir and Moustaffa bragged about how the bombs they threw at a nearby girls' school that day had produced flames that rose more than six feet into the air.

In the wee hours of the next morning, the air was thick with fog when Goha and seven other men piled quietly into a dark green van. The group leader entered last, the doors sliding together behind him to block out the outside world. He informed them that they would be targeting two schools in the area, back-to-back, before returning to the camp. At each site, a whistle would signal when to launch the grenades.

Goha sat with a vacant expression. He wasn't buying the messages from the camp—they were similar to the hot-blooded, one-sided propaganda he'd heard at the *ijtema*. With so many men involved in the mission, it was unlikely anyone would know who threw the grenades or whose detonated. *I've bluffed before in debate tournaments and gotten away with it. I can do it again.*

The driver started the engine, the low whir like a lion's roar in the still night. The hair on Goha's arms stood straight up despite the unseasonably warm temperature. The grenades in his pockets weighed him down like shackles.

They had only driven for a few minutes when the van stopped behind a thicket of trees. The group leader exited first, and as the men followed behind him, he silently pointed to the spot where each one was to be stationed.

Moisture hung in the air as Goha stood behind a tree roughly twenty yards away from the school, scarcely breathing as perspiration dribbled from his face. He startled at a slight rustle, and when he squinted his eyes in the direction of the sound, he saw the silhouette of another man hidden in the nearby bushes.

He strained his ears and heard a distant whistle—the leader's signal—and the next moment, men were hurling their bombs at the school and running back to the van. Goha joined the crowd, his grenades firmly rooted inside his pockets. As the vehicle sped from the site, he glanced out the rear window. Plumes of billowing smoke and amber flames rose higher and higher until they engulfed the entire building.

By the time they reached the second school, no one, including the group leader, had called Goha out. He exited the van and again treaded delicately to his position a few yards away from the property. *No one noticed the first time, so I'm going to fake it again.* He strained his ears for the leader's signal but instead saw two young men cupping megaphones, bolting his way.

"The enemy has seen us. Run away and hide as fast as you can. If you don't run, we'll all be killed!"

Goha spun around wildly. The men shouted and fled in all directions. He spotted an open fence behind the school and darted toward it, tearing through overgrown vegetation, running and running, his pants repeatedly getting tangled and torn from the bushes and weeds. He was panting and dripping sweat from his entire body when he finally stopped.

There was no one around. He fumbled in his pocket for his phone, eventually finding it lodged between two grenades. His hands were clammy and shaky, and the device kept slipping from his fingers. He tried to reach Babrek, but the line was dead.

Unsure of what else to do, he sprinted forward again and didn't halt until he reached a semipaved road. By that time the sky was spitting down rain, so he took shelter under a sprawling oak tree. He dialed Babrek's number again and this time, miraculously, his supervisor picked up the call.

"Goha. I heard about what happened through my two-way radio," Babrek said hurriedly. "Don't panic. I think I know where you are. Do you see a narrow river running parallel to the road on the left?"

"I see it." Goha's voice trembled.

"Do you have your weapons with you?"

"Yes."

"Ditch them into the river. You'll see people heading downstream toward Pir Sahib Ganti Sharif's *dargah*. It has red and white flags on top. You can't miss it. Stay calm and join the crowd. Don't speak to anyone. If someone approaches you, pretend you're deaf. I'll meet you outside the entrance in about an hour. The roads are slick, so you might get there before me." He hung up.

Goha walked cautiously to the riverbank. Seeing no one, he took the grenades out of his pockets and crouched down. He hurled them into the rapids one after the next, five pounds feeling like five hundred pounds unleashed from his body in seconds. In the distance he made out the fuzzy outline of a crowd emerging. Goha pretended to be mesmerized by the flowing currents, and when the group neared, he joined their procession without speaking and avoided eye contact.

When Goha arrived at the shrine, Babrek's car was nowhere to be seen. He followed the devotees inside and imitated their chants, supplications, and rituals for the revered Sufi saint as best as he could without drawing attention to himself.

He came back outside to the sound of thunder booming. As the rain started pelting down, he sat on a bench under a shed in the courtyard in a vain attempt to stay dry. The minutes Goha spent waiting turned into one hour, then two.

His anxiety intensified, and his posture grew taut. *Did Babrek get into an accident? Was he identified as part of the organization and arrested? Oh my God, did Babrek suffer the same harrowing fate as the driver? Is his mangled body in a ditch somewhere in the middle of nowhere?*

Then suddenly there was a break in the clouds, the downpour subsided, and Babrek's SUV approached the shrine. Goha stood and waved him down frantically.

"I could barely see six feet in front of me," Babrek said as he opened the passenger door. "The roads were so bad I almost landed in a ditch. Thank God it isn't raining so hard anymore. Are you okay?"

As soon as Babrek parked the car, Goha retreated to his room without a word. He crashed on his bed and only woke up several hours later from a loud, persistent knock at his door.

"Hey, *yaar*, you going to sleep all day? Time to wake up. I got you dinner." Babrek entered the room carrying a large paper bag that smelled like fried onions and garlic. Goha sat up and rubbed his eyes.

Babrek took the containers out of the bag and Goha scarfed down all the food, barely conscious of what he was eating. He was in no mood to talk about the derailed mission or the ensuing events. He vowed that going forward, for his peace of mind, he would focus on nonviolent, pleasant thoughts even if he were coerced into carrying out actions completely disconnected from them.

"Looks like someone was a little hungry," Babrek said. "Hey, it's too bad your first mission went astray. It wasn't your fault. You'll still get the bonus I mentioned before."

He picked up the containers and tossed them into the bin in the corner. "You're due for a trip back to Karachi, and the organization will pay for a business-class ticket for you. Consider it your bonus. You deserve it after everything you've been through."

Goha managed a small nod. He put his arms behind his head and leaned back, releasing a long, drawn-out breath that had been held inside him for days.

CHAPTER 17

Bala was out with his friend Farid when Goha called home the next day to give his parents two pieces of good news: He was coming back to Karachi and had been given a chance to fly in an airplane for the first time.

"That's so exciting, *baita*," Naseebo said. "I'm so happy for you. Also, your *abba* and I have been thinking you should settle down soon and start your own family. *Alhamdulillah*, you're making a good living now, enough to support a wife and children. We can talk about it when you're back."

"I can't wait to see you and *abba*. I've missed you so much." Goha chose his next words carefully. It wasn't the right time to mention Kajal to his *ammi*, the woman who had sacrificed so much for him and loved him with all her heart. "I respect your ideas about my future and happiness—I really do—but I'm still young, and to be honest, the responsibility of providing for a family right now terrifies me." He laughed, hoping his mother would join in, but instead, she let out a huff somewhere between a gasp and a snort.

Naseebo didn't respond. *How had Goha suddenly become so headstrong?* She had never mustered the courage to tell her son the truth about his birth, how he was conceived out of wedlock, how his father had hurriedly arranged a *nikah* with a mullah who was unaware of her pregnancy. In the official version of their story, Bala and Naseebo's common employer at the time, the Cheemas, noticed their mutual attraction and helped arrange a wedding ceremony to make their union official. The narrative went that their baby, Gohar, had been conceived on their wedding night and had arrived a few weeks premature.

In truth, the Cheemas had been blindsided when they discovered their eighteen-year-old, unmarried house servant, Naseebo, had been impregnated in their home by their twenty-two-year-old day laborer, Bala, who was remodeling their kitchen at the time. Incensed at what they considered a breach of trust, they chastised Naseebo and Bala's lack of morality and fired them both on the spot.

Naseebo's fictitious account depicted her and Bala as upright Muslims who had refrained from sexual intimacy before marriage. For Naseebo, it was a harmless white lie that framed how people regarded their family and—equally, if not more important—how Goha perceived his parents. Her story had become even more critical to preserve as Goha reached adolescence. The possibility of her son following in her and Bala's footsteps terrified her; with all their hardships, she couldn't imagine having to deal with her child's dishonorable reputation on top of everything else.

On a fateful day in September, when a mysterious man named Lala Dabir had knocked on their door, they were given the opportunity to start over, to replace their difficult, pathetic lives with comfort and a little bit of luxury. Her beloved Goha was working hard to make it happen, and now the time was approaching for him to marry. The girl he married, Naseebo decided, would be a good-natured, obedient, and chaste daughter from a wealthy family who would help elevate the Hadis' status. With Goha's good looks, respectful demeanor, top grades, religious upbringing, and now well-paying job, he was a great catch by every standard. Naseebo was sure that girls from families of higher standing would be clamoring all over him.

There was a sharpness in Goha's voice she had never heard before, and she wondered if he had ever questioned his parents' moral integrity or the story around his premature delivery. She was unnerved by her son's petulance, especially since she hadn't seen him in so long, and decided to drop the subject for the time being to avoid a confrontation.

From the moment Babrek dropped him off at the Peshawar airport, Goha was in awe. The entire experience—arriving at the terminal; receiving his boarding pass at the counter from the pretty attendant with the long eyelashes, loose head scarf, and shiny nose stud; putting his belongings on the conveyor belt while filing through security; waiting at the gate to board; watching through the window as the gigantic aircraft pulled up—was exhilarating. On top of that, he had earned a seat in the privileged business class, which made him inches away from becoming someone who could wave a magic wand and experience faraway, thrilling new worlds on a whim.

His seat was in the second row next to a gray-haired businessman who wore a pin-striped collared shirt, navy trousers, and polished brown leather shoes. A pair of rectangular, black-rimmed reading glasses rested on the bridge of his nose. When Goha opened the latch of the overhead bin above him, the man put his magazine down on his lap and smiled.

"Hello, I'm Amir." The man appeared to be Pakistani but addressed him in flawless English, accented with a slight British lilt.

Goha responded in English. "Nice to meet you. I'm Goha."

Goha settled into his chair and soon learned Amir was in the business of exporting Pakistani-made sports equipment to the Middle East—soccer balls, volleyballs, basketballs, baseball bats, cricket gear, hockey sticks, and various types of rackets, all manufactured in Sialkot in the province of Punjab.

"And what do you do in Peshawar?" Amir asked.

"I . . . um . . . the work I do is for a charitable group . . . um organization bringing education . . . sorry, educational . . . and socially cultural changes to Pakistan." Goha fiddled with the adjustments on his seatbelt, suddenly conscious not only of the disingenuity of his statement but also his faltering English and heavy Pakistani accent.

Amir immediately switched to Urdu in a clear attempt to put Goha at ease. "I'm happy to see young people like you doing good work," he said. "I'm appalled that girls' schools are being attacked in that area, though. Innocent children are being terrorized. It's outrageous. I have three daughters, and I can't imagine what these poor families are going through. Who in their right mind would want to prevent kids from receiving a decent education? The misogyny of the tribal people along the Afghan border is mind-boggling. What do they think they're going to achieve by leaving half the population illiterate?" He shook his head.

"And don't get me started on how all the civil unrest is ruining our country's image abroad. It's affecting my company and the entire business community. I have an expansive network, and I've heard real horror stories about firms losing major international contracts since this whole fiasco started."

Blood rose to Goha's face. "Yes, it's awful. *Inshallah*, it will all end soon." He pulled the airline magazine from the seat pocket and pretended to be engrossed in it. When the pilot finally announced they were taking off, he hesitatingly glanced at Amir again, thankful to see he had rested his head back and was dozing off.

Goha knew in his heart he was in the middle of the situation Amir was referring to. *God help me—I think I've been lured into selling my soul to the devil.*

As the plane descended into Jinnah International Airport in Karachi, the orange sun hung low and heavy on the horizon. Goha didn't quite know what kind of world he would be walking into, how dramatically his parents' environment had transformed. But he was exhilarated nonetheless to receive their loving embraces and words of encouragement in the flesh, and to be back in the hustling, behemoth city he called home.

When he exited the airport, he was shocked—and at the same time, somehow not at all surprised—to see his parents standing beside a silver Mercedes-Benz A-Class car. When they waved him down, a well-dressed man in the driver's seat eagerly jumped out, flashed a smile marked by stained yellow teeth, grabbed Goha's bag out of his hand, and promptly placed it in the trunk.

Goha was so enamored by the new vehicle he almost forgot to greet his parents. He gave them both a quick hug as his eyes fixed on the car's luxurious exterior, which shimmered alluringly in the fading sunlight. "Wow, *mashallah*. Nice car."

"Isn't it amazing?" Bala said.

The three of them settled into the back seat, with Goha in the middle, and Bala made sure his son was watching before he pushed the button that automatically rolled down the rear window. "Lala Dabir gave us this car to use as a gesture of goodwill. He's taken good care of us since you joined the organization."

"Wait—*ammi* knows about the organization?"

"I do, *baita*. At first I was upset that no one told me, but I understand now the work you're doing is so special and important it initially needed to be kept secret."

Naseebo was wearing a fashionable A-line cotton *jora* in muted yellow, accented with fuchsia paisleys, that Goha had never seen before. The outfit didn't seem like his *ammi*'s style—but then again, she had previously never had the luxury to claim a style. Her wrist was wrapped in two thin, solid gold bracelets, and around her neck was a delicate gold chain with a small Allah pendant in Arabic. She looked remarkably different than the woman he had left behind at the train station just a few short months ago. Goha was used to seeing his mother wear the same few outfits until they wore thin. They were mostly cheap ones she bought in the bazaar and scrubbed endlessly in the worn-out, red plastic bucket in the courtyard in Qasba, ones that faded in the sun when she hung them out to dry. Sometimes she received good-quality used clothing from the wealthy ladies she served, but they were usually ill-fitting and out of fashion. She had applied makeup too. Her cheeks were a rosy hue, and her lips were painted with a shade that matched the print in her outfit. Her face glowed.

Goha stared past Naseebo out the window, unsettled by how the positive intent of his mother's kind words landed on him so harshly. He changed the subject. "Guess what? I learned to drive, so I can run errands for you while I'm here. And," he added, "to be honest, I really wouldn't mind driving this car."

"Of course, *baita*," said Bala, laughing. "We were so excited to see you that I forgot to introduce you to our driver, Omar. He can take you places while you're here, but you can certainly drive yourself around too. You deserve it after working so hard."

The driver turned onto a residential street, and Goha observed a median lined with trees and flowers. The luscious, fragrant smells of tropical jasmine, bougainvillea, and *raat ki rani* wafted into the car. It was a far cry from the crowded gulleys, piles of garbage, and putrid smells he was used to.

Naseebo sighed happily. "Just look at our new neighborhood. It's clean and safe. And the organization gave us a home big enough to accommodate guests. Can you imagine that? Before, the three of us barely had space to sit together. I wish your father and I could have raised you here, but as they say, *der ayad durust aayad*." Better late than never. She patted Goha's thigh.

They pulled up to a gate, and the driver exited the car to release the padlock. The doors swung open to reveal a modest one-level house constructed of white cement, with two pillars flanking a veranda at the entrance. In the front yard, rows of hibiscus flowers were interspersed with tropical trees. A slight breeze rustled their thick leaves to reveal brightly colored pomegranates, mangoes, figs, and guavas hanging tantalizingly from the branches.

When Goha stepped inside the house, he was both unnerved and elated at how different it was compared to the bleak shack he had grown up in. Naseebo sauntered with her shoulders back and head high as she led Goha from one room to the next. She demonstrated the levers of the Western-style toilets, upright ones instead of the squatting, flush-to-the-ground style that he had used throughout his childhood. She turned on dimmer switches and made him touch the high-thread-count linens in the bedrooms. In the living room, she powered on the flat-screen TV using a sleek remote control.

"What's this?" Goha asked, making himself comfortable on the sofa and running his hand over a rough stone on the side table that was the size of a medium *kaddu*, squash. He studied it closely, fascinated by its crevices and shadows. Jagged and smooth wedges protruded from its center like a mishmash of fingers, slender and thick, long and short. Gold and grayish silver pieces blended and contrasted with translucent and solid white ones, which, depending on the angle, let off tiny glimmers of light.

"It's a natural white quartz cluster from northwest Pakistan," replied Naseebo. "I found it at the bazaar. Isn't it beautiful? The *dukanwala* said it radiates energy that promotes healing and balance. When I saw it, I just knew I had to have it."

Goha was surprised his mother had even heard of quartz, let alone decided to impulsively buy a table decoration made of it that was now prominently displayed in their home. It was surreal how his *ammi* and *abba* were so much more knowledgeable and self-assured than the parents he had left behind at the train station. But then again, he surmised, his entire life over the past few months had been like a dream.

"My counters are made of quartz too," Naseebo told him as they walked into the kitchen. She ran her hand along the smooth surface. "I just love it. It looks so good, plus it's durable and easy to clean. These counters were made up north in our very own country. The shopkeeper said Pakistan's mountains are filled with quartz."

She pulled down a small copper pot hanging on a rack above the stove, filled it with water, and stirred in a spoonful of loose black tea leaves from a square tin box. "So what do you think of the house? It isn't nearly as extravagant as the ones in Clifton and Defence, but I never could have imagined living in a place like this. *Subhanallah*, in this neighborhood we're surrounded by decent, middle-class families. And it's all because of you and the good work you're doing. *Allah tumhe hamesha sub khushian dekhai.*" May Allah always keep you happy. Naseebo set down her wooden spoon, her eyes misty and distant as she mouthed a silent prayer and blew on her son to scatter the blessings.

Goha turned away and busied himself by peering into the drawers and cupboards as his mother added milk and sugar to the boiling water. He found them organized and tidy, with cutlery, tablecloths, placemats, kitchen towels, and dishes arranged neatly in their designated place.

"I only clean houses once in a while now, *baita*. I usually spend my days gardening, sewing, and cooking. Sometimes I have lunch or chai with the ladies in our neighborhood."

She turned off the stove, took a metallic strainer out of the drawer, and poured the chai into three white teacups.

Bala was working less too, and he had started taking business courses at a local college, paid for by the organization. "He took classes when you were little, but it became too expensive. Back then both of us had to work—it was the only way we could afford a few nice things."

Just then Bala entered the kitchen. He had changed into collared pajamas and fuzzy slippers that covered the front half of his feet, and their rubber soles made a dull flapping sound with each step. He thumped Goha on the back.

"*Baita*, I worried so much about you when you left Karachi. But look at you now—healthy, happy, and thriving. God has been kind to us."

A solid, dark tan layer of milk skin had formed on the surface of his chai. He blew on it until it congealed at the far end of the cup and took a long sip.

"Your *ammi* and I have learned a few important things in life. We've learned that when you have money, people listen to you and respect you. Money can help even lowly people like us become something in this world. Speaking of which, we're invited to my friend Farid's house for dinner tomorrow night. I saw him the other day, and he told me he bought a big house just outside of Karachi."

He and Bala had worked together as day laborers until Farid went back to school to study business. Goha vaguely remembered meeting him at a couple of worksites he had gone to with his father when he was younger. Bala told him that Farid had started his own construction company after he graduated from college. "He's a sharp man. Really business savvy. He employs a lot of people now, and he's been able to raise the status of his entire extended family. He has a daughter who's eighteen, and we think she could be a great marriage prospect for you."

Goha's eyebrows shot up. Did his *abba* know about the tense conversation he had had with his *ammi* over the phone a few days ago?

"*Abba*, I am sure Uncle Farid's daughter is a very nice person," Goha said. "But I already told *ammi* I'm not ready for marriage. I'm going to bed." He wasn't ready to bring up Kajal and answer the onslaught of questions that would drag the conversation into the night and likely start an argument.

"But you didn't even drink your chai," Naseebo said.

"You or *abba* can have it. It's been a long day, and I'm tired." Goha gave Naseebo a quick kiss on her cheek, then turned on his heel and headed to his room.

The next morning, Goha found his father sitting on a rocking chair on the front porch, a plate of buttered toast and fried eggs sprinkled with salt and pepper in his lap.

"Who made you breakfast?"

"Our driver works part-time as our cook," Bala responded. "Why don't you ask him to make you something?"

Goha sat on the *charpai* beside his father and ran his hands through his hair, still groggy and overwhelmed. He wasn't used to having anyone cook for him except his *ammi*. The kitchen help meant she wouldn't be burdened with preparing meals for them morning, afternoon, and night as she had in their past life.

Bala set down his plate. "Do you want to drive the car to the Sulaimans' place tonight?"

Goha looked at his father warily.

"Don't worry, there's no hidden motive here." Bala elbowed him teasingly. "It's a scenic drive, and they're good people."

Goha crossed his arms against his chest. "Okay. But no matter how hospitable the Sulaimans are, please remember I'm not interested in being co-opted as their future son-in-law."

CHAPTER 18

Goha opened the door of the Mercedes-Benz and made himself comfortable on the creamy off-white leather seat. He had chosen to wear Western clothes—beige slacks and a short-sleeved light blue collared polo shirt, an outfit that presented well but wasn't overly formal. He was conscious of not wanting to appear like he was trying to win over the Sulaimans.

His parents were still inside getting ready, so he took his time adjusting his position, savoring how he could shift the levers up and down until the height and distance from the dashboard felt just right. He started the engine, and it emitted a low, contented purr like it was excited to face whatever adventures the day had in store. He fiddled with the angles of the rear and side mirrors and ran his fingers along the curves of the smooth steering wheel, fascinated at how ergonomically it was designed. He couldn't imagine the extraordinary brainpower and workmanship that went into creating such a high-quality vehicle.

The front door of the house opened, and his *abba* and *ammi* emerged. They were dressed sharply, Bala in a suit jacket and dress pants, and Naseebo in an eggplant-colored *jora* spun with gold *kaam*, threading, and a silky *dupatta* draped loosely around her neck. They looked like one of those couples from the affluent parts of town, the ones who regularly went to concerts, festivals, performances, Western shopping malls, and fancy restaurants. His mother had applied a substantial layer of makeup to her face that made it look a couple of shades fairer than the rest of her body. She had pinned up some of her hair, and gold jewelry—inlaid with deep purple garnets—adorned her ears, neck, and arms. Goha had to blink a few times to make sure it was his own parents.

During the two-hour drive to Gadap, Goha skillfully diverted the conversation away from himself and his time up north. He engaged in small talk and kept the focus on his *ammi* and *abba* by asking them question after question about their house, neighborhood, hobbies, and upgraded new lifestyle.

Farid Sulaiman was a short man with coffee-colored skin and a toothy smile that took up half of his round face.

"*Janab*!" he said to Bala, giving him a warm embrace as he opened the door to their airy, two-story home. "Look at you! A *nawab sahib* has come to visit me. Naseebo *begum*, welcome. And this must be the famous Mr. Goha Hadi, Bala junior. When I last met you, you were just this high." He held his hand three feet above the ground and patted Goha's shoulder.

Farid's wife, Salma, was equally hospitable. "This is your home, so no formalities, please. Farid, why don't you show our guests around before we eat?"

Just then, a plump girl with a single dark braid and the same prominent grin as Farid bounded down the stairs. She wore a forest green and white *shalwar kameez*, the same colors as Pakistan's flag, and cradled a long-haired, flat-faced cat in her arms.

"This is our daughter Gul-e-Shabbo and her precious cat Sheroo," said Salma. "Shabbo's busy these days with the home economics classes she's taking at college."

"I have to confess I'm hopeless at it," the girl said. "*Ammi* is the master of the kitchen, and I still haven't even figured out how to thread a needle."

Everyone laughed, and after the intensity of the past few weeks,

Goha appreciated how the evening started out on a lighthearted note.

"You don't need to be scared of Sheroo," Shabbo continued. "His name means *lion*, but he's far from ferocious. He's always running away and hiding." As if on cue, Sheroo jumped out of Gul-e-Shabbo's arms and darted up the stairs. Everyone laughed again.

Farid held a set of keys in his hand. "Ready to go?"

Gul-e-Shabbo tugged on her father's sleeve. "*Abbu*, can we pick up Razia on the way? She texted me to tell me she wants to hang out tonight. She loves *ammi*'s fried fish."

"Sure, *baitee*," Farid said. "You'll just have to squeeze together in the back seat."

"It's good we're heading out now. After eating *ammi*'s cooking, we'll all be a few inches wider and might not fit," she responded, grinning.

Farid led them to the car and Goha climbed into the back seat next to the window beside his mother. Going to *dawats*, dinner parties, at friends' houses hadn't been a regular occurrence when his family was in survival mode. He peered out at the Sulaimans' vast expanse of agriculture, which, Bala told him, was spread across seventy acres. Gul-e-Shabbo casually mentioned how her friend texted and wanted to hang out—only upper-class, carefree kids did that, ones who didn't have to worry about supporting their families, ones who owned high-tech phones that didn't come with restrictions.

Even their cat Sheroo was a luxury. In the *katchi abadis*, cats and dogs were mostly seen as despised scavengers who roamed the streets living on scraps and often became the victims of hurled rocks. People from the slums kept animals for the sole purpose of providing food—chickens for meat and eggs, cows and buffalo for milk and dairy products. *Did Gul-e-Shabbo remember when her father worked as a day laborer and their family had to make do with basic necessities?* Goha wondered. *Or has she repressed that time from her memory altogether?*

Razia was a tall, lanky girl with high cheekbones and long, curly hair tied up in a ponytail. She wore stylish white bell-bottom trousers, a short, dark green *kurta*, and a crooked smile when she entered the back seat of the Sulaimans' car.

"Look, we match!" Gul-e-Shabbo said delightedly, hugging her friend. "Raz, these are our friends, the Hadis."

"*Assalam-o-alaikum*," Razia greeted them. "Shab, we'll need to wear these *joras* again in August on Independence Day."

"You could go to Islamabad as ambassadors of Pakistan wearing those outfits. The colors are so spot-on you could even lead the parades in them," Goha quipped, and to his relief, his comments came off as humorous, even though to him, they were an awkward attempt to fit into a world that was still far beyond his reach. He glanced at Naseebo, who smiled at him and nodded approvingly.

They drove past papaya and guava orchards and rows of tomatoes, radishes, spinach, and carrots. "Salma is an amazing cook, and I've noticed that using fresh produce really makes a difference in how her dishes taste," Farid said. "See those men?" They all turned to where Farid was pointing at farmers plowing the field. "They're our seasonal employees. We kept them on after we bought the farm from the previous owner."

Back at the house, when Farid, Bala, and Goha went into the living room, Naseebo asked Gul-e-Shabbo and Razia if they wanted to take a walk outside around the property. She hoped to establish a more personal relationship with the Sulaimans' daughter, to show her that this particular *desi*, South Asian, auntie was good-natured, understanding, and loving—all the attributes of a good mother-in-law.

Naseebo had never had a chance to meet Bala's mother, but many of her friends relayed horror stories about never-ending quarrels and disputes with their in-laws. She was eager to break any negative stereotypes Gul-e-Shabbo might hold about Pakistani mothers-in-law, who were often derogatorily referred to as *saases*. In Naseebo's opinion, they had undeservingly acquired a widespread reputation for being demanding, unscrupulous, mean-spirited, and conniving.

"I'd love to, auntie, but first let me make sure *ammi* doesn't need help with dinner," said Gul-e-Shabbo. "Our cook is here, but she likes to have me around when we use the nice dishes."

"Great idea, *baitee*. I'm sure your mother will appreciate it," Naseebo said, beaming at her. Every part of Gul-e-Shabbo's response was perfect—her enthusiastic tone, making it a priority to help her mother in the kitchen, the reference to the cook, using a separate and nicer set of dishes for guests, and her willingness to spend time with an auntie instead of retreating into a room with her friend to gossip. This was a girl who understood the importance of being *tameez-daar*, respectful toward her elders.

Gul-e-Shabbo ran into the house, and Naseebo turned to Razia. "It looks like you and Gul-e-Shabbo are great friends."

"Shabbo's so nice and so full of *ronuk*," Razia replied. "Everyone loves her. We have two dogs who growl at most people, but when Shabbo visits, they wag their tails and play with her. They think she's one of them."

Gul-e-Shabbo ran back outside with her braid flapping, out of breath. "*Ammi* said she doesn't need my help. Our commander in chief, Salma Sulaiman, has it all under control."

Naseebo smiled at her sweetly. With each passing minute, Gul-e-Shabbo was looking better and better as a potential *bahu*. Like them, the Sulaimans had risen out of poverty; like Goha, Shabbo was an only child, a rarity among Pakistanis, and one who had experienced a hard life on the other side of the tracks. If things worked out between the families, Naseebo resolved she would do whatever it took to keep the girl happy. She wasn't going to be a critical, demeaning, and jealous *saas*, the vicious kind who patronized her daughter-in-law and made her life a living hell. Given Farid's newly acquired wealth, a union between the families would elevate the Hadis' status, and the last thing she wanted was to drive Shabbo away and jeopardize that.

"Shabbo, you are so helpful, fun, and friendly," Naseebo said as they strolled together in the front yard. Razia had gone to the bathroom inside the house, and Naseebo was taking full advantage of their few minutes alone. She had deliberated whether to use Gul-e-Shabbo's nickname to address her and had decided that she would, to demonstrate her affection and hopefully forge a bond between them. "Your future husband will be one lucky man." She gave her the biggest smile she could muster.

It was the perfect time to deliver her next strategic words, when no one else was within earshot. "Goha's just a year older than you, and he has a great job up north. It probably sounds funny coming from me, but don't you think he's handsome? You two seem to get along so well." She cleared her throat. "Anyway, I wanted to be sure to talk to you first, before your Uncle Bala and I approached your *ammi* and *abbu* about potential arrangements."

Gul-e-Shabbo's cheeks flushed. "Auntie, thank you for your kind words. I'm flattered you think so highly of me. Actually, my parents have been discussing a *rishta* for me to my mom's cousin's son. He's in his third year of medical school. We've known each other all our lives, and we get along really well."

"Oh, I see," Naseebo said, her voice flat.

Just then the patio door opened, and Salma emerged. "Please come inside—dinner's ready!" she announced cheerfully.

Naseebo plastered a smile on her face. She adjusted her *dupatta* loosely over her head and chest and walked into the dining room with her head up. Formal place settings had been laid out, and aromatic dishes adorned the table: bone-in *mutton pulao*, fried pomfret, white chicken *korma*, beef *shami* kebabs, *achar sabzi*, homemade tandoori *rotis*, flatbread, and a salad made with fresh vegetables from the farm. The men took their seats at one end of the table and the women at the other, and as they passed around the food, everyone lavished praise on Salma for her hard work and exquisite presentation.

As Naseebo had anticipated, everything Salma prepared was scrumptious. She glanced at Goha and Gul-e-Shabbo periodically during the meal in hopes of catching them exchanging shy, flirtatious smiles, but the two of them and Razia only appeared to be engaging in casual, friendly banter. However, she was still determined to offer a *rishta* to the Sulaiman family. *Even if there's no attraction right now*, she thought, *couples can grow to love each other over time.*

Over dinner, the Hadis learned that Farid Sulaiman's construction company had grown substantially over the past year. He had been able to acquire the farm from the profits of his business, and since he now had several supervisors handling the firm's day-to-day operations, he spent his newly acquired leisure time staying current on South Asian news and politics.

"What are you doing these days, son?" Farid asked Goha.

Bala jumped in, saving Goha from explaining his nebulous work for the umpteenth time. "He's working for a welfare organization in Northern Pakistan. Their goal is to bring about social and political changes that will improve our country," he said proudly, patting Goha on the back.

"Fantastic. We need more young people like you to stay in Pakistan and help our country prosper instead of going overseas, where the grass always seems greener. If all our bright, ambitious kids leave, how will our nation progress?" Even during Pakistan's worst times, Farid told them, he never considered uprooting his family, even though he'd recently been blessed with enough money and influence to move abroad if he wanted to.

"How's the law-and-order situation up north, *baita*? I've been reading about an influx of terrorist activities. Apparently, they're a big concern."

Goha shrank. *How many times will I have to dance around this subject?*

"I think a lot of the news has been exaggerated by the media," he said finally. "A few people are causing trouble, but unfortunately, they're tarnishing the image of the entire area."

"I'm glad you don't think it's a large, organized group," Farid responded. "I worry about youngsters being recruited and brainwashed into terrorizing others by ignorant people in the tribal areas. At one point I thought those people had valid ideas, but they've become so violent and extreme that I don't give them any credibility now. To be honest, I don't know the real extent of it—I only know what I see on TV or read in the newspaper."

Goha didn't respond and was relieved when the conversation moved on to the benign topic of *masalas* Salma used to marinate the fried fish: paprika, cumin, turmeric, salt, lemon, chili, garlic, and coriander.

On the drive home, while Goha and Bala marveled over Farid Sulaiman's remarkable catapult from his scanty beginnings, Naseebo sat in the back with her head against the headrest, quiet and reflective. Her exchange with Gul-e-Shabbo gnawed at her to the point where she felt she would erupt if she didn't get it off her chest.

She waited for a break in their conversation before shifting the topic. "I had the most lovely time with Gul-e-Shabbo this evening," she started casually. "She told me Salma's nephew is in medical school. There may be something going on between them, I'm not sure. But I don't think that should stop us from offering them a *rishta*. Shabbo would make a great wife for you, Goha," she continued, oblivious to his growing discomfort. "Her complexion is a little dark, and she's on the chubbier side, but I'm fine with that. I love that she's studying home economics, and I think her personality is adorable. Don't you think the Sulaimans were the most gracious hosts this evening?"

"*Ammi*, for God's sake!" Goha clasped the steering wheel. "What does that have to do with anything? There are millions of good hosts around. Is that the reason you want me to marry Gul-e-Shabbo? So I can be part of a family that throws nice *dawats*?"

Naseebo turned her face to the window, her eyes stinging.

"Oh wait, I know . . . you have another requirement too. The family of the girl I marry needs to be rich, right? Shabbo is an only child, so she'll inherit all her father's wealth. I know how important that is to you."

Naseebo's jaw tightened. So what if she wanted to join the privileged class, to have money and a more comfortable life? The wealth possessed by many elites was passed down over generations—they had personally done nothing to earn it, nothing to deserve it. Was it a crime to desire the status and reverence that society superfluously bestowed on them simply for being born into the right families? Wasn't that what all lower- and middle-class Pakistanis prayed for day and night? She said a silent *dua* that Goha would remember the importance of being *tameez-daar* and the hadith where the holy Prophet Muhammad said *jannah* lies beneath a mother's feet.

But Goha didn't stop, even as they pulled into the gate and entered the house. "I can't believe you're clinging on to this crazy idea, even though you know Uncle Farid and Auntie Salma have picked a partner for Gul-e-Shabbo from their very own family. You're embarrassing yourself and all of us, *ammi*. If you don't quit it, I'm going back to Peshawar. I mean it. Good night."

He marched to his room and shut the door.

That night, Goha had a vivid dream about his *ammi* bustling around in all her glory as she planned in excruciating detail his wedding to Gul-e-Shabbo. Old and new friends flocked to the new house, offering their hearty congratulations and *duas* for the bride- and groom-to-bes' health and happiness as Goha passively and helplessly stood by. The dream was so realistic it took Goha several minutes to come out of his unconscious state to comprehend that the buzzing in his dream wasn't his mother's voice, but his phone in real life. He turned over groggily and picked it up. It was Babrek.

"Hey, *yaar*, I don't want to alarm you. But I heard a local police officer will be coming to your parents' house. You need to answer questions about Saber's disappearance from a city magistrate."

Goha sat straight up, forgetting all about his dream and the heated exchange with Naseebo the previous evening. "Why? I thought the FIR I did for Nek took care of everything."

"I'm not sure why, but I do know these things can drag on. Don't worry, it's a routine inquiry, and we have the right contacts. The police have other suspects too. Turns out Saber made quite a few enemies." Their connection with Nek had come in handy—the inspector had arranged for Goha to meet with a magistrate in Karachi instead of Peshawar to make it more convenient for him, Babrek said.

"Anyway, how's it going with you? What have you been up to in Karachi?"

Should I tell Babrek about my parents' new house with quartz countertops and upright toilets? Their fancy car with automatic windows and high-tech gadgets? Or how they're determined I marry into a rich family so they can solidify their wealth and become part of the upper crust?

"The regular stuff. It's been busy, but everything's good."

CHAPTER 19

Goha was sitting on the couch the next afternoon, captivated by the vast array of colors reflecting off the quartz cluster, when Bala walked into the room and told him the driver was taking him and Naseebo to a shopping mall to pick up groceries.

"A mall?" Goha asked, surprised.

"There are so many more international foods there," Bala replied. "I've really acquired a taste for Japanese udon noodles, of all things." He chuckled. "Why don't you come along? Your *ammi* and I are planning to visit your *mamoos* afterward too."

"I'd love to, but I have work to do for the organization." This lie didn't bother Goha. He was fond of his three *mamoos*—his mother's younger brothers—who were all jovial, even-tempered, and had managed to carve out decent lives for their families as shop owners in high-traffic areas of Karachi. Goha enjoyed playing with his younger cousins too. It had been awhile since he had seen his extended family, but he was in no mood to answer their questions about his work up north.

In the past, his parents got their food and other necessities from cheap, unassuming storefronts or local vendors rolling unstable, portable carts brimming with their wares through the gulleys of the *katchi abadis*. In the new house, convenient packaged foods lined the kitchen cupboards—sterile boxes of American cereal infused with artificial colors and flavors, Styrofoam cups of dried instant noodles, individually packaged granola bars, jarred tomato and cream sauces, various combinations of canned fruit in sugary syrup, tinned meat and sausages, and even pricy European chocolates.

Inside the shantytown, at any time of the day or night, people were shouting, motorbikes were screeching, and the *adhan* was blaring overhead. Steps away from their shack, Goha could get his hair trimmed by the local barber, barter with the electronics store owner, or spend hours jostling with his friends as they competed with each other on a beat-up video arcade or pinball machine. Men were roasting fresh corn or frying meat-filled samosas amid a swarm of flies in the alleyways, the aromas mingling with the stench of wastewater. The undefined boundaries within the labyrinth of makeshift housing led to inevitable community bonding; more than once, Goha had found himself in someone's living room when he made a wrong turn. He was surprised to find himself missing the overstimulation and chaos of his unpretentious former life.

He moved outdoors to enjoy the greenery in the front yard and took out his phone to call Kajal when he heard a vehicle stop outside the house. When he unlocked the gate, a dark car with the words "Karachi Police" prominently painted in white block letters was parked on the side of the road. A man with a familiar face stood beside it. It took Goha a minute to discern who it was, and when he did, his posture relaxed.

"*Assalam-o-alaikum*, Goha," Inspector Nek said.

"*Wa 'alaykumu s-salam*, Inspector Nek. Babrek told me someone from the local police would be coming by, but I sure am glad to see you here instead."

Nek gave him a tight-lipped smile. "I was asked to come to Karachi since I prepared the FIR for this case. I've arranged for you to see Magistrate Dildar Baga in North Nazimabad. If you're ready, I can take you there now."

Goha shoved his hands in his pockets and kicked a rock on the road, stalling. Though Babrek had given him a heads-up, he was still disconcerted that the inspector knew the location of his parents' new house and had showed up without notice. His surly attitude didn't help matters either. Still, since his *ammi* and *abba* were out and blissfully unaware of the situation, he figured it was a good time to get the questioning over with. He nodded.

"Good. His office is closed for repairs, so he's conducting business from home. It's about a twenty-minute drive from here."

From the outside, Magistrate Baga's house presented itself as a small, well-kept hotel with manicured lawns, palm trees, and a paved walkway leading to polished cedar doors at the main entrance. A mustached guard stood at the gate, attentive and unsmiling, and led them inside and down a hallway lined with ornate mahogany furniture, brocade wall tapestries, imposing oil paintings, and porcelain vases reminiscent of eighteenth-century Europe. When they reached a set of frosted French doors, the guard rang the bell. The doors swung open to reveal a gigantic room covered in thick oriental carpeting.

In the middle of the room sat the magistrate on a light green velvet sofa. He was dressed in a magenta-colored velour robe and matching slippers, and in his hand was an etched crystal goblet filled with a rich amber liquid. He set the stemware on a silver tray and stood when they entered.

"Hello, Israr. It's been a long time. And this must be Gohar Hadi. I believe your name means *gemstone*? Your appearance certainly lives up to your name." He let out a high-pitched titter. "I've been waiting for you. Please have a seat." He gestured at the space on the sofa next to him.

Baga picked up a small gold bell with a wooden handle from the table beside him. Within seconds, an androgynous, gangling young attendant came running in from an adjoining room wearing makeup, fake eyelashes, and an ankle-length, flowery orange dress.

"Nagina, please take Inspector Nek into the next room and pour him some tea."

The attendant nodded dutifully, curtsied, and led the inspector out of the room.

As soon as the door closed, the magistrate took Goha's hands in his own. The stale scent of fermented grains was heavy on his breath. His long, straight hair was slicked back behind his ears. Bags swelled under his eyes, and tiny red blood vessels crept down his bulbous nose. His perfectly manicured fingers slithered across Goha's skin.

"Goha, my dear. You look worried—don't be. I'll take good care of you. I won't be asking you any questions. This is all just a formality."

He rose, went behind the bar in the corner, picked up a decanter with the amber spirit, and held it up.

"Would you like a drink? I'm having scotch. I also have French wine, vodka, rum, gin, and brandy. What can I get you?" He opened a cabinet behind the bar to reveal dozens of bottles of liquor in various shapes, colors, and sizes.

Goha blinked.

"Why are you surprised? Magistrates can have a little fun, too, can't they?" He smiled broadly and let out a gleeful, demonic chortle. "I'm throwing a party tonight, so I'm well stocked. I would love for you to come. The bar will be open, and there will be other treats too. I promise you'll have a great time." He winked at Goha.

Goha had never tasted alcohol. From what he understood, alcoholic beverages were prohibited to everyone other than non-Muslims and foreigners. Some teenagers from his school had boasted about crashing A-list underground parties—secret gatherings by invitation only where pricy booze supplied by local bootleggers flowed freely, where women in miniskirts and men with gelled hair bumped and grinded on a dance floor and the air was thick with smoke from a smorgasbord of illicit narcotics. But unlike in America and Europe, where liquor was commonplace and part of the mainstream culture, in Pakistan it couldn't easily be found in public markets or casually consumed out in the open.

Goha was flummoxed when he considered how many illegitimate channels the magistrate must have tapped into to possess so much alcohol. And what were the other "treats" he was referring to? Psychedelic drugs? Hookers? Or maybe things that were far beyond

Goha's naive imagination. He had heard about the corrupt and unscrupulous behavior of government officials, but this was the first time Goha had seen it up close in person. It made him sad to see scumbags like Baga fast becoming the country's new elite.

"I'm not into those kinds of parties, sir. I believe you have read me wrong. Very, very wrong."

Goha stood up swiftly and found Nagina and Inspector Nek across the hall.

"We need to leave," Goha told the inspector.

Nagina's big, soulful, liner-rimmed eyes pleaded with Goha. She reached for his hand. "Please don't leave. Magistrate Baga likes to get to know the young men he meets. He doesn't mean any harm."

"Nagina, I'm not interested in getting to know the magistrate or, frankly, anyone he associates with."

Nagina turned away.

"I didn't mean you, Nagina," Goha said gently. "Now listen to me. I don't know how you ended up here, but if it wasn't your choice, I can try to help you find a way out. Call me if you need to." He pulled out a receipt from his pocket, grabbed a pen from the table, and scribbled down his cell number.

Inspector Nek drove Goha back home in silence. He barely acknowledged when Goha exited from the police car and sped away the instant Goha closed the door. When Goha entered the house, he was relieved to find his parents were still gone, which meant he wouldn't have to lie about his whereabouts.

The next morning, before Bala and Naseebo woke up, Goha called Babrek to fill him in on Inspector Nek's surprise appearance and his shady encounter with Dildar Baga. Even though the magistrate hadn't interrogated him, it was possible the murder investigation could escalate without warning, and Goha decided it was best to cover his bases.

"I'm not surprised," Babrek said after hearing Goha's account. "It's no secret Baga likes handsome young men. He's very capable of creating problems for you, so don't tell anyone about the meeting. Trust me, the magistrate isn't someone you want on your bad side." Baga was well connected to the highest officials in his department, and commonly known as one of the most unscrupulous, underhanded judges around, Babrek said.

He paused, and Goha heard him light a cigarette.

"I'm a little surprised Nek came all the way from Peshawar and showed up at your door. Anyway, I'm glad you called because I need to tell you something." He said police and paramilitary were cracking down hard on certain groups in the area, and it was best if Goha extended his stay in Karachi for at least a couple more weeks.

Babrek's update left Goha jumbled. He was relieved that the police were taking action, and he fervently hoped they were targeting the type of ultraconservative leaders who had spoken at the *ijtema*. But a clampdown could mean a financial setback for him and his parents. On a personal note, hanging around longer in Karachi meant dealing with his *ammi*'s incessant nagging about Gul-e-Shabbo and postponing his reunion with Kajal.

He lay back and closed his eyes, hoping to catch a couple more hours of sleep. But just as he was dozing off, his phone buzzed.

"Goha, it's me again. I just got some unexpected and confidential news." There was urgency in Babrek's voice.

"Everything okay?"

"I'll tell you when I get to Karachi. I'm flying in tomorrow." He hung up.

As Goha deliberated what news could be so important it required Babrek to jump on a plane right away and travel across the country, Naseebo opened the door and strode into his room.

"*Assalam-o-alaikum!*" she said buoyantly. She opened the curtains, unleashing a million speckles of sunlight. "How are you doing, *baita*?"

Goha crooked his arm over his eyes to block out the blinding light.

"I'm fine, *ammi*."

"Sometimes you seem all right, but overall, you haven't been yourself. Your *abba* and I are worried about you."

She sat at the foot of his bed, still smelling faintly of the rose-scented *attar* she had applied to impress the Sulaimans.

"I hope you didn't mean the things you said the other night. Farid and Salma really seemed to like you. I think they would seriously consider a marriage proposal from us. Why won't you consider it?"

Since he had come back to Karachi, Goha hadn't found the right time to break the news to his parents about Kajal. But he had reached a point where his mother's relentless badgering made him close to exploding.

"I know how much you want me to marry Gul-e-Shabbo. She's seems like a nice girl. She's really funny."

Naseebo's eyes brightened. "Yes, *baita*!" she exclaimed. "She was a delight to talk to and so much fun. If it works out, you and Shabbo could live in Karachi, close to us. I'm sure Shabbo would be an excellent homemaker, but your *abba* and I could certainly help raise your children, our grandchildren, *inshallah*. I would be a *dadi*—can you imagine that?" She laughed. "It would make me so happy. And you don't need to worry; I won't be one of those annoying, difficult *saases*."

"*Ammi*, I need to tell you something." Goha managed to keep his tone even-keeled. "You don't seem to be hearing me, so for the hundredth time, I'm not interested in marrying Gul-e-Shabbo. I'm in love with a Kalash woman I met up north."

"Oh Allah. So that explains your moodiness. There's another girl involved." She raised the back of her hand to her forehead. "Kalash? What do you mean by Kalash? Do you mean she is *qalash*, wretchedly poor? *Ya Allah*, what have I done to deserve this?"

"*Ammi*, for God's sake—it's not *qalash* with a *qaaf* but Kalash with a *kaaf*. Kalash people are a fascinating tribe that live in northwest Pakistan. They may have descended from Alexander the Great's invading army. A lot of them look more Western European than South Asian. Their culture, customs, religion, and language are completely different than ours too."

"So this girl you met is not Muslim or Pakistani? *Hai Allah.*"

"I just told you her community lives in Pakistan and has for centuries, and that makes them just as Pakistani as you and me. They're not Muslim, but they're hardworking and honest, and that's what counts."

Naseebo sniffed.

"Kajal is thirty, and she was in a relationship with a man who pretended to be religious but treated her like garbage," Goha continued, determined not to be emotionally blackmailed or let his mother's unyielding perspective dominate the conversation. "I'm telling you her age and history so you don't think I'm hiding anything from you."

"*Ya Allah.* Really, Goha? You are my only son, my only child. Your father and I have sacrificed so much for you. How could you do this to us? You want to be with a divorced woman who is ten years older than you? This is preposterous!" Tears glistened on Naseebo's cheeks.

Goha gritted his teeth and waited for his mother to compose herself.

"Goha, sometimes young people think they're in love, but it's really just infatuation. You said yourself, Kalash people have nothing in common with us. Plus, they live so far away. So how will this girl work out with our family? Have you thought about the future?"

Goha gave her a surly look and didn't respond. A strange, unfamiliar feeling came over him—resentment toward his mother for being so patronizing and judgmental.

"Does she have any children?"

"No," he said sullenly.

"Even so, this just isn't right. There are plenty of girls from good families in Karachi for you to choose from. Your future wife should be someone from here, someone who's younger than you and has never been in a relationship before."

"When you say someone, you mean Gul-e-Shabbo, right? You're bent on us somehow finagling our way into their family so you can raise your status."

Naseebo's eyes narrowed. She folded her arms across her chest.

"*Ammi*, you're living in a dreamland. Wake up. People get involved in all kinds of relationships before they're married and sometimes even while they're married. And for your information, those relationships aren't always between men and women."

Naseebo let out a small gasp, and for a second, Goha lamented dumping the news about his girlfriend and the reality of unconventional sexuality norms on his mother all at once. But once he got started, it was like a massive balloon had burst.

"I'm not the first person in the world to be involved with an older, divorced woman. You need to accept my decision and welcome Kajal into our family, or you may never see me again. Also, I'm telling you straight: If you keep going on about the Sulaimans and Gul-e-Shabbo, I'm moving into a hotel."

"I can't believe how *budtameez* you've become. It was so hard for me and your father to send you away, and now you've come home and shocked me with this news." She leaned her back against the wall, and when she spoke again her voice had lost its harshness. "Let's talk to your *abba* and get his opinion. I'm sure the three of us can work something out."

Goha sighed loudly. "*Ammi*, I'm not intentionally being *budtameez*. I am trying to stick up for myself and for what I want. There is nothing to work out. I will gladly let *abba* know about Kajal and tell him I want to be with her."

"How are you so convinced that Kajal is the right girl for you? You haven't even told me about her family. Who are they? What do they do?"

"Kajal's parents are farmers who grow fruits and make butter, cheese, and other dairy products. They sell them up north in the Bumburet Valley. That's where they live."

"I don't know where that is."

"It's close to the city of Chitral." Goha closed his eyes and shook his head. His mother wouldn't have a clue where the city was located or how to find it on a map.

"Have you met them?"

"No. But I hope to soon, *inshallah*."

There was a pained expression on Goha's face. Naseebo saw a cynicism in him now, a determination to make his own decisions and take charge of his future. The few months he had been gone had transformed him from an innocent boy into a strong-willed, opinionated young man. She felt her insides soften.

"*Baita*. You're my heart. If you want to marry this Kalash woman and spend the rest of your life with her, all your father and I can do is pray she is the right choice for you and our family."

Goha pulled his mother toward him and held her close, breathing in her natural scent combined with the flowery *attar*. "*Ammi*, I would never do anything to intentionally hurt you. I'm sure Kajal will be just like your own daughter. She is amazing and stunningly beautiful. She makes me so happy. I can't wait for you to meet her."

He released himself from his mother and left the room to fetch them glasses of water.

CHAPTER 20

The next morning, Babrek called from the Karachi airport and asked Goha to suggest a quiet, secluded spot where they could meet. The Katrak Bandstand in Bagh Ibne Qasim, the largest urban park in Clifton, was one of the richest areas of Karachi, and a place Goha had occasionally hung out on weekends. The park was cleaner and far less crowded than most parts of the city, and he was confident they could talk freely in the wide-open space.

The driver was out for the day, and Bala would have readily handed him the keys to the Mercedes, but after hearing the edge in Babrek's voice the day before, Goha opted to hail down a rickshaw instead. Though luxury vehicles were plentiful in Clifton, Goha wasn't *bewakoof* enough to drive up in a flashy car, especially since Babrek's information was apparently so sensitive it needed to be delivered face-to-face.

Goha sat on one of the pink Jodhpur steps of the iconic domed structure, taking in the scenic seafront below. A few couples were out on romantic walks, a group of coed teenagers horsed around, and young parents chased their small children. No one seemed to notice or pay attention to him.

He was fully absorbed in watching strangers and envying their seemingly normal, uneventful lives when he felt a tap on his shoulder. In the couple of weeks that Goha had been in Karachi, a grayish stubble had formed on Babrek's chin that made his face look older and more weathered.

Babrek took a box of cigarettes out of his *kameez* pocket. "I wish I had more time, but I need to catch a flight back to Peshawar today. So I'll get right to the point. Inspector Nek was arrested by the Federal Investigative Agency."

"What?"

"It was all a setup, Goha. You were framed." Nek knew Goha had killed Saber all along, Babrek said. The inspector had been playing dumb when he interviewed Goha, hoping Goha would confess the crime so he could get it on record—that's why he started taping the conversation. If Goha had admitted it, Nek would have gotten a nice payout from someone he worked closely with. "One of your favorite people—Dildar Baga."

There was no question Baga could afford to pay Nek for the confession, Babrek went on, tapping the ashes from his cigarette on the step as Goha sat in stunned silence. "Baga's been living the high life on a steady flow of cash from sex trafficking. He was the head honcho in a criminal chain that kidnapped and smuggled destitute kids." Some of them stayed in Pakistan, he said, and others got sent to European and Middle Eastern countries to work as prostitutes.

An image of Baga's spindly adolescent attendant, Nagina, flashed across Goha's mind. "But . . . how did Baga know I killed Saber?"

"They were in cahoots, and Saber's house was bugged. That's how Saber knew about your affair with Kajal too."

Baga and Saber had always played together in the same nefarious circle, Babrek said. "Saber told the magistrate about you, and Baga suggested that my uncle invite you to his house during the storm. When Saber jumped into bed and started intimidating you, Baga thought you'd be so scared of ruining your reputation you'd do whatever sexual favors Saber wanted—and later, whatever Baga wanted." Then, when Goha strangled Saber, Baga had freaked out—but he had also been intrigued by Goha. "He fancies young men, and you showed you weren't going to take any crap. You presented yourself as clever and hard to get, and that made you extra appealing."

Baga told Nek, and they both figured that if Goha confessed to the murder when the inspector came to the rooming house, the magistrate would be able to hold it over Goha's head. "Baga wanted you to be indebted to him forever. That's why he offered Nek big bucks and even flew him to Karachi on a private jet so he could stay involved with the case and try to cajole you." But by the time Goha and Nek got to Baga's house, the inspector had become fed up with the whole thing. He figured he wasn't getting the payout and likely realized too late he didn't want to associate with Dildar and his fellow slimeballs. So when Goha had said he wanted to leave, Nek agreed right away.

"I actually feel bad for Israr," said Babrek. "When I knew him in Peshawar, he tried hard to avoid the corruption and scandal that surrounded him. It's too bad he fell into Baga's trap." Anyway, the two of them would likely get to know each other well during their time in jail, he said.

"I know this is a lot to take in, but I have some good news too." Apparently, Goha had a guardian angel who had protected him and looked out for his best interests throughout his time with the organization. According to Babrek, his angel tapped into conversations and had proof of all the despicable activity that had gone on at his expense.

"In case you're wondering, your angel's name is Lala Dabir."

Lala Dabir? The discourteous, unpredictable man who barged into our shack in the middle of the night? The one who convinced my abba to send me away and set this whole crazy series of events into motion?

"Wow." It was the only word Goha could manage to utter.

A few days after they met in Karachi, Babrek called Goha to tell him the organization wanted him back in the tribal area outside Peshawar. In the wake of federal government clampdowns, a slew of recent recruits had unexpectedly left, and they desperately needed more foot soldiers to carry out scheduled assignments.

Goha dreaded participating in more missions that bore even a faint resemblance to the previous ones. But he was anxious to see Kajal again, and he knew how difficult that would be if he stayed in Karachi. Now, as he exited the Peshawar airport, Babrek stood outside his SUV. The car was noticeably more battered than the last time Goha had seen it. There was a dent in the front bumper, scratches on the doors, and a crack in the windshield that started with a hole and expanded out like filaments of a spider's web. He was about to ask Babrek what caused the damage but got distracted by the sound of road crews shoveling and grinding in the distance.

"The main highway was vandalized," Babrek said, following his gaze. "We'll need to take local roads back to the rooming house instead of our regular route."

"Who did it?" Goha asked, a familiar anger rising in him that only seemed to manifest while he was up north. *And how many innocent people were killed or injured?* he almost asked Babrek, but the exorbitant cost to repair the road, combined with the inconvenience it posed to travelers, was more than enough for him to bear. "Do the authorities have any suspects?"

"I don't know," Babrek said, without diverting his eyes from the road.

I'm sure you do, though. Goha was once again frustrated at Babrek's reluctance to openly discuss the organization's destructive actions. *I'm not tiptoeing around important subjects anymore*, he thought. *I'm putting it all out on the table.*

"Babrek, I told my parents about Kajal and our relationship," he blurted.

There was a drawn-out silence.

"I only want what's best for you," Babrek said at last. "Now, if you don't mind, I'd like to talk about your upcoming duties with the organization."

Goha was taken aback by Babrek's brusque response. It was unclear to him whether Babrek fully accepted the major role he expected Kajal to play in his life. But he let it go, appreciating everything Babrek had invested in him and respecting his position of authority. He had returned to Peshawar to continue supporting his family's comfortable lifestyle, and if that meant carrying out more missions, that's what he would have to do.

"Tonight a driver will pick you up and take you to another camp. This time you'll be on your own."

"What will I need to do?"

"You'll be given incendiary devices to use at a girls' school."

Goha couldn't control his eruption. "Why, Babrek? Why? Why is it always girls' schools that are targeted by the organization?"

"This one is an old building, and it's a safety hazard for the students," Babrek replied, unfazed by Goha's rising pitch. "The curriculum around here is questionable. A lot of people think it's tainting innocent young minds."

Goha folded his hands together, pressing down so hard his knuckles turned white. "I may sound blunt, but I would think you'd be a big proponent of educating girls and helping them take control of their lives after what happened to your *ammi* and sister."

"Yeah. I guess it's complicated. I believe in educating girls, but sometimes I think my mom and my sister would still be alive if Amina *baji* hadn't gone to school and fallen in love with her teacher. She had liberated ideas. They were too progressive for our environment. She wanted freedom, and it cost her her life. And my mom's life too."

"Your dad's control and anger issues are what cost your sister and mom their lives," Goha countered. "Amina simply wanted to make her own choices and be with the person she loved."

"I suppose you're right, Goha. I can always count on you to make me see things differently. People tend to blame victims more than abusers and perpetrators, and I guess I'm guilty of that too."

Babrek said the mission was scheduled before the students arrived. "So, like the last ones you were assigned to, no one will get hurt if all goes according to plan."

Goha sighed, resigned to how the conversation had abruptly pivoted yet again. "Okay. But how will I get back to the rooming house?"

"Don't worry, *yaar*. You won't be abandoned. The last thing the organization wants is to lose more members. Someone will be at the camp to pick you up and bring you back as soon as the operation is over."

The next morning, Goha was already awake when the group leader called his name. He was in his own room this time and had only seen a couple of other men wandering around since the driver had dropped him off after dark the previous evening. He stumbled out of bed and out the door, squinting and raising his hand to his forehead to shade his eyes from the dazzling sunlight.

A stout man with drooping eyelids, steely eyes, and a round belly approached him.

"Goha Hadi? These are for you," he said, handing him two small incendiary bombs. "Tomorrow morning at eight, you will hide them in your pockets and ride one of those bikes to the school." He pointed at a group of motorcycles lined up along the side of the bunkhouse.

The man instructed Goha to follow a road that led to the school and leave the bike on the grass by the veranda. "Calmly walk to the principal's office on the other side of the building. She arrives early and will likely be the only one there. Tell her you want to enroll your younger sister. Complete the forms, come back to the yard, and throw a bomb at the bike so the grass catches on fire. Like this." He threw a device at a nearby pile of straw and wood chips, and seconds later, flames burst into the air. A couple of attendants rushed toward the fire, spraying it with extinguishers.

"If the first one doesn't ignite, throw the second one. Then hide in the bushes. The principal will have a chance to leave the building when she hears the noise and discovers what's going on."

"What if someone sees me?"

"They won't suspect you since you just signed up your sister. You'll see the same SUV that brought you here. Get in the car right away so you can leave the scene."

Goha nodded dutifully as the smoldering, glowing orange embers danced and crackled like shapeshifting jinns against the hazy sky.

Later that evening, Goha placed the bombs on his bedside table. Before turning out the lights, he muttered a *dua* he pulled from the recesses of his brain related to *sabr*, patience. There was no turning back now, only somehow pushing through.

Several times during the night, he woke up groggy and became startled when the metallic surfaces of the devices shone eerily in the dim light. He had a lucid dream about them, too, where he arrived at the school on the bike and saw Kajal outside the building. Then Babrek appeared, and just as he was about to hurl the weapons, both of them started shouting at him, but he couldn't understand what they were saying. He woke up with a start in a damp sweat.

When the auburn streaks of dawn faded, the sky transformed into a cloudless, immaculate blue. Goha woke up with his head throbbing, anxious to get the mission over with so he could leave the scene and forget about the whole thing. He quickly put on his green camouflage fatigues and went outside. Fresh droplets of dew covered the ground, shining deceptively like tiny glimmers of light. Myna birds chirped in the crisp air, and he found himself irritated by their cheerfulness, which made everything seem normal. He mounted the first motorbike in the row and started the engine. It was a low hum, but to Goha, the sound was like a rocket exploding. The bombs in his pockets pressed against his thighs and constrained his movements.

When he arrived at the school, there were no cars and no people. He parked by the veranda as instructed and walked to the back, stealthy as a leopard. The building stood like a stalwart, dark and quiet. All the lights were out. He cupped his hands between his face and the window to block the glare, mist forming on the glass from his shallow, nervous breaths. He detected the shadow of a large office chair and a desk piled with papers.

Thankfully, the principal hadn't arrived yet, and he wouldn't have to interact with anyone. He peered around the corner of the building and, still seeing no one, treaded as softly as he could back to the bike. This time, as the lone person on the mission, there was no way to avoid doing the deed. He took a few steps back and recoiled when his foot cracked a twig. His pounding heart verged on bursting through his chest. He scanned the grounds a full 360 degrees, then took the device out of his right pocket, pulled the pin, and hurled it at the bike. It sailed through the air and landed hard, instantly catching fire on the grass. He stumbled back, the lingering weight on his left side making him sway unsteadily like a drunk. *I'm getting the hell rid of this one too.* He pulled the second contraption from his pocket and flung it at the burning blaze.

Simultaneously sick to his stomach and satisfied he'd had the guts to follow through with it, Goha hastily retreated behind the nearby bushes. The noxious smell of charred rubber and metal permeated the air. He turned away from the school with his hands pressed tightly against his ears, unable to face the damage he had caused, and waited.

From the corner of his eye, he glimpsed an SUV approach from behind. He ran to it, yanked open the door, and jumped into the passenger's seat. He barely had a chance to close the door when the driver gunned the engine, leaving behind a murky trail of dust.

Goha was sprawled on his bed face down when Babrek rapped on the door and called his name.

"Hey, congratulations." Babrek came inside the room and sat on a chair. "I heard you did great."

"Thanks," Goha said gloomily.

"I need to tell you something, though. Unfortunately, I have some bad news."

Goha bolted upright. "What is it?"

Babrek kept his eyes focused on the wall above Goha's head. "Your devices killed a few people. We don't know exactly how many, but it seems a girl and her mother were among them. They were on the other side of the veranda."

"No. No!" Goha clenched his hair in his fists. "I can't do this anymore. This is murder, Babrek, whether you want to admit it or not. Tell me what I need to do to leave the organization."

"Listen to me." Babrek placed his hand on Goha's arm, and Goha jerked back. "What happened wasn't deliberate. Islam emphasizes the intention of our actions, and you didn't intend to kill anyone, okay? There's no way you could have seen them. The flames caused part of the roof to collapse, and they happened to be walking underneath it. These things happen, Goha. It's called collateral damage, and it's common in military operations. That's just how it goes."

"Military operations?" Goha rose angrily and threw his hands in the air. "No one told me I'd be involved with military operations when I joined the organization. I'm sorry, Babrek. I can't be involved with this work anymore—I want out."

Goha went to the bathroom, shaking, and came back with cold water running down his face.

"Goha, don't make rash decisions that could jeopardize your family's future. What happened today could've happened to anyone. There's a big difference between murder and accidental death. Don't confuse one with the other and beat yourself up about it. This was an accident."

I'm not buying it, Babrek. The organization has copious amounts of blood on its hands. And now so do I.

CHAPTER 21

Over the next few days, social media channels and traditional media outlets alike buzzed with news about philosophical differences and hostilities brewing between different factions of the organization.

Of the two major groups, one was made up of militants who arrogantly and defiantly claimed responsibility for the school bombings and deaths. Calling themselves "*Muhib-e-watan*" or "The Patriots," they declared they would do whatever it took to invoke the social, political, and educational changes they deemed necessary to restore Pakistan to its purest state. The second group, "*Sukoon*" or "Peace," claimed its goal was to restore Pakistan's cultural heritage without strife, violence, or the loss of innocent lives.

When Goha had initially questioned Babrek about the internal conflicts, he had said the media overemphasized the differences, and overall, the organization operated as a unified body. However, Babrek finally accepted the reports were true when, because of the discord, the group's activities were put on hold indefinitely.

"You should go back to Karachi," Babrek told him. "The infighting isn't pretty. No one here who's involved with the organization is safe."

"I'm worried about Kajal too. Bumburet isn't that far away."

Babrek nodded. "Contact her as soon as you can and advise her to leave the valley." He paused. "Maybe Kajal and her family could stay at your parents' house until things settle down."

Goha gave Babrek a small, grateful smile. "That's a great idea, Babrek. Our families could get to know each other that way. What are you planning to do?"

Babrek rubbed his chin. "I'm not sure yet. I think I need to stay here a while. The leaders on both sides are stubborn. But I'm hoping to help negotiate a compromise."

Goha rested his back and one foot against the wall outside the Peshawar Cantonment railway station. He had eventually gotten through to Kajal when she was in Mingora visiting friends. Yansing and Timuk didn't want to leave the valley, she told him, but she promised she would do her best to convince her parents. The plan was for the four of them—Goha, Kajal, and her parents—to meet up in Peshawar and take the lengthy train ride to Karachi together, but after Kajal returned to Bumburet, Goha had been unable to reach her to confirm the arrangement. He hoped in earnest it would all work out since, after talking to Kajal, he had finally managed to convince Bala and Naseebo to host her family.

What if Kajal's parents decided not to come? Or what if they came, got to know him, and didn't like him—or simply decided to dissuade Kajal from choosing another Muslim man? He reasoned that if they already had a negative impression of Islam from Muslims who considered them infidels, Kajal's experience with *Maulvi* Saber must have made it worse. It was certainly plausible that they wanted Kajal to pick a man from Bumburet who would bear Kalash children, one who understood their unique customs and traditions and would keep them alive as their tribe faced the dire threat of extinction. It was even possible that they already had someone in mind for their treasured daughter.

As he brooded over the real possibility he could lose his soulmate and true love, two women in flowing multicolored dresses appeared in the distance, accompanied by an older man. His surroundings became a blur as the younger face got closer.

"Goha!" Kajal cried breathlessly, running toward him. "It's been so long!"

The creases on Goha's brow disappeared. His mouth turned up at the edges and quickly widened into an open-mouthed grin as Kajal rushed into his arms.

Men passing by on the street stared at their overtly affectionate reunion, but Goha didn't care. He hugged Kajal tightly and then held her back at arm's length to take in her appearance. She was more ravishing than he remembered. As her parents approached, he could see Kajal had been blessed with the most attractive features of both.

"Goha, these are my amazing parents, who I call *aya* and *dada*. *Aya* and *dada*, meet my boyfriend, Goha."

"Your daughter is the most amazing woman," Goha said, letting go of Kajal and putting one arm around the older woman and man, who, he vowed and prayed with all his might, would one day soon be his *saussral*, in-laws. "I'm humbled and so honored to meet you both."

The day Goha had called Naseebo from Peshawar to ask if Kajal and her parents could stay with them until the situation up north died down, she reluctantly agreed, in large part because she didn't think her son would take no for an answer. Most people thrived on gossip, and rumors from inquisitive neighbors and her brothers' families were inevitable. But if questions arose, she had already thought through and rehearsed a series of vague, noncommittal responses. There was a chance things wouldn't work out between Goha and Kajal, so there was no need to overshare information about the mysterious, unconventional family and why they were visiting.

Now, Naseebo stood outside her closet, deliberating what kind of first impression she wanted to make on Goha's potential future in-laws. It was a significant meeting that had the potential to shape the families' interactions well beyond the initial encounter, and as Goha's mother, her role was paramount. *Sophisticated, yet welcoming. Elegant, yet accepting. Personable, yet discerning.* At long last, she landed on a pistachio green organza silk *jora* with a scooped neckline and delicate silver stitching. Goha told her Kajal and her parents were simple and nonmaterialistic, but she had no intention of lowering her standards. Regardless of who he ended up marrying, this was an excellent opportunity to present herself as a gracious woman of means from a reputable social class.

As the train pulled into the station and passengers began disembarking, Naseebo leaned into Bala, scanning the crowds eagerly for her son's face. She eventually spotted him at the far end of the platform, assisting a slender white woman and her parents with their bags. She left Bala behind, her pace quickening as she headed toward them.

She embraced Goha and kissed him on the cheek, but it was the youthful female face that had her transfixed. Naseebo was unable to take her eyes off Kajal's beautiful features and fair skin. "My son said you look like an American movie star, and he wasn't kidding," she said before she could help herself.

"And he can't stop telling me how crazy he is about you," Kajal replied, giving her a hug. "It's lovely to meet you."

Bala caught up to the group and greeted Kajal's father with a handshake. Naseebo approached Kajal's mother, who, she noticed, had made no effort to wash up or fix her face before getting off the train. Her lack of makeup accentuated her age spots and wrinkles, and as they embraced, the older woman's body emitted a vague, unpleasant odor reminiscent of animals and outdoor labor. Her dress, although striking and distinctive, was constructed from scratchy wool, a far cry from the high-end, brand-name *joras* in the boutiques Naseebo had occasionally started visiting that were made from double georgette, crepe, taffeta, and French chiffon.

She wasn't optimistic about it, but she hoped at the very least,

Kajal and her parents would appreciate her tastefully decorated home and the scrumptious meal she had labored over for them.

Naseebo had directed Omar to take out her special Sindhi block-print tablecloth and fancy dinnerware for the guests. When she walked into her dining room, she was pleased to find he had followed her exact orders. Puris, halwa, omelet, kebabs, and *chana chaat* had been placed in the middle of the table on fine porcelain serving dishes, surrounded by table settings featuring plates with gold lattice borders. Kajal's parents appeared simultaneously overjoyed and unsure of what to make of the new environment; Goha, meanwhile, had never looked happier.

But Naseebo, although pleasant and graceful, was chastising herself for the praise she had heaped on Kajal at the train station and on the car ride home. *It will probably get to her head, and if Goha ends up marrying this woman, she needs to understand her position as a bahu.* The discrepancy between Kajal's *aya* and *dada* and the type of people she wanted for her son's *saussral* was abyssal.

When they were all seated, Bala stood at the head of the table. "Goha, Naseebo, and I are thrilled to have you all here. I should let you know that while I'm trying not to take it personally, I think this is the happiest I've ever seen our son." Everyone laughed except Naseebo. She poked Goha in the ribs.

"*Khoobsurti har cheez nahi haye.*" Beauty isn't everything, she said to him when the others were engaged in conversation. "You found yourself a cover girl, but your *ammi* will be the one filling your stomach."

"Well, at least you'll get to show off your beautiful, fair-skinned *bahu* to your respectable new friends," he whispered back in her ear teasingly.

<h1 style="text-align:center">CHAPTER 22</h1>

A couple of days later at breakfast, Kajal shared incredible news: Kasim Zaidi, the husband of her best friend Nargis, who worked for the Karachi Police Department, was still alive after having gone missing a year earlier.

Goha stopped eating midbite, the buttered toast he was holding suspended in the air. "That's unbelievable, Kajal."

"Remember how she told us she thought Kasim *bhai* died in a suicide bombing? It turns out that information was wrong. I had her number, so I called her to check in. She told me that Kasim was actually kidnapped by Baloch separatists." Since Pakistan's founding, insurgents from Balochistan—the nation's largest, most sparsely populated, and least-developed province—had revolted against the central government, arguing they were economically marginalized and impoverished compared to the rest of the country. In the commotion of the terrorist activities, the rebels had believed Kasim was working against their party. "They kept Kasim *bhai* isolated until they learned it was a case of mistaken identity. Then they let him go and dropped him off outside of a police station. I honestly can't believe this. My friend lost precious time with her husband, but he's finally coming back."

"This calls for a celebration," Goha said.

"Absolutely. Nargis *baji* said Kasim was relieved but weak. She's flying to Quetta today to bring him home."

Nargis's arm was affectionately interlocked with Kasim's. She reached over for another samosa and put it on his plate. "Eat more, *jaan*, you need to get your energy back."

They were sitting on the Hadis' porch on a breezy Sunday afternoon, and as they drank their chai, everyone—Goha, Kajal, Bala, Naseebo, Nargis, and Kajal's parents—was focused intently on Kasim, who was relating harrowing stories about his time in captivity.

"The repercussions from terrorist attacks extend far beyond the victims and their families," he was saying. "Terrorists create big problems for lots of other innocent people too. I was simply trying to do my job to restore order after a suicide bombing, and things got so out of hand that a mob of separatists thought I was sabotaging their efforts." They didn't believe him when he tried to explain that his work had nothing to do with them. "I felt like I was in a horror film," Kasim said.

Now he had experienced firsthand what it meant to be in the wrong place at the wrong time. "With God's grace, I survived, but many people in similar circumstances don't. The torture I endured and not being able to communicate with my family for months on end nearly killed me. My wife and parents had no idea if I was alive or dead. And now poor Nargis is worried about some of her other family members who recently went missing."

Kasim's words were interrupted by a buzzing inside Goha's pocket. "Sorry, Kasim *bhai*," Goha said. "Hold on—I'll just be a minute." He stepped into the house, away from the group.

"Hello?"

"Goha, this is Lala Dabir. *Assalam-o-alaikum*. I hope you remember me."

Goha sucked in a lungful of air. He hadn't heard from Lala Dabir since he had initially left Karachi, which, at that point, felt like a bygone era. Lala Dabir—the man who had led him down a path filled with potholes, landmines, abuse, death, and despair. Lala Dabir—the man who had lured him out of his sheltered childhood and forced him to face jarring and often cruel realities. Lala Dabir—the man who had ignited a chain of events that led him to question almost everything he had previously believed to be true.

However, Lala Dabir was also the man who had helped ease life's burdens for his beloved parents. The man who had sparked a series of experiences that would be seared into Goha's conscience forever. The man who had helped Goha discover an unexpected comradeship over time with an unlikely companion, Babrek, and deep, compassionate love with a woman he never could have imagined meeting, Kajal. The man who had saved him from a life tied to the corrupt, scandalous world of Dildar Baga, and who was, according to Babrek, his guardian angel. Goha's focus shifted to the quartz display and its tiny glimmers of light.

"I could never forget you. *Wa 'alaykumu s-salam.*"

"Babrek told me you're staying with your parents in Karachi. I have some news I think you'll be happy to hear."

"You're welcome to come over tonight, Dabir *sahib.*"

"See you all tonight then, *inshallah.*"

Goha hung up. Regardless of the nature of Lala Dabir's news, that evening would be the perfect chance to tell him he wanted out of the organization once and for all, especially since Babrek wasn't around to make him second-guess his decision.

There was an obvious change in Lala Dabir's demeanor when he arrived at the Hadis' house that evening. Gone was his on-again, off-again rough, abrasive style and distinctively husky whisper. Dabir presented himself as easygoing and accommodating, and when he spoke, it was in a submissive, appreciative tone, like a servant to a benevolent master. Like he was someone who had seen the dark side of life and was simply grateful to still be alive.

Goha led Dabir, Naseebo, and Bala into the living room, excusing them from Kajal and her parents and closing the door behind them.

"Dabir *sahib,* we would still be living in the slums of Qasba if it weren't for you," Bala started. "I don't know how we can ever repay you."

"And in return, you gave the organization your most valuable possession—your most cherished son." Dabir looked at Goha fondly. "Goha *baita*, I know your time up north wasn't easy. But I can see how much you've changed and matured. You were an innocent teenage boy when I met you, and in just a few short months, you've become a wise, confident, experienced young man."

He reached for the glass of water Goha had set in front of him.

"I came here to share some news with you all. The friction inside the organization has gotten worse—the differences between factions have intensified. Any goodwill and amity that used to exist is gone. The only thing leadership agrees on now is to disband."

Goha leaned forward with his elbows on his knees and his hands folded, absorbing Dabir's words. Clearly, Babrek's hope to mediate and help leadership reach a compromise hadn't happened.

Dabir said he always valued preserving Pakistani culture, especially since their country was so susceptible to outside influences. But he never condoned violence or terror as a way to get there. In fact, he said, he'd always renounced those things, even if it wasn't a popular stance to take.

He stroked his beard wistfully. "People from poor economic backgrounds can unknowingly get trapped into carrying out illicit and inhumane activities. I come from poverty like you, and years ago, I was so desperate that I was willing to do anything to escape from my situation." When bin Laden had allegedly been killed but no evidence had been brought forth, Dabir accepted the prevalent notion that Pakistan had been used as a political pawn and betrayed by America and the West. He was attracted to outrageous ideas and lured by easy money. "It was only after I got pulled into the web that I realized how hard it was to get out. I was told I had a duty to recruit others. So I did, and it helped me relieve my guilty conscience. It made me feel better to know that other decent, hardworking people like you were involved too."

Goha, Bala, and Naseebo exchanged glances.

"I got persuaded into believing things that aren't true, like women are stupid and inferior to men. Those kinds of ideas take our already patriarchal society to an extreme. Naseebo *behan*, you have my utmost respect. I consider you my sister. If I said or did anything to offend you, please accept my sincere apologies."

Dabir said top leadership had passed a unanimous resolution to let employees and their families hold on to the assets they received from the organization. "That means you get to keep your house, car, and cash," he said. "And I have more good news. Field workers like me, Babrek, and Quezed will get additional money based on our work and level."

Goha looked at his parents, whose appearance seemed to reflect his own shock, elation, and befuddlement. It sounded like the mental and physical anguish he had endured over the past months had finally, miraculously, come to an end without the dramatic exit he had envisioned. However, he was unclear why Dabir didn't mention his name in the list of field workers who would receive bonus compensation.

Lala Dabir eyed him with a grin. "Goha, you look puzzled. Are you wondering about Quezed?"

"Well, I . . ."

"Babrek and I used that code name to talk confidentially about someone we're both very fond of, someone who prevailed through great ordeals and came out stronger than ever. That someone, *baita*, is you."

"Me?"

"Your name means *gemstone*, and the English letters *que* and *zed* are the symbol for quartz. Several varieties of quartz are abundant in the mountains up north, and many are considered gemstones. Some people say the mineral is indestructible, so it became the perfect name for you. You're a resilient young man, and God's grace has been on your side."

Dabir pulled out a folder from his bag. "My lawyer will transfer the house deed in your name. And this is for you," he said, handing Goha a banker's check.

Goha had to blink a few times to make sure he wasn't seeing extra zeros. But in spite of the bountiful payment, he was still unsettled, like a half-constructed house missing its foundation.

"Dabir *sahib*, you're offering me a lot of money. But I need you to know that I can't be part of the organization anymore, even if it resurfaces. I won't be part of it ever again—in any capacity. I simply can't do it." He swallowed. "If that means I have to return the check, I'll give it up."

"The money is yours with no strings attached. It's all in the paperwork. You have no more ties to the organization. Not now. Not ever again."

Lala Dabir stood. "The cell phones are yours to keep too. You all have my number, and I have yours. Please don't be strangers."

As Goha got up to see Lala Dabir out, twilight blanketed the sky with burnt orange, golden yellow, and azure, merging in a warm, delicate unison. The quartz crystal in the corner caught his eye, its protruding pieces reflecting the colors and glimmering in the fading light.

Lala Dabir bid them a warm *khuda hafiz* and walked out the door.

CHAPTER 23

During the mild spring days, Goha treasured his time showing Kajal and her parents around Karachi. They marveled at the Mazar-e-Quaid, the imposing final resting place of Pakistan's founder Muhammad Ali Jinnah; strolled through local parks; collected shells at the beach; explored shopping venues and bazaars; discovered art galleries and museums; and tasted a variety of foods from local restaurants and street vendors. Sheikh Samir said there was *barkat* in opening one's house to guests, and Goha was grateful his family could now do so without financial strains.

It made Goha happy to witness his parents being hospitable and generous toward Kajal's family, even though his *ammi* didn't hesitate to occasionally pull him into a corner to make a disparaging comment or two about their simple habits and lack of sophistication. At some point he would have to secure a good job and a steady income, but Goha was in no hurry. If they were careful about spending, the money from Lala Dabir would be enough for him and his parents to live comfortably for a few years. Eventually, God willing, Goha envisioned buying a house in one of the most affluent areas of Karachi, one that was spacious enough for his *ammi* and *abba*, Kajal's *aya* and *dada*, and guests. He imagined that when he and Kajal had children, both sets of parents would play a big role in raising them. Kajal's parents didn't want to leave Bumburet, but as they grew older, Goha anticipated they might want to spend time in

Karachi's moderate climate during the cold months in the valley. He planned to be the type of son-in-law they cherished and loved like their very own son.

The traumatic incidents Goha had experienced up north were losing their intensity, and he was relieved when his parents eventually stopped pressing him about the work he did for the organization. The day he came to their house, Lala Dabir had spoken about the hardships Goha faced and implied the organization was involved in illegal and inhumane activities. Since then, Bala and Naseebo hadn't brought up the subject, and Goha figured they were either in denial or simply didn't want to know the details. In any case, he concluded it was best to put the past to rest.

After Dabir's visit, Goha hadn't had a chance to discuss with Babrek the fallout from the organization's disbanding. He was eager to talk to him and properly catch up. What was Babrek up to in the aftermath of the failed unification efforts? How had things changed after he received his payout? Goha was hopeful that maybe, finally, the next time they chatted, he would receive some candid insights into the organization's inscrutable inner workings.

One afternoon, just as everyone was finishing chai in the dining room, Goha's phone started vibrating. He was hoping to hear from Babrek but was equally pleased to see Lala Dabir's number on his screen. He went into the living room to answer it.

"*Assalam-o-alaikum* Dabir *sahib*! How are you doing?"

"Goha, I'm afraid I have some terrible news."

Goha barely recognized Dabir's croaked voice. "What is it, Dabir *sahib*? What's wrong?"

"Babrek is no more. He was killed two days ago."

"*Ya Allah*, no! What are you saying?"

Dabir stifled a sob, and several agonizing seconds passed before he spoke again. "From what I understand, a small, extremely conservative faction of the organization believed he was a government spy. I don't know if that's true—I guess it doesn't really matter at this point. When certain people are convinced that someone's a threat and needs to be taken out, there's no reasoning with them. They shot him in the head in cold blood."

Goha's words came out as a barely audible whisper. "*Inna lillahi wa inna ilayhi raji'un.*" To God we belong and to Him we return.

"His *janaaza* is tomorrow. I'll be flying to Peshawar tomorrow to attend."

"Dabir *sahib* . . . I'd like to go too. I want to pay Babrek my final respects."

"I think you should stay in Karachi. The people who took Babrek's life have no humanity left in them—they're even attacking funeral processions. You're about to start your life with Kajal, and you have responsibilities toward her and your parents. But I don't want you to have regrets. You can come to Peshawar if you must." Like Lala Dabir and Goha, Babrek had received a big sum from the organization. Dabir said he would be giving most of that money to Goha since Babrek's immediate family members were deceased and he had recently told Dabir that Goha was his closest friend.

Goha put the phone down and squeezed his eyes shut. His time with Babrek played through his mind like an emotion-packed TV drama. The abusive start and the serious, painful confrontations. The feelings of anger, confusion, and frustration. The exchanged perspectives and sincere attempts at empathy and understanding. The fun, lighthearted moments. The unwavering support and loyalty. And at the end of it all, a relationship that felt as unbreakable as the quartz in the mountains of Northern Pakistan, as solid as the crystal cluster shimmering on the table in front of him. Goha stayed in the room for a long time, his head buried in his hands, overcome by a strange jumble of loss, emptiness, sadness, heartache—and even a surge of relief.

With swollen eyes and wet cheeks, he dragged himself into the adjoining room to relay the news.

The question of whether he should book a last-minute flight to Peshawar bounced around in Goha's head that night until he finally heeded Dabir's advice. It simply wasn't worth the risk—he could pray to Allah for Babrek's soul and high place in *jannah* from anywhere; plus, he didn't feel comfortable leaving Kajal and her parents behind in Karachi. Once everything settled down, he vowed to make a special trip to Peshawar to visit Babrek's gravesite.

Was Babrek really a government spy? From the beginning, he had been infatuated with the organization and ready to defend its nefarious actions, but maybe it was all a farce and Goha had been oblivious to the signs. He had been puzzled by Babrek's joyful reunion with the army officer, General Zafar, when they were helping earthquake victims in Mingora, and by his obsession with Pakistani news and foreign relations.

When they had met in Karachi, Babrek conveyed what seemed like insider information about the underhanded dealings of Inspector Nek and Dildar Baga. Plus, Babrek lived in the country's capital, Islamabad, for a couple of years as a minor under *Maulvi* Saber's care. Is that where it all began? Babrek didn't fit the profile of the organization's leadership—he was far more intelligent and open-minded than the bigoted presenters at the *ijtema* and the group leaders at the camps. He'd seemed surprised to hear about the government raid following the *ijtema*, but maybe he had been faking it. Was his involvement with a covert government operation the reason for all his secrecy? Now that he was dead, Goha didn't know if he would ever uncover the truth.

Goha found himself awake before dawn. In the stillness of the night, he slipped out of his room and treaded softly into the kitchen. A daily English newspaper that Kasim had brought over was lying on the dining table. He unfolded it and started scanning through it, turning the pages slowly to minimize the rustling.

A couple of articles grabbed his attention. In the first, he learned about a new school that was scheduled to be built outside Peshawar to replace one destroyed in the recent attacks, with funding from the Pakistani government and local and international donors. The second was a tribute to victims of the strikes, listing the deceased in alphabetical order by last name. His breath grew rapid as he skimmed the article, a piece that personalized and memorialized the innocent lives lost, that imprinted a permanent, bloody stain on the organization even as it disintegrated.

"Pervez Abdullah, twenty-five. Altaf Baig, thirty-five. Dawoud Bhatti, twenty." He mouthed each name silently, his eyes darting down the list, and halted abruptly. "Gulnaz Durrani, thirty-three. Naima Durrani, nine."

"Durrani . . . Durrani . . ." *Where have I heard that name before?* Then it came to him in a ripple of panic.

There was stirring in the guest room, and a few minutes later, Kajal emerged, rubbing her eyes.

"Good morning, *janoo*," she said, pulling out the chair beside him. "You're up early. I hope you're all right after hearing the shocking news about Babrek."

Goha put down the newspaper and tried to steady his voice. "Kajal, did Nargis *baji* have people in her family named Gulnaz and Naima?"

"Gulnaz is her cousin, the one she was visiting up north when I introduced you to her. Nargis told me she and Gulnaz took a stand for female empowerment by keeping their maiden names when they married. Gulnaz's husband died a couple of years ago—she became a widow at a young age. Naima is her older daughter, who is nine, I think, and she also has a set of younger twin girls. They all adopted *Durrani* when their father passed away."

"Oh no."

"What?"

"When Kasim came to the house, he said Nargis was worried about a couple of people in her family who had recently gone missing. I think he was talking about Gulnaz and Naima. They were killed recently, and I probably had a hand in it." He covered his face with his hands. "I can't believe this."

"Oh, Goha." Her tone conveyed sympathy, pity, and a touch of anger he had never heard in her voice before.

"The organization said it wanted to bring systemic changes to Pakistan. But they never said what kind of changes or how they would cost so many innocent people their lives. This is all too much, Kajal. I have to do something to make things right. Oh Allah, please have mercy on me and help me make things right."

As the first faint light peeked through the window, he folded the newspaper, took Kajal's hands in his own and squeezed them, and headed to his room to say his *fajr namaz*.

That afternoon, Kajal disappeared inside the living room to talk to Nargis. She emerged several minutes later with watery eyes and held out her phone to Goha.

"Kasim *bhai* wants to speak to you."

Goha dreaded speaking to anyone, let alone someone so close to the victims, about the senseless deaths he was unwittingly involved with. He hesitatingly took the phone from her and stepped away.

"Kasim *bhai*, I want to express my deep sympathy to you and Nargis for the death of Gulnaz and Naima. May Allah give you *sabr* during this difficult time." Goha cringed at his words as soon as they left him. To him, they sounded trite and rehearsed, perhaps even insincere. *Kajal is so close to Nargis that she must have told her I was likely involved with the mission that destroyed her cousin and niece. And if Nargis knows, Kasim knows too.* Goha feared being rebuked and reprimanded at best, or at worst, accused of being the killer of a guileless woman and her child who were simply trying to go to school.

"Thank you, Goha," Kasim said. "This is a trying time for our family. I'm concerned about Nargis—she was close to Gulnaz and crazy about her niece, Naima. But since we got news of their departure from this world, I've been thinking a lot. I spent twenty-five years in the Karachi Police Department, and I saw scores of young men like you get lured into organizations that carry out criminal activities that go against the teachings of Islam.

"Unfortunately, these types of organizations prey on families like yours. Sometimes kids want to rise up and do something to escape their poverty. Some feel lonely and just want to belong somewhere. Some kids are attracted to being part of something bigger than themselves. Some are influenced by friends or relatives. Some are lured into thinking their life will become easier or more meaningful if they join a group that does things in the name of God. And sometimes it's a combination of several of these factors."

Most leaders of those organizations were *jahil*, ignorant and illiterate, Kasim said. "But they're masters at riling up youngsters about perceived injustices and convincing people that their mission—to preserve our true Pakistani heritage through extreme, violent actions—is virtuous. I'm shattered by our family's loss, but the last thing you should do is feel guilty when an entire network—one that's much bigger than me and you—is at play here."

As Kasim spoke, Goha felt the weight of a thousand Himalayan mountains lift off his shoulders.

"Kasim *bhai*, in your time of grief, you're putting things into perspective to make me feel better. You don't know how much your words mean to me."

"I have seen you follow in the footsteps of our prophet and act with generosity, love, and kindness," Kasim replied. "You have a bright future ahead of you, *inshallah*. The most all of us can do is learn from our mistakes, pray we have the *himmat* to look forward, and move on with honorable intentions."

CHAPTER 24

When the unrest up north eventually subsided, Kajal's parents—overwhelmed with the sprawling coastal city and Naseebo's over-the-top hospitality—said it was due time for them to return to their farm and the simplicity of their Kalash lifestyle. Goha and Kajal, concerned about their welfare over the long journey, at the last minute decided to join them on the Khyber Mail train to Peshawar. For Goha, it was also a timely opportunity to take care of important unfinished business.

The four of them had just returned to their sleeper car after a filling meal of mutton curry and steamed basmati rice in the dining car. Goha felt for the box; it was still there, nestled deep and secure inside the pocket of his jeans. The romance of the golden hour was starting to filter through the windows, casting shadows tinged with a toasty saffron glow. Goha had seen enough movies, had envisioned the scene enough times in his mind to know exactly how he wanted it to play out. That day, it wouldn't be Bala and Naseebo who approached a suitable family for a *rishta*. This was his time.

He got down on his knee in front of Kajal. "Kajal, you are the most beautiful, loving, and compassionate woman," he said. "My life has completely changed since I met you." He wobbled to the side as the train swayed.

Kajal clasped her hands, her eyes shining.

Goha grasped the guardrail and turned to Kajal's father. "Uncle, your daughter is the woman of my dreams. With God's help, I'll do my very best to keep Kajal safe, happy, and healthy. Can you hear me?" By this time, Goha was shouting to make himself heard over the train's vibrations. A few curious children poked their heads in and giggled.

"What I'm trying to say to you, Kajal, is that I can't wait to spend the rest of my life with you. With your parents as witnesses, I would like to formally propose to you. Will you marry me, Kajal?"

The train came to a hasty stop just as Goha popped the question. His voice echoed throughout the car, and he tumbled into the aisle. Kajal burst out laughing, and several passengers sitting nearby stood and started clapping at Goha's comical and endearing show of affection.

Goha got up, grinned sheepishly, brushed himself off, and ran his hand through his overgrown hair, which had recently started falling into his eyes. "That wasn't exactly how I wanted it to go. Let me try this again."

He took out the small velvet jewelry box from his pocket and opened it, revealing a quartz engagement ring studded with diamonds and sapphires that matched the color of Kajal's eyes. He took Kajal's hand and gently placed the ring on her finger.

Kajal's face glistened in the afterglow of the sunset. "Oh, Goha. With my dear parents as witnesses, yes, I will marry you. Yes!"

Goha approached the front desk of the hotel in the Qissa Khawani Bazaar, the very place he had stayed with Babrek when he first arrived in Peshawar. Though it had only been a few months, it seemed years had passed as Goha had stood by idly in that same spot, blissfully unaware of what his future up north held.

When their train journey had come to an end, Kajal's parents took off in a rental car with a driver for the second leg of their long journey home to Bumburet. Now, as Goha checked himself and Kajal into the deluxe hotel room he had booked for them, the discomfort and dread from his original visit there were gone. Goha had spent weeks restraining himself from Kajal in Karachi despite the smoldering inside him. Since they hadn't yet made their union official, being intimate with her seemed inappropriate and disrespectful, especially under Naseebo's watchful gaze and with both sets of parents around.

That night he would be alone with her at long last, in a luxurious hotel suite no less, and the engagement ring on her finger put him more at ease with the situation. He also had time to process Dr. Khan's wise words and found himself in a calm mental space where he had almost completely forgiven Babrek for his transgressions. He decided he wasn't going to dwell on Babrek's bad qualities; the Prophet Mohammad said overlooking character flaws would be rewarded in the afterlife. It was incumbent to forgive and forget the sins of the deceased, Sheikh Samir told his students.

As they entered their room on the fifth floor, Kajal smiled at Goha suggestively and kissed him tenderly on the lips. Goha's body grew hot as he pulled open the sliding door to tuck their bags into the closet. When he turned toward the bed, Kajal had undressed and was lying between the sheets, beckoning him seductively to join her.

Goha didn't need to be asked twice. He stripped off his clothes and joined her in bed, murmuring loving words into her ear and running his hands up and down her smooth skin as she quivered in delight. They pleasured each other for a long time, discovering and savoring the contours and details of each other's bodies.

When Goha finally entered Kajal, it removed all doubts about his virility. Sparks erupted from the heavens, and the world spun harder and faster as they reached a climax together in a passionate sweat.

The next morning, Goha asked the hotel concierge to call for a taxi. "Please take us to the Peshawar Education School System on Kohat

Road," Goha told the driver as he and Kajal climbed into the back seat.

The woman at the front desk was busy filing papers when they stepped into the building.

"Goha Hadi? Welcome. Ms. Kundi's expecting you. Please follow me."

She led them down a corridor where plaques engraved with the names of donors—companies, individuals, and groups who had given generously to schools in the area over the years—were mounted to the wall on rectangular brass plates. Outside the corner office hung a nameplate that read "Ameera Kundi, Head Administrator of Girls' Schools." A petite woman wearing horn-rimmed glasses, loose cropped pants, and a mid-length *kurta* sat obscured behind a desk. Her presence expanded when she stood to greet them.

"*Assalam-o-alaikum.* Ameera Kundi. Thanks for getting in touch, Goha. It is a pleasure to meet you in person." She extended her hand.

"*Wa 'alaykumu s-salam*, Ms. Kundi. This is my fiancée, Kajal."

"Please have a seat. Can I get you both something to drink?"

"Thank you. We just had breakfast at the hotel."

"That's right. You came in from Karachi yesterday. That's a long journey."

"Yes. But it was important for us to meet with you."

"Of course. How can I help you?"

Goha took a deep breath. "Ms. Kundi, I know schools in this area have faced a lot of hardships lately." He glanced over at Kajal, who gave him a small nod of encouragement.

"I'd like to offer you a proposition. I received a substantial sum of money from an organization I used to be a part of, and I want to donate a portion of it to your schools. Ideally, I'd like to divide it into three parts. The first will go toward repairing damages caused by recent attacks." He cast his eyes downward, unable to hide his remorse, and took a moment before continuing. "The second will go toward breaking ground on a new school I read about in the newspaper. I believe it's scheduled to be built outside Peshawar to replace one that was decimated. And the third will go toward compensating teachers and staff, who must be shaken from all the unrest and mayhem. Does that sound feasible?"

"It absolutely does. It's not every day that we receive an offer like this, especially from someone who isn't an active part of our community."

"It's the least I can do." Goha paused.

"I'd also like to pledge a donation from my friend Babrek. He was killed recently, and he supported causes that uplift women and girls after his mom and sister died. I think your schools are a great way to honor his memory."

"Have you considered how you want to use the money from Babrek?"

In truth, Goha had spent several hours on the train thinking about it. "I'd like it to go toward a couple of scholarships for bright, dedicated students who might be facing hard times at home. Like maybe they're being abused or struggling with their purpose or identity. Could that be arranged?"

It could, Ms. Kundi said, but the stigma associated with those kinds of sensitive topics might pose a challenge. "A lot of kids won't open up because they think they'll get in trouble if they share information that their families consider shameful," she said. "Most are being raised in conservative environments, so I get why they're scared. Plus, some are so poor they're simply trying to get through the day with enough to eat."

"I have a joint degree in teaching and psychology, and I've been wanting to put it to use," Kajal said. "Maybe setting up mental health counseling would help?"

"We could certainly try."

"I just thought of something else too." Kajal told Ms. Kundi about her parents' farm, and the vast quantity of fruit, nuts, wheat, maize, and beans grown in Bumburet. "There might be a way for my family to provide surplus food from the valley to poor and malnour-ished students in Peshawar," she said.

Ms. Kundi appeared overwhelmed at the young couple's benevo-lence. "What you both have proposed for us is tremendous," she said. "After all the atrocities, your visit here feels like angels have descended upon us. If it's okay with you, I will arrange to have plaques engraved with your names to hang on our donor wall."

"Thank you, but that's not necessary," Goha said. *The left hand shouldn't know what the right is doing*, Sheikh Samir told his students, quoting a *hadith* that encouraged Muslims to be humble and avoid seeking praise when helping others.

"I do have a request, though. May I suggest a name for the new school?"

"Of course."

"I'd like it to be called 'The Naima Durrani School for Girls' to honor a victim of one of the attacks. I'd like to propose a name for the scholarships too. Can we please call them 'The Babrek Azam Memorial Scholarships?'"

Ms. Kundi pulled out a paper and pen from the drawer and scratched down the names. "I would be happy to recommend those to our board," she said.

"Wonderful," Goha replied. "Thank you, Ms. Kundi. We'll be in touch."

He placed his hand on his heart, nodded gratefully, pulled the chair out for Kajal, and got up to leave.

EPILOGUE

Two Years Later

Goha leaned back in his top-grain brown leather chair, his hands cradled behind his head. Out the window from his office on the eleventh floor lay the cityscape of Peshawar, the busy frontier city that had recently become his and Kajal's new residence.

He rolled his chair around and glanced out the door into the lobby. Hamza, his receptionist, was tidying up his desk. Above it hung a large, polished silver sign with black rivets. It had been secured to the wall just a week ago by two young workers who fretted over making sure it was centered and readable from all angles: Sulaiman and Hadi, Ltd.

When Farid Sulaiman had asked Goha to join his construction company as partner and chief operations officer to help set up a regional office in Peshawar, Goha was hard-pressed to say no. The business was thriving, and since it was based in Karachi, it meant he could visit his parents, relatives, and friends regularly.

Overall, Goha felt he was living the life he had dared to dream about as a teenager in Qasba. Since their wedding in Karachi, his emotional connection with Kajal had only grown stronger; it made their day-to-day interactions and lovemaking easy and effortless. On the work front, Goha had acquired a cadre of conscientious associates and was starting to build a roster of influential contacts. He didn't have to worry about competing with Karim, Gul-e-Shabbo's husband and Farid's new son-in-law, who was fully engaged in an internal medicine residency at the Dow Medical Center in Karachi.

Goha's phone hummed, and a familiar number popped on the screen. He picked up on the first ring. "Ms. Kundi, *assalam-o-alaikum*. Yes, everything is ready for tomorrow. The team's done a great job."

To Farid's surprise and delight, Goha had managed to secure a contract with the Peshawar Education School System to build a girls' school in the area just days after he joined the firm. For Goha, the contract was a way to immediately prove to Farid he was willing to work hard in spite of his connection to Bala and was worthy of the position despite his young age and limited experience.

Goha's phone vibrated again. It was Kajal.

"Are you ready for the big event, my love?"

"I think we're all set. The only potential hitch is the weather. The forecast for tomorrow is stormy. How are you feeling?"

"Better than yesterday, for sure. The doctor's appointment went well, and I haven't vomited since waking up."

"Good. Have you heard from Nargis?"

"I called her earlier. We're coming to the ceremony together."

"How are *aya* and *dada*?"

"Not great. Still reeling from the insurgency. They said it was awful. Drones flew over the valley, and all the lights went out. No one was allowed to enter or leave the village. And they still haven't heard from Timuk."

Two weeks prior, newsrooms in the area had been in a frenzy when militants from the tribal area released a video demanding the Kalash community accept Islam or prepare for violent attacks. The Pakistani government swept into the valley and attempted to force the extremists out, but they gained strength by luring a group of unsuspecting, uneducated men into their fold. Kajal's eldest brother, swayed by the scare tactics and fervor, had abandoned his family to join them.

Goha opened his desk drawer. A business card from Pakistani Army General Zafar Malik lay face up. It was one of Babrek's few keepsakes he had found at the rooming house. A couple of years had passed since they met briefly in Mingora, but it might just be the time to get back in touch with his deceased friend's contact, who would likely have the authority to pull some strings.

"I'm sorry to hear that. I'm going to call someone I know who might be able to help us get Timuk back."

The following day, Goha stood outside the school, struck by the curved archways, pristine white marble tile flooring, and ornate gating. The air was warm and misty, and the gray clouds signaled a potential downpour at any minute. But even in the dreary atmosphere, the building was ravishing.

It was an open-air concept designed at no cost by a top architect from the culturally rich city of Lahore, with outdoor walkways and spacious, modern classrooms. In the courtyard, a three-tiered quartz water fountain spilled lavishly into a shallow basin, its drops gleaming like miniature diamonds. Goha had been impressed with the laborers' agility and speed. Every time he had driven by the site since they had broken ground a few months earlier, there was remarkable progress. That meant the school was ready for students sooner than anticipated.

The ribbon-cutting ceremony was scheduled to start in the playground area at 2:00 p.m. Farid was en route to Dubai to meet with a materials supplier, and without him there, it was Goha's responsibility to make sure nothing got overlooked. So far, everything was going smoothly—a crew had set up a food tent close to a wooden podium; workers were hauling folding chairs out of a truck and arranging them in neat rows on the lawn; soothing instrumental sitar music emitted from a nearby speaker. They expected the event to draw a significant turnout; the agency he hired had proven to be adept at generating buzz and showcasing the school as a symbol of the community's resilience and progress. Over the past few weeks, both he and Farid had spoken on prominent TV and radio shows and had been interviewed by reporters from local, regional, national, and even international publications.

Goha walked back to his car and pulled his *janamaz* out of the trunk. He wanted to say a special prayer on the property before guests arrived, to ask Allah to guide him and Kajal on a path of serving others, to protect the students and administration, to always keep the learning environment happy, productive, and safe.

Just as he was finishing up his *dua*, his phone buzzed. It was a number he didn't recognize.

"Hello?"

The voice on the other end was distinct: a high-pitched inflection that transported him back to several lifetimes past. "Goha? This is Nagina. From Dildar Baga's house in Karachi. Do you remember me?"

A jumble of mishmashed images—a police car, oriental carpeting, a green velvet sofa, a crystal decanter, a gold bell, elaborate furnishings—flittered through Goha's brain. "Of course, I remember you, Nagina. What a surprise to hear from you."

"I know it has been a long time, but I never forgot how kind you were the day you came to the magistrate's house. When you left, you said I should get in touch with you if I ever needed help."

"I did say that, Nagina."

"After Magistrate Baga was arrested, I moved to Peshawar. I heard on the news you're opening The Naima Durrani School for Girls, and I'm planning to attend the ribbon-cutting ceremony today. I would like to enroll as a student."

"Nagina, you have my word that you'll be signed up as our very first student. The event starts in an hour. See you soon."

By 1:15 p.m., a trail of cars had begun entering the gated campus like a continuous, winding rope. Politicians and representatives from domestic and international NGOs milled around, making small talk and helping themselves to mango sherbet, cocktail samosas, chicken sandwiches, and chocolate biscuits on an expansive, buffet-style table inside the tent. Reporters from TV stations set up video cameras on tripods behind rows of chairs, and newspaper and magazine journalists strolled around, typing notes into their phones or scribbling them into their pocket-sized journals. Photographers with sophisticated cameras strapped around their necks snapped pictures of the people and grounds from different vantage points.

At 1:30 p.m., Goha's car pulled up, and Kasim exited from the front passenger door wearing a pressed collared shirt and a suit jacket. The driver opened the back door, and Nargis and Kajal emerged in elegant, brightly colored *shalwar kameezes*. Two small girls with ponytails, wearing pastel blue-and-white–checkered dresses and glossy white shoes tumbled out after them, giggling and bouncing up and down in excitement.

Goha walked over to them. "Kasim *bhai* and Nargis *baji*, I can't tell you how happy I was when Kajal told me you were moving to Peshawar. It's an honor to have you join us today with your sweet girls."

"Can we go to school here?" The twins chimed in unison.

Goha laughed, crouching and putting one arm around each of them. "We'll make absolutely sure that you do."

"Goha, this opening comes at exactly the right time for us," said Nargis, dabbing her eye. "The twins are about to reach school age. Gulnaz would have been so pleased. She was the biggest proponent of educating her girls. I can feel my dear cousin and niece's presence with us today."

Goha met her eyes and nodded, unable to speak. As the girls skipped over to the tent, he swallowed the lump in his throat and turned to Kajal. He put his hand tenderly on the curve of her belly. "Did you find out?" he asked her softly.

"It's a girl," Kajal said. "And I think I already know her name. *Noor*, which means *light*. Our baby girl will be our guiding light. And I can't wait for her to go to school here one day."

A small smile formed on Goha's lips. It was almost two o'clock. The wind shifted and the clouds opened, swathing the school grounds in a faint, hopeful, pale yellow light.

ABOUT THE AUTHORS

Aqueel "Al" Athar grew up in Karachi, Pakistan. He received his PhD in clinical microbiology from the University of London and previously worked as the head of microbiology labs and director of infection control at the Calgary District Hospital Group in Calgary, Canada. His teaching positions included adjunct professor at the University of Calgary and faculty member at Benedictine University in Lisle, Illinois. Aqueel is an active Rotarian who has served as president of Rotary Clubs in Canada and the U.S. He has penned several books in English and Urdu. Aqueel has two grown, married daughters (Yasmin Ahmed and Tanya Athar-Jogee) and four grandchildren. He currently lives in Bolingbrook, Illinois, with his wife, Ansa.

Tanya Athar-Jogee was born in Calgary, Canada, and currently resides in Austin, Texas. She completed her undergraduate degree in journalism from Concordia University in Montreal, where she won the award for the most outstanding journalism graduate in her class. Tanya also holds an MS in Integrated Marketing Communications from Northwestern University in Chicago. Her op-eds on social issues, culture, faith, and identity have appeared in *Newsweek*, *Common Dreams*, *Truthout*, and other national publications. She has also written features for *Dawn*, the oldest and largest English newspaper in Pakistan. Tanya is married with two children and a cat. *Tiny Glimmers of Light* is her debut novel, co-authored with her father.

www.ingramcontent.com/pod-product-compliance
Lightning Source LLC
Chambersburg PA
CBHW031032310726
48969CB00007B/1953